STROKING PRIDE
A SONS OF SATAN NOVEL

CREA REITAN

DRAGON FIRE FANTASY

Stroking Pride

A Sons of Satan Novel

Copyright © 2022 by Amber Reitan writing as Crea Reitan

www.facebook.com/LadyCreaAuthor

Cover Copyright © 2022, Mythical Worlds Publications

Editing by Hatters

All Rights Reserved. No part of this publication may be reproduced, distributed, or transmitted in any form or by any means, including photocopying, recording, or other electronic or mechanical methods, without the prior written permission of the publisher, except in the case of brief quotations for review purposes.

This is a work of fiction - all characters and events portrayed in this book are fictitious. Any resemblance to actual persons, living or dead, places, or events is purely coincidental and not intended by the author.

Dragon Fire Fantasy, Inc.

dragonfirefantasy@gmail.com

ISBN:

ASIN:

Version 2022.10.11 - P.NA

❀ Created with Vellum

For Lady Fury, who shares my obsession with demons. This is what we've been waiting for!

This is a work of fiction, a paranormal romance that begins in our world and then takes a violent turn when our heroine winds up in Hell. This is a story within the shared world of Sons of Satan and is accompanied by six other stories.

Though this isn't a particularly dark story, there are dark elements from time to time. There is brief glimpses of torture and death, as well as violence. However, that is not the focus of the story.

This is Nuke's story, told primarily from her POV. However, this is also Malak's story, as well as the other demons they're surrounded with. Each character and relationship dynamic is just as important as those with Nuke.

Having said that, this is not a single-lady-gets-all-the-men story. This is a polyamorous romance, a whychoose reverse harem that concentrates on all relationships being equal and just as important as each man's is with our female lead. This is equal parts MM and all the girly holes getting filled by each man.

If anything that you just read bothers you, it isn't what you're interested in, or you find might be triggering, please do not read this book. Otherwise, enjoy this sinful story that shows what trust and humility can do for the prideful!

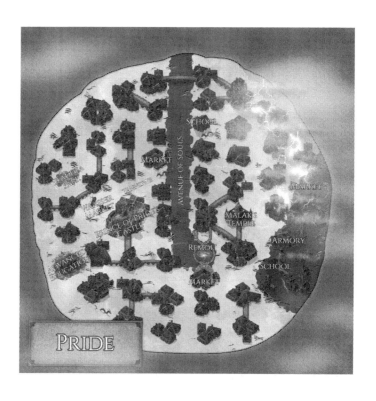

CHAPTER ONE
MALAK

The shrill screaming that penetrated my closed window and set my jaw on edge made me sigh.

Kingsley yawned as he got to his feet and threw open the balcony doors. The screeching sound made me cringe, but before I could snap at him to close it again, his frown caught my attention.

With another sigh, I pulled myself up to join him on the balcony.

My estate sat surrounded by a large moat that led into the main throughways of the city. Because so many of the main waterways led to and from my home, it was always a busy port outside. There were many short taxis and longer public boats. Even a few historic rides that shined in the sunlight.

On the nearest bridge is where the commotion originated.

"A pridefall," Kingsley said. "Maybe multiple. It's hard to tell from here."

There were several for sure. I'd like to say the pridefalls were a newer anomaly but since my damned father vanished in the night, Pride has been getting chaotic. The magic runs wild and becomes more untamed the longer I am unable to wield it.

One such effect of that is the pridefalls.

There were almost a dozen demons battling them. I counted three. Based on their colors, the sin they fell to was lust. I rolled my eyes. Shocking, for sure.

"This is getting out of hand," Kingsley said, turning back inside.

I watched a while longer, wondering if I needed to interfere. Everything burns, after all. But I'd just finished having the last remnants of a fight scrubbed off the bridges in my view. Scorching them again would just irritate me.

"You need to do something about this, Malak," Kingsley said when I didn't answer him.

We've been through a dozen 'queens' and they all fail to be what I need them to be. And without my queen, I cannot control the magic. Fuck, I can't even touch it. I can feel it running rampant and disrupting my city. But I can't do a thing about it.

And I've spent a whole fucking lot of resources and time trying to. What I wouldn't give to be able to take hold of my magic before one of my brothers handles theirs. My one consolation was that none of them were any closer than I was.

Which was fortunate. I'd be an asmodai's ass fin before I let one of those fuckers take the reigns of Hell. Fuck that noise. Just what Hell needed was a lazy fuck like Bee on the throne commanding all of Hell. Or Sorin who can't think of anything but sex for more than a solid minute.

And don't get me started on the slow fuck, Tharul. By the time he made it to the throne, Hell would have frozen. At least that was a bit of a consolation. He's not got the speed to make it there. Smart man, but that was his only saving grace.

"Malak," Kingsley said, trying to make me pay attention to him.

I didn't want to think of the ways I was failing right now. What kind of prince am I if I can't get this shit together? How can I take my true throne without the magic of pride to back me up?

And seriously, I needed a fucking woman to get me there!

A hand on my lower back had the tension in my shoulders releasing. It slid up my back, following my spine, before Bael leaned against me.

"As much as he's a pain in the ass, King's right, Malak. We need to find your queen," Bael said.

I sighed, leaning against the railing as I watched laraje drown one of the pridefall so the crowd only had to concentrate on two. Six per pridefall. It shouldn't be this difficult. But a normal, unimpressive kimaris suddenly became as strong as a devourer or a nybbus when they fell from pride and into a different sin. The really curious thing was that despite what sin they fall to, they became exponentially more dangerous and powerful. Running on adrenaline and lacking pain receptors.

It didn't matter which sin, though. Sloth was as strong as wrath. And lust, which was turning into a more frequent issue, apparently, was just as deadly. The two pridefalls have taken out five of the demons around them. I shook my head, readying myself to set some assholes on fire. Fortunately, an oriax climbed onto the bridge and started taking bites out of the pridefalls.

I smiled, wondering if I should call Zyphon out here to watch what an oriax could do if they actually took the time to master their control. The one there was massive, which meant he could probably find me my queen without trying too hard.

I raised a brow and turned away. Part of the issue was that I didn't want a queen. I wanted to rule Pride on my own. But fucking *Daddy dearest* refused his sons that possibility. We all must find our destined queen in order to finally get a handle on our magic.

At least my brothers are just as miserable about this as I am.

Bael followed me in, shutting the doors behind us. When I stopped, he was at my back again, resting his face against my shoulder as he looked at the other three with me. Kingsley was in my chair, something that made him smirk as he looked at me with challenge.

Hayt lounged in another chair. But Zyphon was tapping away on his phone, seemingly oblivious to what's going on in the room.

"How about we make this interesting," Zyphon said, looking up from his phone.

"Make what interesting?" I asked.

"Finding you a mate."

"I don't need-"

Demons often misinterpreted what the queen was. They're not a mate. Just a partner that was able to control the magic with me.

"You need a mate," Zyphon said, talking over me. "And finding one you can easily manipulate has failed thus far. You're the prince of pride, Malak. You need a proud woman to rule this place with you."

"No," I countered. "I need someone strong enough to touch the magic and that can open the pathway up for me. Then I don't need her."

"And thus why every woman has failed at becoming queen," Kingsley noted.

Sometimes, I hated that man.

"Malak, if you keep fucking around in this, one of your brothers will find their queen first. I'm sure I'm not the first to have figured out that your queen has to be directly in-line with your sin."

Bael chuckled. "Lazy fuck's been researching."

"I'm not lazy," Zyphon said, rolling his eyes and leaning back in the chair, the front two legs coming off the floor. "But sitting around here scowling at the pridefalls or harassing you to find a queen wasn't getting us anywhere. Finding a weak human woman to attempt at shaping her into a strong enough puppet has failed gloriously every time. So, yeah, I stopped paying attention to what you were doing and started trying to find a solution."

"What's the solution?" Hayt asked.

"The proper motivation." Zyphon clicked off his phone and pocketed it. "We need prideful. A woman who knows her worth and makes sure the world knows it, too. But someone honest and generous and loyal. Her positive traits need to balance her pride."

"I'm not sure that's motivating at all," I said, crossing my arms. Bael's hand slid around my waist, resting on my stomach. He was trying to soothe me. I dropped a hand to rest over his and he hugged me tighter. I fought the smile that touched my lips. He was a good man. A frightening fucking demon, but a damned good man.

"That's where the wager comes in," Zyphon said, grinning. "The five of us go to earth and hunt around for the perfect queen. *Not* someone easily controlled or manipulated. A true queen of pride that will be a partner to Malak and allow them both to get this place under control."

"What could you possibly offer that could make me seriously want to look for this?" I asked.

"You should want to look for it anyway," Kingsley said. "Six brothers, Malak. You have six brothers you're in a race against to find your queen first. Zyphon just told you the kind of woman you need to get there and you're *still* being a whiny pain in the ass."

"You know, your presence isn't required in my life, fucker." I narrowed my eyes, the room changing in hue as my darker side pulled to the surface.

"You say that, but you never kick me out," he countered, a smug smile lingering on his face as he leaned back in my chair, making himself comfortable.

I licked my lips as I stared at him. Reaching for his soul. Reading it. Seducing his desire out-

"Nope," Kingsley said, breaking eye contact and looking away. "Not happening. My desires are my own."

"Anyway," Zyphon said, steering us back to the topic at hand. "Aside from being the first to control your ring and making you the rightful ruler of Hell, a place that really only makes sense for pride to control anyway, I've thought about what we could all take advantage of that would lead us to hunting down the best candidate for the job. And I've come up with an idea."

The grin on his face almost has me ending this before he could finish. Something about it made me incredibly uneasy. I wasn't going to like this.

"Well?" Kingsley prompted as Zyphon waited.

But Zyphon was waiting for me to tell him to finish or to fuck off. That he was right, they were all right, and I was running out of time meant that I really needed to get serious. Generally speaking, the five of us head to Earth to

find a woman together. We don't put much thought into it. Not really.

And yes, I always chose someone I didn't like. Someone who had no place in my circle of Hell since their pride didn't even register on the scale. That had never been a trait we cared to seek out. We were looking for someone who wouldn't get in my way.

"What's the winner get?" I asked, tension making my shoulders stiff.

"To fuck your queen as if she were our own," Zyphon answered, his grin sadistic.

Hayt immediately raised his brows, tilting his head to the side in interest. Kingsley nodded, licking his lips. Even Bael, still wrapped around me, smiled against the back of my shoulder.

"You don't really think I'm going to agree to this, do you?"

"Yes," Zyphon said. "I can already see that you acknowledge the need to get serious about this if for no other reason than not to let Adrian or Lorcan on the throne." I scowled further. Princes of greed and wrath, respectively. Adrian would try to take over Earth, just to expand Hell, never being satisfied with what he has. He needs more, more, more. And Lorcan would be just as likely to keep war in Hell since the man thrives on rage. "With the prize being your wife, your queen, as our winning token, we will be assured that we will try to find that queen. And your assurance will be that *you* find your queen so you can keep her to yourself. It's a win-win."

I wasn't sure that I was going to consider this a win-win.

Minutes ticked by as I stared at Zyphon, willing him to take it back. That he was right told me he's been thinking about this for a long time. He pinpointed what we needed to look for in identifying the queen of pride *and* he found a driving force to assure we were all on the right path to putting forth our best efforts in finding said queen.

"Fine," I said. "Bet's on. Find me my queen and the winner gets to fuck her as if she were his own."

"Hold up," Kingsley said. "Are we talking a one-time fuck or-"

Zyphon shook his head before I could nod. My hands clenched into fists, the one over Bael's tightened between his fingers. "No, no. One time fuck isn't enough of a motivating factor." I grit my teeth, already anticipating his next words. "Winner gets to have her with Malak indefinitely."

A growl filled the air. With everyone's eyes on me, I realized it was my growl. I was ready to break out of my skin.

"Still on?" Kingsley added.

Bael's hand tightened around me. He kissed my shoulder, nuzzled his face into the back of my head until I released a breath. Fuck them if they thought they could have my queen.

"Yes," I said, my jaw aching from how I clenched my teeth. "I lay out the rules. We have three days, seventy-two hours, and then we bring the information for our best candidate back. One person. You get to choose one. And a winner is only determined if that woman successfully controls the magic in pride, I can control the magic in pride, and she rightfully becomes my queen. Only when all three points are met does a winner get to be chosen."

"And you don't just get to fuck the queen. She has to agree," Bael added.

"It's going to be a game of encouraging her and

seducing her," Hayt said, his smile growing the longer he thought about it.

I hated this already.

"We start at dawn." Pulling free from Bael, I left the room, needing to get myself under control. This was going to end badly. I could already tell. It's not that I haven't enjoyed women with them before. We shared often. Men, women, food, bloody sacrifices. These were my true brothers. Not the imbeciles that share my father's blood but my *brothers*.

But we're talking about *my* queen. My fucking queen!

I was confident in presenting my find. A government official with confidence enough that she could convince the public that she had the power to reroute a damn river. But she was kind, often volunteering at nursing homes and veteran's homes. She was highly educated, had three dogs, and owned an apartment complex. Her tenants had only good things to say about her.

In all honesty, she was a diamond in the rough. There weren't many government officials like her.

Kingsley found an actress who certainly was off the charts as far as arrogance was concerned. She had obtained some of the top roles in the industry and had a rule about donating 15% of all her earnings to various charities. Humble to balance out her arrogance. But the more I looked at her, the less I thought it was arrogance at all.

She was just good at what she did. In all the videos of her that we watched, she was rather humble.

Thankfully, that put Kingsley off the running.

Bael found an athlete. And boy was this chick strong,

quick, and conceited. Her game talk was fierce. The commercials she did were hilarious and the little candid reels we watched showed that her haughtiness was not faked. Even when she was unaware that she was being watched, her self-assuredness was top notch.

But she lacked any of the balancing traits that Zyphon said were needed. She kept her money for her own, which by all means, do. She earned that shit, and in quite a physical way. She didn't volunteer and she had no real friends or acquaintances.

That was too bad. Of all of them, I think I'd mind least of all to share my queen with Bael.

The girl Hayt showed us had the rest of the room fading away. My lips parted as I stared at the images he presented us, telling us about his find. Anuka Hauptman goes by Nuke. She's a high-profile model recruiter with a weakness for frappuccinos and cookies. Many candids showed her with her little compact hand mirror as she checked her hair and makeup.

There were equally as many pictures of her with the same guy and girl as they laughed in various backgrounds. And her bank records show that she pays for her younger sister's college education, her supplies and electronics. She recently bought a brand-new car for her mother.

I missed who came after that. All I caught was Zyphon's pick was a fashion mogul. It didn't matter. I found my queen. It was time to bring Anuka to Hell.

CHAPTER TWO
ANUKA

His body was great. Perfectly toned, smooth, well-defined muscle structure. His coloring was great, too. Tanned but not to the point where he looked fake. His hair was a gorgeous shade of brown that had streaks of honey in it.

Even his eyes were a unique shade of hazel that I could play up. And his teeth were perfectly straight and white. Not blinding white. There's such a thing as too much, and when they start to glow in the daylight- no. That's a hard pass for me.

But I didn't like his face on the whole. I could tell that's what his concern was too. That was his least confident feature. The poses he was best at and moved toward naturally, did not highlight his face at all. In fact, more often than not, it was half hidden.

Finding the entire package was difficult. I've been doing this for years and I know that a confidence sharp enough to cut glass is the key strength necessary to have when one part of your body isn't perfect.

This guy was my best candidate, but you can't grow the

kind of arrogance overnight to sell that face for top dollar. Perhaps I can just sell him for his abs? He'd make a phenomenal romance cover model. The hornballs that buy those books only care about the bodies. They almost always look past the face. Even when they think they're looking at the whole package.

Speaking of packages. If theirs was perfect, that could outdo almost anything. No six pack? That's okay, he's got a thick dick. Face leaves something to be desired? Did I mention he's long, too?

Why did I care about their package? You wear the right clothing, and you can sell that image too! It's all about working your assets. And as a model, you spend your life being judged. Might as well use everything you have to your advantage.

I must have been staring at this guy for too long, frowning, because my assistant pushed a different headshot to me.

"If you don't like him, you don't like him," Malcolm said. "Don't push it, Nuke."

He was right, of course. But I was one client away from making a million dollars this year. Just one. But only if it was the right one. Otherwise, it was two of these guys. To get top dollar, I really needed to focus all my energy on a single person, not split my attention between two.

I sighed, dropping the full body shot and turning to the headshot Malcolm pushed toward me. "I like this one less."

He chuckled. "No, you don't. You're just pouty right now."

Malcolm's been my assistant for years and he was damn good. Before finding him, I was going through assistants as fast as I changed my underwear. It was sick. I'm high maintenance, which I freely tell them up-front.

Still, no one could hack it after a few days of seeing just what that entailed.

Until this angel came along. I've never once had to so much as tell him he did something incorrectly. It's like he was made for me. Well worth the $100,000 I spend on his salary every year.

The one he pushed back toward me was a young woman, barely legal age. She had that baby look about her too, which directly contrasted with how she chose to model, which was barely clothed. Tastefully, yes, but she *looked* so damn young, I wasn't sure I was willing to sell that.

Yes, there was a market for that, but it's personally against my morals. I wanted someone who looked mature and like they've lived a life, while also being flawless, confident, and sexy as fuck. Not asking for a lot.

Aside from her age, I didn't like the shape of her eyes. And her eye color was your everyday run-of-the-mill blue. Nothing special about it.

"Okay," Malcolm said, pulling the headshot from me. "You're going to make her picture cry if you keep glaring at her like that."

I snorted, tossing my hair over my shoulder. Pulling out my compact travel mirror, I clicked it open and gazed into it. My eyes were dark today. Though it wasn't biologically possible, I felt like their exact shade changed depending on my mood. They were charcoal gray. The combination of their rare color and the shade I kept my hair dyed – deep red/purple – I wasn't a face you quickly forgot.

Of course, I took great care of the rest of me, too. I spent a good amount of time hiking to counter my weakness for mocha frappuccinos and cookies. I couldn't exactly sell perfection if I didn't look the part, now could I?

Assured that I hadn't so much as a sweat streak, I clicked it shut and looked at Malcolm. "I think I'm going to take a break from this today. Maybe tomorrow I'll see things differently."

His smile said he didn't believe that, but he nodded. "I'll renew the audition notice."

"You're too good to me." I stood and kissed his cheek on the way by.

My studio was on Madison Avenue in downtown New York. It didn't matter what time of day you walked outside, it was always busy. There were always lights, whether it be from the sun or streetlights, car lights, or windows. The city never sleeps.

I tended not to carry a bag. Although I haven't often felt unsafe, usually keeping to the busiest parts of the city, it was my motto not to give a thief reason to look at you. My apartment and studio were both keycoded so that I didn't need to carry keys. If I couldn't pay with one of the apps on my phone, I wouldn't shop in that location.

Therefore, the only things I had in my pockets were my compact mirror and my cell.

I stopped at a coffee shop and ordered a pastry before sitting at one of the small tables to watch the passers-by outside. Maybe I'd get lucky and find perfection walking down the street. That would be too convenient.

My phone rang and I answered it without looking.

"Nuke Studios."

"Hey, Sister."

I grinned, turning away from the window. "Hey, Jessie. How's school?"

"It's great. We're getting to the dissection section and, thankfully, they have an option to dissect digitally. I could never bring myself to cut open a real animal.

I scrunched my nose. "No, I agree. I'm glad they have that option for you."

My sister was nineteen. Her dream had always been to be a biologist. She didn't know what she wanted to specialize in, but she loved biology in general. Our mother was a single mother and only ever just barely made it by. Anything more than a community college looked out of reach for my sister.

So when I started making serious money a few years ago, I determined that I'd pay for her schooling and that I'd start to encourage my mother to accept my help. She lived in Terrytown. You know, Sleepy Hollow. Although she mostly walked around the small town, it limited her on where she could go. I bought her a car a few months ago, telling her it was a birthday present just so she couldn't deny it.

I loved taking care of them both. Spoiling my family was one of the joys in my life. It was always my driving force for finding the next big shot. The next face and body that I could sell to billboards, television, and fashion.

I'd already outdone myself this year, but I was so close to my first seven figure year, I *had* to get it!

"How's the pretty faces?" Jessie asked.

I laughed. "Meh. I think I'm running out of pretty faces to sell."

Jessie giggled. "There are eight billion people in the world, Nuke. There's no way you've found them all."

"I've found the only ones that are worth anything. I swear, there's usually some massive flaw that I just can't work around."

"I think your standards are far higher than industry standards. A six on your scale is off the charts gorgeous anywhere else."

I always thought she and Malcolm would get along great. He's told me those exact words many times. Except he says my threes are off the charts. Jessie's standards were high, too.

"Be that as it may, if I find a ten in my book, that means I can sell their first contract for well into six figures. Even a nine I can scrape 100,000 for." I sighed. "But enough about business. What else do you have going on?"

"Well, the campus has been noisy since they're remodeling one of the dorms right now. From what I can tell, it's going to be pretty cool. I think I'm going to sign up for a marine biology course next year, just to check it out. And maybe geology."

"Sounds fun. Which are you most looking forward to?"

She sighed, "I don't know."

I found myself watching outside again, absently tracking people as they walk by. Judging them. The way they held themselves. The way they walked. The way they watched people in turn.

"I think marine biology," Jessie answered eventually. "I know it's just an intro, but we have a marine bio lab on campus, and I'll be able to check out the seals, turtles, and penguins they're nursing. And sometimes they have a stingray."

I smiled at her excitement. That I could give this to her was everything. "That sounds great, Jessie."

"Yeah. Will you come visit next semester? Check it out with me?"

"Absolutely. It's been a while since I visited you. We're about due for some sisterly fun."

I was distracted when a man across the street caught my eye. He was stunning but it wasn't the reason I spotted him. My gaze had flickered over him several times. Meaning he'd been standing there for a while.

Standing there staring at me.

"Had any hot dates recently?" Jessie asked slyly.

I laughed, turning away from the window. He wasn't staring at me, just staring in this direction. I doubted he could even see me through the glare on the window. "No. I think I've ruined myself for dating. No one will ever be good enough."

"Nuke, that's sad. You don't want to be alone forever, do you?"

It wasn't something I thought about seriously. My life was pretty busy or at least full of people and events that took my attention. It didn't occur to me that I could get lonely.

"I'm really focused on finding one more client this year," I told her. "And then I'll examine whether or not I'm lonely."

"No, you won't," Jessie said, and I could hear her eyes rolling in her voice. "Then you'll be focused on next year. You should hand over more responsibility to Malcolm so you can focus more on you."

"You've been talking to mom, haven't you?" I asked, narrowing my eyes. Mom had literally just said this to me two nights ago.

"No. Well, yes. I talk to mom all the time. But if I sound like her in this instance, it's because we both know you well enough to know that you're always going to be focused on the next project. You will always put yourself as a last priority."

"Not true, Jessie. I'm very high up on my priority list. However, I'm certainly not lonely enough to want to seek company for more than a night or two. If I was, I'd do something about it."

"Promise?"

I smiled. I was nine years older than Jessie, but sometimes she acted like the older sister. "I promise." Getting to my feet, I threw away my napkin and set the dish in the bin before I headed onto the sidewalk.

The man across the street was still there. Still staring. And as I moved, it became apparent that he was, in fact, watching me.

Did I know this man? Had I rejected his audition? I've never had a run-in with an angry model before.

No. This man wasn't a model. There was something dark and dangerous about him. Something that said I ought to get somewhere safe.

"Jessie, I need to stop at the store. Call you later?"

"Sure. Love you, Sister."

"Love you too." I hung up and kept my finger poised over the emergency button that would immediately dial the cops.

There were never enough police in a city this size but there were usually one or two close no matter where you were. I hurried down the street, catching his reflection in large windows as I went. He was still following me.

Maybe I should just confront him. See what he wants. Make a scene so he'll go away.

Instead, I dipped into The Morgan Library and Museum. As soon as I was inside, I scanned the app on my phone and moved to lose myself in the aisles. It wasn't the easiest place to get lost in since it wasn't a normal library with rows and rows of books. It was filled with old texts, safely locked away in caged bookshelves.

The architecture of the building was just as amazing as

what was inside. Tall ceilings with painted frescoes, and stone infrastructure carved in Old World beauty. But there wasn't anywhere to hide.

This was a bad idea. Okay, I'll just slip into the ladies' room for a while and then leave through the side entrance. With a plan in place, I headed into the ladies' room and then further into a stall. Shutting myself in, I waited, calming myself down with a routine check in my little mirror.

Ugh, my expression gave away my stress! How frustrating. I took a couple deep breaths as I arranged my hair and brushed my cheeks with my fingers, I leaned back against the stall wall and waited.

The door opened as I slipped my mirror back into my pocket. The tapping of high heeled shoes moved through the room, and I tracked her by the sounds of her footfalls. To a stall. Doing her business. To the sink to wash her hands. To the dryer. Out the door.

I yawned and stretched my back. When I got home, I was going to throw myself on the couch and take a nap. Get into some comfortable lounge clothes. Text my sister to tell her I'll call her tomorrow. And just relax the rest of the day.

Minutes went by in the silence, and I was confident that the danger had passed. If there had been danger. It was probably my imagination. The man walking in the same direction as me probably wasn't even the one who had been watching me from across the street. I was just imagining the stress.

I opened the stall door and walked to the sink to rinse my hands. Even though I didn't use the bathroom, I always feel like I need to wash my hands when I'm in a public bathroom. You don't know what kind of germs are here.

Another yawn escaped me, and I looked up into the

mirror. A yelp escaped my throat as I spun around to face my stalker. Yep, I was calling him a stalker.

"Hi," he greeted, a smile on his face. His hands clasped behind his back as if to make himself appear less threatening.

Right.

"I don't carry money on me," I told him. "Nor do I wear jewels. I have nothing you'd want."

He tilted his head to the side. "On the contrary. You have exactly what I want." He advanced on me, and I swear, there were four more shadows in the room.

The man reached for me, and I dodged him. Before I could scream, the lights cut out and a hand wrapped over my mouth. I kicked, flailing blindly as I tried to wrench myself free.

"I suspect this will be less painful if you stop fighting," the man said, and I screamed all the louder.

Not that it helped. It was as if he'd taken my voice and I was under a ton of fluff. I was making noise but for all the good it did me, I may as well be silent.

The mirror shattered and the man sighed. "I should have just brought a dagger. I hate leaving a mess behind."

The emergency light finally kicked on in the bathroom. I blinked rapidly as my eyes adjusted. My vision cleared just in time to watch the man bring down a shard of glass and embed it into my chest. The hand fell away from my mouth and then another was covering it. Warm liquid filled with a gross metallic tang dripped into my mouth and down my throat as I weakly tried to get away.

No point. I was dying. And this psycho man who thought he was a vampire was feeding me his blood. Great. Just the way I wanted to die.

CHAPTER THREE
ANUKA

I woke up gasping, my hand going to my chest. Without opening my eyes, my fingers brushed against my shirt.

Sighing in relief, I relaxed. Just a dream. My shirt wasn't even ripped.

Yet, I almost gagged at the taste in my mouth. It tasted like I'd bit my tongue so bad that it bled, and I haven't brushed my teeth yet. That coppery gross taste of old blood lingered on my tongue.

Taking a breath, I opened my eyes. And then opened them wider when five faces hovered over me. It was almost comical at first. They were around me like I'd passed out and they were waiting to see how I'd fair. I felt like I was in a cartoon or a comic book.

Then I recognized the man who had attacked me.

Bolting upright, the five of them scattered back so I wouldn't slam my head into theirs. I scampered off the lounge. The room spun and the floor came at me before hands caught me. I wrenched away and ended up on the floor anyway, but I didn't fall. The hands let me go but only after I landed safely on the ground.

I took a minute to let my head settle. To force the walls to stop rolling over. After a deep breath, I looked up, shifting until I could find the man who had followed me into the bathroom.

But I was distracted. We were not in the bathroom anymore. It looked like old architecture where there were decorative elements on the wall and ceiling, that were all painted a dark charcoal color. But as if the room was made for me, there were also pops of purple everywhere. The rug. The table. A flower. A blanket.

I didn't know what to demand first.

My head hurt. I needed some Advil.

Before I could speak, one of the men approached me, crouching down to get closer to eye level. He was attractive, with dark eyes, light hair, and a strong jaw covered in unmanicured hair. His white button-down shirt was open revealing a perfectly smooth, hard torso.

"Hi, princess," he said. "The dizziness will pass in a minute."

"Did you drug me?" I asked, thankful that my voice was steady. I looked down, noting that my shirt was in fact in one piece. No rips or tears.

"No, of course not," he said.

"You say that as if you're appalled and yet, you've moved me somewhere while I was passed out."

He smiled and it transformed his features to something almost sexy. My heart stuttered before I shut that down. Whoever these men were, they weren't good people.

And then I thought maybe I was seeing things. When he shifted his head, I swear there were horns on his head. Just for a second. Enormous ribbed horns that started at the back of his skull and twisted around to the front, like he was a bull.

I shifted backward, staring at him warily.

"I am appalled," he said, "though not surprised since Malak's ability to woo a woman is fucked."

Someone behind me snorted.

"I'm Hayt."

I raised a brow. "Hate? The opposite of love?"

He chuckled and my heart stuttered again. That sound, so deep and inviting.

Fuck.

"Yes but spelled slightly differently."

I nodded, wondering what kind of parent names their kid that.

"That's Zyphon. Bael. Malak. And Kingsley." He gestured to the men surrounding me, waiting for me to look at the one he was pointing to before telling me their name.

"Where am I?" I asked.

"Well..." he said, getting to his feet and offering me his hand. I raised a brow. He thinks that after he told me their names that I trust him now? He can't possibly be that naïve. When I didn't give him my hand but remained where I was, Hayt smiled, turning his attention away.

Following where he was looking, my gaze landed on Malak. The man who stalked me into a bathroom.

"My home," Malak said.

"Stalking. Assault. Abduction. What other crimes can I pin you with?" I asked.

"Murder," he answered, frowning. "In order to get you here, I killed you."

My breath caught. The phantom pain of glass being plunged into my chest made me shiver. And then...

"Are you going to try and tell me you're a vampire?" I asked, scowling at him. How fucking unsanitary if he really did try to drown me in his blood.

The appalled look he gave me had the others chuckling. I'd have laughed if this wasn't an extravagantly fucked-up situation.

"No," Malak said. He closed the distance between us and hauled me to my feet, his hands on my upper arms. I swayed and he held me still until I could balance on my own. Then I pulled away and stared at him, demanding an answer. "I'm the son of Satan, Anuka. One of the strongest demons in existence."

Delusional. I see. "Right. And these guys are your slaves?"

The various bursts of laughter and scoffing had Malak grinning. "They fucking should be, but sadly, no."

I pinched the bridge of my nose. "What was so important that you murdered me- wait." I looked up at him in horror. "You *murdered* me?"

Malak nodded. Absolutely no remorse on his face.

The world shifted again, my vision condensing to focus on just him. My breath caught as tears stung my eyes. Was it fear I was feeling? Helplessness, maybe?

Whatever it was, I threw my weight into punching him in the face. More laughter broke out until I continued trying to hit him. Kingsley pulled me off him, but I struggled to get free and continue attacking him.

"You asshole," I shouted. "I was paying for my sister's school! I was getting ready to buy my mother a house. I was so damn close to making a million dollars. And you took all that away!!"

The laughter stopped and finally their smiles fell.

No one spoke. I was so pissed that I actually let my tears fall. How would my sister continue to finish school? Who was going to pay for it? What would happen to my business? To Malcolm? I'd built that damn thing from the ground up.

Angrily, I wiped at my face and then froze. Fuck. Usually the makeup I wore was waterproof but I'd been killed so who knows what my makeup looks like right now.

Without thinking about it, I reached into my pocket, moving away from Kingsley so he wasn't touching me, and pulled out my mirror. The phone was gone. Probably lost back in the bathroom. I inwardly flinched. I could only imagine what stories would circulate about my disappearance.

Clicking the mirror open, I lifted it and froze. My hair was a fucking wreck but that's not what made me stare. Turning my head to get a better look with a different angle, I reached up with my free hand.

"Horns?" I asked in disbelief. "You gave me fucking horns?"

Not just horns. They were small and blunt, maybe two or so inches, and they glowed with a purple fire that danced.

"What the actual fuck?!"

"No, I didn't give you horns," Malak said. "Your soul chose the type of demon you became when I brought it here."

I shook my head, still not believing this. "What kind of demon am I?"

He didn't answer. When I looked up, he was staring at me. I was glad to see that he had a bright red mark on his face where I solidly landed that first punch.

"I don't know," he answered. "I'm thinking perhaps a shax, but they don't have horns. The energy around your horns is reminiscent of their race, though."

I shut my mirror and stuffed it into my pocket again.

Rubbing my temples, I tried to decide what to do. Five big men – demons – that I couldn't outmaneuver. Especially not on their turf. I couldn't overpower them.

"Why am I here?" I asked.

"Will you sit?" Hayt asked. "You're swaying and I worry that you're going to fall again."

I glared at him, but he wasn't wrong. I was definitely swaying. After looking around, I found myself back on the lounge I'd awoken on.

"I'm Malak," Malak said, placing a hand on his chest. There was a slight uplift to the way he stood, as if he were straightening his shoulders. I rolled my eyes. "I'm the Prince of Pride. Years ago, my father, Satan, decided he was going to be an ass and cursed my brothers and I that we'd be unable to rule our lands with the magic belonging to it until we found our queens. Only then could his heir be named as the next ruler of Hell. You are my queen. I've gone through many women to find the right one. Meanwhile, Father has disappeared, and my brothers and I are in a race to be the first to find our queen. What I need from you is for you to be able to touch and control the magic here. Once you do, I will have access to the magic too. Then I'll be the king I'm meant to be, and you my dutiful queen."

This was a joke, right? Did Malcolm set this up? Or my sister, maybe? She was constantly on me about doing something other than work.

When it was clear that he was convinced of his ridiculous story, I snorted. "There's so much wrong with that, I can't decide which question to ask first."

Bael moved towards me cautiously and took a seat next to me. He gently touched my hand as he looked at me imploringly. "It sounds fantastical, I know. But we can prove at least some of this to you."

"Oh yeah?"

"The fact that Malak killed you and you're alive, for starters," Kingsley said.

I didn't point out that since they'd managed to knock me out, and there wasn't actually any evidence on me that proved I'd been murdered, this could all just be an elaborate prank. I was choosing to ignore the horns on my head right now. I'd explain those away later.

"I'm a devourer, a demon who eats souls," Bael said. "I can show you."

"By eating my soul?" I raised a brow.

He smiled and he reminded me of a neighbor. The kind that was cute and didn't know it. Sweet and kind and oblivious that people around him thought he was gorgeous.

Oh, wait. I hadn't realized I thought he was. Further proof to my assessment of him.

"Of course, not."

"You're going to turn into a demon?"

"No," he said, smiling. "I'm always a demon. But sometimes we parade around as humans so as not to terrify the people of Earth into thinking the world is ending."

"Right. Okay. Prove away."

I stared in growing horror as the sweet man beside me slowly morphed into something... well... demonic. Terrifying. His body mass increased by like three or four times. His skin turned sallow green with red marks that looked like a toddler dragged a paintbrush all over his body. He had two nasty sets of horns coming out of his head and periodic spines along his shoulders and down his arms.

But his face... that was what nightmares were made of. It was both skeletal and covered in flesh with glowing red eyes in black sockets. His teeth... well, I didn't know what a soul was made of, but those teeth looked like they could tear apart anything.

That it happened before my eyes was the part that truly petrified me. Green screen? Or was I hallucinating? Back on the idea of drugs.

His image faded back into the boy next-door as he watched me with a careful smile. I realized I'd moved away from him when he wasn't nearly as close as when he sat down.

For a minute, I just stared at him. What was I supposed to do with this? Seriously!

"Do you all look like that?" I asked.

Bael shook his head. "We're different races of demons. So we look different. Have different abilities. Different amounts of power."

I nodded. "And me? As a- what did you say?" I looked back at Malak.

"I don't think you're actually a shax," he said, "but maybe. They don't have horns but the energy surrounding your horns is very shax-like."

"A shax feeds off pride," Hayt said. "Like a vampire, though there's no biting involved. They use one's pride as an energy source."

I frowned. Maybe it made sense if my soul chose that. I made reading someone's pride a career.

"How can I go home?" I asked. I didn't miss Bael exchanging a look with Kingsley. As did Hayt and Zyphon. But Malak kept his eyes trained on me.

"You don't go home," he said. "You're trapped here until you can control the magic. And if you don't, you die here."

"I thought I was already dead."

"You die again. I brought you back to life with my

blood. But if you die here, unable to wield the magic, it's permanent."

"You're scum," I said, leaning back into the lounge.

Kingsley snickered, a grin spreading across his face. Malak's eyes narrowed.

"So, tell me about this magic."

"Each circle of Hell has its own magic," Zyphon said. "It's both the same and different depending on which circle you're in. It needs to be controlled or it starts tearing apart the fabric of the circle and causing all kinds of chaos. And it's certainly been left unchecked for far too long. We have the appearance of pridefalls, which are pride demons who have succumbed to a different sin. They turn into base monsters set on destroying everything around them. There are other nuances but that's the idea."

"And how am I supposed to control it?"

"I like that she's asking questions," Hayt said. "That's promising."

Zyphon smiled. "We don't know. The curse that Lucifer left on his sons is vague at best. And thus far, all the sons have been interpreting it how they feel it would work best for them. When in reality, what they want is the furthest thing from helpful."

Malak pressed his lips together, glaring at Zyphon.

"They're not your slaves and they clearly don't think you're too clever," I said to Malak. "So who are they to you?"

Kingsley laughed. Although Zyphon and Hayt tried to hide their amusement, I didn't miss their smiles. Bael was the only one that frowned at me.

"Believe it or not, they're friends," Malak said. "They're getting close to being tossed out, though."

I sighed, got to my feet, and looked at his smug face with a frown. The arrogance in his stance, the self-importance in his gaze, the haughtiness in his precisely disheveled hair. He thought he was special. Important. Perfect. His arrogance was almost a tangible thing.

"Is that it?" I asked, glowering. "You'd never make it as a model. Not even a social media model." I looked at him up and down, taking in his whole appearance. "You'd be lucky if I could turn you into a thirst trap."

The indignation on his face was only slightly satisfying as I crossed my arms in annoyance.

"And you think you did me a favor," I said, narrowing my eyes, "by killing me to make me your fucking queen of this hellhole?!"

"Yes," Malak said. "You're a queen. How is that not better than the life you left behind?"

"I'll tell you what," I said, turning for the closest door, thankful when the world remained upright. "You've clearly not gotten anywhere on your own, and will obviously be no help given the lack of success you've told me about. So you boys sit tight. I'll take care of this on my own."

CHAPTER FOUR
ANUKA

I got to the door before they caught up. It didn't stop me and thankfully, no one put a hand on me.

"Where are you going?" Malak demanded.

"To find competent demons to help me," I answered.

The silence that followed me, including their footsteps faltering, made me smile. I was only slightly distracted by the extravagance of this place. It really was breathtaking in an all-around obnoxious way. And seriously, the pops of purple were amazing.

"Where do you think you're going to find help that we can't give you?" Zyphon asked.

I shrugged. "It can't be that hard."

One of them growled behind me. I tended to think it was the prince himself. I wasn't stroking his ego. But really, they've been stuck under this curse for how long? Enough that many other women have come before me.

Besides, if I couldn't leave this place until I controlled the magic here, I was going to put goddamn reins on it and ride it like a fucking bull. I was getting home to my sister and mother. And if these demons were useless, I was going to find people who weren't.

I turned down a hall and found stairs leading down. Based on the glimpses I'd caught out windows that I passed, I was willing to bet we were up a couple floors at least. So I started down them, skimming my hand over the railing as I went. Both to make sure I wouldn't suddenly get dizzy and fall to my second death, but also because they were so smooth.

As soon as my feet hit the bottom floor, a chorus of arguments broke out behind me. But I'd spotted the door and didn't stop moving until I reached it. With my hand on the handle, I turned around and watched as the five demons stopped short.

Apparently, their agitation (and perhaps my little truths that they took as insults) had made some of their human features fade. Many of them now sported horns. Glowing red eyes. A flickering skeletal tail that moved with the annoyance of a cat's. Kingsley had massive wings that look like they'd been torn apart in a shredder. Swiss cheese in wing form, right there. And Zyphon? He had three fucking tails, all of which were whipping around in irritation.

"I clearly get under your skin," I noted with a pleased smile. "Look. It sounds like you've had plenty of time to get the magic under control and you've failed." I held up my hand when several of them tried to protest, stopping them from speaking. "Evidence states that you're not the best candidates for the job. It's nothing personal, even if I am pissed that you murdered me to be your ridiculous queen without my permission. I built my life on judging people worthy and I'm sorry, you don't make the cut."

"You know nothing about this place," Malak growled.

"Even if I'm trying to accept your logic and look past your treasonous insults, how do you expect to find the kinds of demons that could help you in a place you haven't even seen outside my house?"

"As I said, I made a life out of judging people. And if I fail, you're no worse off, right? You just start again with a new woman you have no regard for."

There was no argument though many frowns remained on me. When a minute passed and they didn't speak, I turned the handle and opened the door.

Then stopped short.

If it wasn't for the architecture and the odd purple glow at every line and corner, I'd say I had been transported to Venice. There were no streets but waterways branching off in every direction, cutting through city blocks. The water went right to the sides of the building and in some areas, the doors were at water level.

There were many boats like those in Venice, though their shapes were different. They looked older and not as sleek. There wasn't a motor in sight or hearing. Yet they moved with speed and agility along the smooth surface.

And can we just talk about the water for a minute? It had beautiful, crystalline clear channels. And under the surface were mermaids and...

Was that a fucking water dragon?

"Damn," I whispered.

"Will you at least let me show you around?" Kingsley asked as he stepped out the door and to my side.

"No," I answered, turning to walk down the stairs toward the cobblestone path. There was a bridge that connected this piece of the city with the next. City block? Is that what I'm supposed to call these parts that were broken up by water?

"Anuka," Kingsley called.

I waved him off. Actually, I was surprised that they let me walk out at all. And again when they didn't follow me when I said no. Demons that respected boundaries, yet were quick to murder me to get what they want. It was a strange conundrum.

I paused at the peak of the bridge and looked into the water. There was a group of mermaids – were male mermaids called mermen? – that swam under the surface. One of the guys spiraled around as he moved. The water was so clear that I could see the sun glisten off their scales.

They were an enchanting mixture of blue and purple scales and hair. Even their eyes.

"This place was made for me," I murmured as I walked down the opposite side of the bridge. I paused there to look around.

Where would I find a whole bunch of people? A bar? Did Hell have bars? Meeting halls? This architecture looked old-school. Ancient gothic spires and decorative elements. Maybe that meant they had a tavern or pub.

I scanned the opposite shore as I walked, careful to make sure I wasn't headed in a direction that would end and I'd have to either swim across or try to figure out how to charge a boat ride to the prince of Hell.

The population in the water was heavy with mermaids. But there were also the water dragons. And then some hybrid thing that was perhaps a cross between the two. It had wings, fins, maybe some suction cups. Its wings looked like granite. Their bodies a smooth marble.

Maybe they were gargoyles?

These two species tended to make up a lot of the bodies within this heavenly water city. But then there were those with grayish skin and strange blue-purple hair. I swear, there were smokey purple tentacles surrounding them.

Absently, I touched one of my horns. Maybe they were one of the races of demons that Malak had said I could be. A shax? Should I ask one?

Interspersed less frequently were more frightening-looking people who definitely brought to mind the image of a demon. And then there were those who looked human, which, based on what I'd seen in the prince's house I just left, they were likely some of the nastier demons in human bodies.

I watched them, seeing where they were headed. When I found several go into a single door, I decided that was my destination. It took me a moment on the path to find a course over the many bridges but after I mapped out my route, I spent the walk admiring the city.

Even the most demon-looking had their own beauty to them that somehow blended in and made the whole area look enchanting. Though most of the buildings were abutted right up to the water, there were some channels that had walkways alongside the water. And those usually led to a bridge crossing.

I paused on another bridge as I watched some domestic activities. Demons snapping their wash over a balcony. Hanging flower boxes being tended. Even the scent of dinner cooking wafted to me through the air.

Taking a deep breath, I closed my eyes for a moment and listened to the sounds. The talk and the movement of water. The clanking of dishes and the snap of a towel.

When I looked at the water, one of the mermen had poked up his head, giving me a flirty grin. I smiled back and carried on. Just one more bridge and I'd be on the correct city block. I watched in the opposite direction, on the thin walkway were lines of tables for two at a restaurant.

"This is not what I thought Hell would look like," I muttered. "It's so... human."

I turned back and found I'd made it to the building I was aiming for. There was a large demon outside, one of the freaky kind. I paused a dozen steps away and waited to see what he was asking for when someone approached. One demon was acknowledged as he walked past with a slight bow of the head. Another was asked for an ID.

Frowning, I thought I'd take my chances.

"ID," the big demon asked me. His eyes were like burning sapphires.

"I'm the newly murdered queen-elect," I told the man. "Besides that, I didn't realize they issued IDs in Hell."

He frowned at me. "I can't let you in without an ID."

"I just told you who I am, and I watched you let a man in without one," I demanded. "Do you really want me to go get the worthless demons I just left so they can make you let me in?"

"Worthless-"

His words cut off as something in me flared, bringing with it a sting as though I'd just stuck my finger into a light socket. Just for a second. Enough that I felt the jolt run through me.

"Sorry, Your Majesty. You may go in," the demon said, taking a step away from me.

So, he felt it, too then. Good to know. "Good idea," I told him. But I paused, feeling how rude that was. "Thank you for reconsidering."

He bowed his head, and I stepped inside.

Yep, definitely a tavern of sorts. Not a modern bar. At least not like one I've been in. There was a fire burning in a large hearth at one side of the room. A long bar that took up almost the entire length of one wall. And more than a dozen round wooden tables throughout the rest of the room.

And the patrons were mostly of the more badass-looking demons. Not the common ones that I saw plenty of; ones that looked human. While others were a cross between the two. They were littered around tables, along the bar, and some were dancing where a man was playing a weird instrument I didn't recognize. The tune was nice and haunting. I wasn't sure the dancers were really feeling the beat since their movements were a lot more quick and sensual than slow and rhythmic.

I moved throughout carefully studying everyone while being mindful not to stare. I caught many curious watchers as I moved, many eyes tracking me as I wove slowly through the space.

The guys said a shax can feed off pride as a source of energy like a vampire does blood. I wondered if they felt it. I didn't see anyone feeling any differently when I walked past them, nor did I feel any different. I was willing to bet I wasn't a shax.

Curious that I made my own species of demon. And all I had to show for it was a set of sexy little purple fiery horns. There are worse things in the world, anyway. Worse looks.

My gaze caught on a man standing against a beam, arms crossed over his chest as he looked around the room. His eyes were dark crystalline blue that reminded me of the water outside. His hair was messy, and a quiet smile played on his perfectly kissable lips.

But what caught my attention beyond that he was good-looking was the way he was reading the room. By the way his eyes lingered on someone, it made me think that he was learning something about them. Judging something about them.

And since he was in this room, I thought it safe to assume he was a badass of some kind.

Decision made, I headed his way, keeping my measured pace as I went. He spotted me when I was halfway to him, a bright red flash ignited his pupils before dying down. Yep, badass.

Standing in front of him, I smiled, enjoying the way his gaze drifted over me and a different kind of smile touched his lips.

"I'm Nuke," I introduced. "I was recently murdered to be your new queen but since I think the idiots in charge are about as capable as a ladybug, I'm looking for more competent demons to assist me in learning to tame the magic that's running rampant. Are you interested?"

Amusement lit his face though it was still relaxed in that lazy, sure way that someone entirely confident in themselves is. He didn't speak but nodded.

"Great. I'm looking for more demons. Two more maybe? Any suggestions?"

His gaze swept away, and he nodded in the direction of the bar and although he still didn't speak, I knew who he was referring to without him giving me any further indication. There was something still and haunting that hung about the demon. Sitting on a stool in a suit and watching the bartender mix drinks with a little bit of flair in throwing the bottles, I could see those around him were eying him warily. And they weren't sitting nearly as close to this demon as they were pressed shoulder to shoulder with others at the bar.

"Yep, I can see his... appeal. I'll be right back."

The man I needed a name for nodded and I made my

way down the bar. I didn't need to squeeze myself in between this man and the one next to him. There was far more than a person's body width before the next stool.

He turned to me when I pressed to his side. A brow raised in surprise. As if making a point that no one touched him.

"Hi," I said, smiling into his dark eyes made darker by the light hair on his head. It was in direct contrast to the dark scruff on his face. Yet, I didn't think either were dyed. That was just him. "My name is Nuke and I'm the recently murdered queen-to-be. I need demons capable of helping me learn the magic here since the prince is lame. That man in the corner suggested you might be interested in helping me in addition to him."

He looked beyond me, a curious smile hinting across his mouth. "Eko?"

I blinked a couple times. "I don't know what answer you want from me."

His dark eyes landed on me again, his smile spreading. "The man in the corner? Right? Probably didn't speak at all?"

"Sounds right, yes."

"That's Eko."

"Ah. I was wondering how I'd get his name from him if he didn't speak."

This new man chuckled. "He speaks. Sometimes he doesn't shut up."

I grinned. "Good. And you are?"

"Rhyl."

"Okay, Rhyl. Are you interested in helping me?"

"I definitely have some questions but it sounds more entertaining than anything else at the moment."

"Awesome. Thank you."

Rhyl nodded. I looped my arm with his and pulled him to his feet, leading him back towards Eko. Eko remained amused as he watched us approach. When we were together again, I turned back towards the room. "Okay, demons. I need one more. Who's the next biggest baddie?"

This time Eko pointed. I tried to follow where he was indicating but it was clear that he was signaling for someone dancing.

"Alright, which one, Eko?"

"Blonde wearing a purple dress."

I turned to look at Eko because that hadn't been Rhyl's voice. I grinned at him and made my way to the dancers but paused when I tried to find the woman in a purple dress. It took me more than a minute to find said person, but it wasn't a woman. A man with white blonde hair and equally light eyes was wearing a loose purple dress and dancing in the group. His hands were all over everyone, and theirs were on him in turn.

I glanced back at Eko. Him? Really?

As if I'd asked the question out loud, Eko smiled and nodded.

Sighing, I turned back. By the time I was facing the dancers again, the blonde man in a dress had spotted me and was watching me with a sexy smile. And the way his hips moved was almost hypnotizing.

He shimmied and gyrated his way through the crowd toward me and offered me a hand. I took it but when he tried to pull me into the dance, I dug my feet in until he tilted his head. Then I tugged him away from the dancers.

Curious, he followed. His eyes never left me as I fumbled my way back to the other two. Since I wasn't doing a good job watching, I wasn't at all surprised when I backed straight into one of them. A hand landed on my hip. This new man moved into my space, the heat from his body making me sweat. And suddenly, as if I haven't been touched in years, my entire body came alive with heat in my blood.

Focus!

"My name is Nuke," I said.

The new man tilted his head, both his brows raising. "Nuke. Like a nuclear weapon?"

I nodded. "Yep."

He grinned and it was enough that my pussy clenched around nothing. "I'm the newest trial queen, but I'm going to make it happen. I need help from men who are more competent than the ones who murdered me."

"Queen," he repeated. "The demon who murdered you was Malak?"

"Correct."

His smile grew and he licked his lips. "I see. You don't find them adept in pride's circle of Hell?"

I rolled my eyes. "I'm far, far from their first attempt at finding a queen to get the magic under control, something they readily told me."

"There've been a dozen or so to my knowledge but maybe more," he agreed, nodding.

"And they've all failed. Which lends me to believe that they aren't capable of doing what I need in getting the magic in my control. Therefore, I'm hunting down my own team of demons."

His smile was almost radiant but there was certainly something behind it. Something I didn't know.

"Sounds like a good time," he said, nodding. "I'm in."

"Your name?"

"Revan. A name you'll know all too well before long."

"I don't know what that means, nor do I care. As long as you're more capable than they are."

He chuckled and once again heat seared through me as he leaned in. "I assure you, I'll be an asset to your merry little crew, Nuke."

I smiled at him before pulling myself away from between him and whichever of them was at my back. Looking at the three of them, I smiled.

Would you look at that. It took me less than an hour to find demons that would be useful to me. And they were pretty to look at. Even in a purple dress. Time to take a nap. I was still fucking tired.

CHAPTER FIVE
ANUKA

Stepping back outside, I paused. It hadn't occurred to me to look at the building I'd left. Malak's house. Since he was a prince, I expected a castle. Something dark and ominous, especially given how the inside was covered in dark charcoals with pops of purple everywhere.

But what I was looking at took up three city blocks. There were tall tunnels that went under and through the house. At the angle I was standing, I could see two sides. Enough to know that the place was enormous and that there was likely a labyrinth of tunnels of waterways under it. Even as I stared, one of the larger boats slipped into one and disappeared.

It was seven stories at its tallest peak from what I could see. Dark stone. The windows looked like they had a black sheen over them. And deep purple accents.

"Okay, not that I'm complaining because I love purple, but my first question for you is why is everything purple?" I asked, catching sight of one of the mermaid's hair. "Even the people."

"Purple is the color of pride. And it happens to be Malak's favorite color," Revan answered.

"Also, that house is massive," I added as I stared in reluctant awe at Malak's estate. It wasn't a castle or even some kind of fortification. It was a mansion. Some enormous estate.

He chuckled, draping an arm over my shoulders. "It is. Let's get back. Can't wait to see how this is going to go."

I glanced at him. The glint in his eyes said that I was going to be in for a show. I started walking before Revan caught my arm.

"Where are you going?"

"The path back is that way." I pointed, dragging my finger through the air to trace the path.

They were all smiling at me. Amused.

"I barely convinced them to let me in this place." I gestured to the bar or club or whatever it was we just left. "I wasn't going to try and figure out how to charge Prince Purple for a boat ride," I said. "Besides, this place is really pretty. It gave me time to look around."

"It's pretty," Rhyl agreed. "But there are darker sides that are becoming more problematic."

"Exactly. The longer the magic goes untamed," I said, nodding. "And thus why I sought out demons who would be useful." I let them lead me down to the side of the water to flag down a boat. A long canoe of sorts with high ends. "My understanding is if you look like a man, you're actually a badass demon. What kind of demons are you?"

"I'm an uvall," Rhyl said. "I see the past, present, and future in a continuous stream."

I stared at him, eyes wide. "Then you can tell me how to get the magic. Right? Tell me how I succeed!"

Revan laughed, pulling me against him and hugging

me. I smiled, leaning into him. It has been a long time since I've let someone hold me. It felt nice. This camaraderie.

"I love your confidence, Nuke."

"If you're already convinced you're going to fail, you likely will," I told him. "Besides, failure is not an option."

"Why's that?"

"I have a sister and mother to take care of and I can't very well do that if I'm dead."

The smile that lingered on Rhyl's lips was demure. Still amused, as if everything was slightly funny to him. "You think Malak will let his queen leave Hell?"

"You're under the impression he has a choice in the matter. I assure you, that's not the case."

Revan laughed again, kissing the side of my head. "You're already my favorite person."

Glancing at him over my shoulder, I asked, "And the kind of demon you are?"

He grinned. "Judgment Day." His smile turned dark and wicked. A glint of glowing alien green flashed in his eyes. "I determine the everafter of your soul."

Did the way his voice drop and become eerie as fuck make every hair on my body stand on end? Fuck yes, it did. I shivered, despite trying to keep it in.

That made me turn my attention to Eko. But our conversation paused as one of the canoes stopped at the edge of the waterway in front of us, allowing us to climb in. Revan was our voice and told the man where we were headed.

When we were settled for our few minutes' ride back, I looked at Eko again.

He ducked his head, looking up at me through his lashes. The smile on his lips was sweet, if not a little shy.

"Vessago. I can make an echo of your sins and soul to examine. And to torture you with."

I shivered again, looking at him wanly. Letting my gaze flicker between the three, I determined that I had indeed gathered some baddies. How they were going to help me control the magic, I didn't know. But I was positive it would happen.

I chewed on my lip, staring at the big house as we approached. House. Mansion. Extravagant monstrosity. Whatever.

The boat stopped in front of a set of stairs that descended into the water. As I stepped out, I looked down at them and saw that they continued into the depths. As if the ground was lower at one point. Maybe it wasn't always filled with water?

Revan led us to the two massive doors looming overhead. They were easily four times the height of an average man, coming to a sharp peak in the middle. The door handles – large rings - were at the height of my head and bigger than my face. There was a panel above and below the handles that were intricately carved with stereotypical Hellish scenes of death and torture. But the top halves of either side were different. One was a depiction of the sun rising and the other was... of the universe?

Revan opened the doors, pushing them in with little effort. We didn't need both doors open but he wasn't settling on just one. I assumed they were either lighter than they looked or well-greased. This wasn't the door I'd exited out of but somehow, the five demons who orchestrated my death were there waiting for my return.

None looked less pleased than Malak, though it was his disapproving scowl that I watched more than the curious array of emotions that flitted over the others' faces.

"Good news," I announced. "I found demons that haven't failed at this a dozen times already."

Maybe I was poking a beast. I was sure that a string of fire wound its way around Malak as he glared at me. His hands were fisted together, even where they were tucked across his chest. He stood rigid and furious.

"You can't just leave-"

I waved him off. "I can and I did. I've found what I'm looking for. Now, if you don't mind, I was exhausted *before* you murdered me, and a lot of bullshit has happened since then. I need a nap."

"Wait," Zyphon said. "What are you going to do with them?"

His expression was probably the most curious. Especially since three tails, wings, and horns were fighting to break out of his body. The look on his face didn't say he was angry though. There was turmoil, something he was fighting to keep inside.

"How did you find *them?*" Bael asked warily.

I glanced at the three demons I'd brought back. Eko's amused smile hadn't left as he watched everyone like this was high entertainment. Rhyl's was almost the same, though his gaze didn't look focused until it landed on me. But Revan was grinning wickedly.

"There's a place that didn't want to let me in," I said, waving towards the outside wall. "Filled with demons who look like men. I figured that was a good place to start and I scored right away. Met Eko first and he pointed out Rhyl and Revan. Do you know each other?"

Revan chuckled, shifting his dress so it wasn't so loose against his body, but showed off the hard planes of his abdomen, his thick legs, and the package that ran along the side of his thigh.

The shivers that raced over my body were very different this time as I turned back to the demons who killed me. It might just have been Malak who actually did the murdering, but something told me they were all involved somehow.

"So... a room would be nice. Or I can stay with one of them." I stuffed my fingers in my pocket, a hand immediately curling around my compact. It was such a small thing, but it brought me some comfort. Something from my life. Something that was mine and always brought me assurance.

"I'll show you to your room," Hayt said, stepping forward. "Unless you'd like a tour first."

"I wasn't exaggerating when I said I was tired. I want a nap."

He nodded and turned, pointedly ignoring the men I had with me. He gave his men a look I couldn't interpret in profile before heading down the hall. Hayt offered me a smile, urging me to follow him.

Too many halls, doors, and stairs later, Hayt pushed open a set of large double doors. Not nearly as big as the ones out front, but these were surely ten or so feet high. They swung open freely and he backed away.

The floors were white. The walls and curved architectural beams were a deep plum. The ceiling was painted to look like a cloudy sky. The furniture was in rich purple tones, interspersed with white to break it up and make it look sophisticated as opposed to gaudy. Touches of black metal and gold splashes brought it together.

And the room just went on and on. I spied a balcony that looked enormous. And a spiral staircase that went into the ceiling.

"This isn't Malak's room, is it?" I asked. It couldn't

possibly be a guest room. Too lavish and large. Besides that, I assumed if I was supposed to be his queen, that meant he had plans.

"No," Hayt said. "It's your room. The queen's."

"Okay, thanks."

He nodded and took a step back, still pointedly ignoring the men who had followed me in. "And them?" This time when he spoke, his words were stiff.

"They're my demons, thanks. They'll stay with me."

Hayt's shoulder's stiffened to match his tone. "If you need anything, just say one of our names in the hall and you'll be attended to."

"A map of the city," I said. "And maybe of this ostentatious house would be useful."

He smirked at that. "I don't know that there's a map of the house, but I have no doubt you'll be directed where you're interested in going without issue. A map of the city I can have sent up."

"Thanks."

He nodded, holding my gaze as if he were waiting for me to ask the right question. When Revan draped his arm over my shoulders, Hayt's lips pressed together. After another bob of his head, he backed out of the room and shut the door behind him.

"I'm not sure that was the show you were looking for," I said to Revan.

He laughed. "Oh, but it was. And just the beginning, too." He let me go and turned around to examine the room.

"Explain," I demanded as I began opening doors to see if there was clothing in here. I was distracted by the bathroom. Pretty sure it was the size of my entire apartment back in New York.

"Not much to explain. I have a history with them," Revan said as he dropped onto the couch.

"What kind of history?" I continued to stare at all the features of the bathroom, wondering if I wanted to wash the day away before my nap or not.

"Zyphon and I were lovers for a long time. And though I've had relations with all of them, since that's kind of how they roll, Zy and I were very close." I turned to look at him, narrowing my eyes. He grinned. "Malak was jealous. That came between us and Zy chose Malak." He shrugged.

Though I studied him for several minutes, I didn't see that it bothered him. He was looking out the balcony doors with a pleased smile. Like the last twenty minutes had been the highlight of his day.

He shifted and his dress rode up his leg. It was loose on him again, since he wasn't pulling it tight, but I could still see the way his dick lay across his thigh.

"Do you always wear dresses?" I asked.

The other two men were wandering around the room, peeking in drawers and doors as I was. Revan looked at me, a wicked smile on his lips again.

"Nah. This was because I lost a bet. But I enjoy the way my junk swings. It's very freeing."

I laughed as I opened a drawer, sighing when I finally found clothing. I pawed through it until I selected a pair of shorts and a tee shirt and headed for the bathroom once again. I stripped immediately, setting my mirror on the vanity, and used a washcloth to run over my body. Too tired for a shower or bath right now and I wanted to enjoy this experience so it would need to wait.

I quickly pulled the clothes on and stepped up to the sink to wash my face. In a drawer I found a toothbrush still in its packaging and toothpaste so I could finally get the gross taste of blood off my tongue.

And then I paused. I looked the same except for the horns on my head. And if I was being critical, they were a little big. Not nearly as delicate as I'd have preferred when choosing horns to wear for a party or something. But they were cute. And they didn't actually take anything away from my appearance. In fact, I kind of liked how they enhanced my eyes. How they flickered as if they were covered in a glow of magic fire.

Running my fingers over them again, I sighed. It was clear that I wasn't dreaming. This was real. I was murdered, fed some arrogant jackass's blood, and brought to Hell. All because the prince is lame as fuck and cannot get his own magic under control.

Leave it to a woman.

I smirked. That's fine. I got this. And I'll do it without him getting in my way.

Brushing my hair over my shoulder, I entered the bedroom again. Revan was on the balcony now, his purple dress pulled against his body as the wind took it. I shook my head. When I turned toward the bed, I found Rhyl and Eko leaning against different pieces of furniture as they watched me.

"So, I guess I don't really have a plan for you outside of helping me. That bed is huge though, so I don't mind sharing. And there's a whole bunch of furniture here so you're welcome to stay if you want to," I told them.

"Would you like us to stay?" Rhyl asked.

Biting my lip, I nodded. "I realize I know you just as well as I do them, but I feel a little more secure in that you didn't kill me and trap me in this Hell. And you're willing to help me without knowing anything about me. And you haven't asked for anything in return." I almost added 'yet' at the end of that. But I didn't want to put that thought in their heads. They're demons. Who knew what they'd actually ask for?!

"I'll stay," Eko said, nodding towards the bed. "Nap. We'll talk when you're rested."

Rhyl nodded his agreement and I relaxed. I didn't ask Revan, but he seemed happy enough to be along for the ride even if the only reason was to let his presence harass the others. I was sure he'd help between doing that.

Finally feeling a bit of peace, I climbed into the bed, sinking into the mattress and blankets. For Hell, this was probably the most comfortable bed I've ever been in. I wouldn't mind spending eternity within its warm embrace.

CHAPTER SIX
BAEL

We were already tense when Nuke left. Kingsley tried to follow her, but she blew him off. On the one hand, I loved the look of shocked rejection on his face when she told him no and gave him her back. On the other hand, how could we make sure she doesn't run into trouble alone?

She was brand new in Hell! And we hadn't even tried to convince her to wear a crown.

On the bright side, I've never been more convinced that this was the queen we've been waiting for. I was nearly convinced of that by the way Malak stared at her picture when Hayt presented her to us. But now that she was here, I was dead set positive she was the one.

Glancing at Malak as he stared furiously down the hall where Hayt led her and the three demons she brought home, I was a little less convinced that she was going to be able to unlock the magic for him.

That begged the question – can she control the magic without him? Does she somehow need him to touch the magic? And what if she can rein it in but somehow that doesn't help Malak if their relationship is... nonexistent?

"How did she manage to find Revan?" Zyphon asked.

I glanced at him. He was as devastated as Malak was furious. I could feel the fire burning under Malak's skin and the chill followed from Zyphon's mood.

"There are more than 100,000 demons in Pride. Why him?" Zyphon said, dropping his head back against the chair.

Malak looked his way and frowned. "There are more important concerns right now."

"Fuck off," Zyphon said halfheartedly. That he said it at all made my eyes go wide.

It made Malak stare at him, too. As if trying to determine whether he'd actually heard the words. They weren't said with any venom, and he hadn't actually opened his eyes. But he's never told Malak to fuck off before.

Hayt interrupted whatever might have resulted from that brief confrontation, if that's what it was, when he returned from showing Nuke to her room. He rubbed a hand over his face and dropped into a chair.

"Now what?" Kingsley asked. "We have your queen but I'm not sure she's interested in being yours at all."

"Your approach could have used a little improvement," Hayt pointed out.

Malak sighed heavily, frustrated, turning around to look at me as if I had an answer. I pressed my lips together. I wasn't sure anything I could say would be helpful right now.

"I need some strategy," Malak said through his teeth. Admitting he needed help without actually saying so.

"You think she's the right one, then?" Kingsley asked.

Our prince didn't answer right away. When he did, I thought it was grudgingly. "Yes. Maybe if I'd had any confidence that this curse was reversible I might have put some effort into actually talking to her before I brought her here. But all I wanted when I saw her-"

He didn't finish. Kingsley did for him.

"Was her." He smirked, enjoying seeing Malak this way. Wanting someone who wanted nothing to do with him.

Malak didn't agree but neither did he argue.

"Zy?" Hayt said. Zyphon opened his eyes but didn't pick up his head. The hurt that we thought was gone was almost glowing in his eyes. Having to choose between a man he loved and Malak had cost him a lot. I didn't think their relationship would survive that. And really, it was a shell of what it had been. Zyphon was here. He did his part because he loved Malak deeply. But since Malak forced him with an ultimatum, Zyphon hasn't gone anywhere near Malak. I always thought if Revan showed up again there would be a showdown and this time, Zy wouldn't be staying.

But he'd buried everything deep enough that we never saw so much as a hint of that turmoil. I think we thought he was over it, even though he's never fully forgiven Malak for being forced to give Revan up. Glancing at Malak, I could tell he saw the same thing I did. And those old wounds were split wide open unknowingly by the woman who was supposed to fix everything.

"What?" Zyphon answered, his voice dull.

"Ideas?"

He'd always been the best among us to put forth a solid plan that was successful more times than not. I think we'd come to rely on that.

"For what outcome?" The disinterest in his voice was thick. There was little other emotion there.

Hayt looked at Malak for an answer. I wasn't sure Malak's voice would be a good thing right now. Maybe he knew that because he looked at me in turn.

If Zyphon was the one who gave us successful plans, I was the one who usually determined what was the highest priority. The problem was, right now, I wasn't sure what it would be.

"I think we need to make it all equally important," I said. "Help Anuka reach the magic and learn to control it. I know she doesn't want us around but if we impress upon her that only the *queen* can actually use the magic, it will emphasize that she needs to know more than just magic. Those demons might be able to help her with the magic, but it will be us who helps her become queen." I paused, glancing at Malak. "And to be queen, she needs the king. So somehow we need to get her opinion of Malak to improve."

Zyphon pressed his lips together. Right now, might not be the best time to suggest something like that.

"But primarily, I think we should let the three demons she found ease her into Hell and help her with the goals she set out. I think if we try to overstep, it'll be counterproductive to what we need. So while they do their thing and we maybe somehow try to mend our own bridges with her, we continue to concentrate on what's breaking down in Pride."

"Fine," Zyphon said, getting to his feet and turning down the hall. "I'll let you know when I have an idea."

We watched him walk away. Only when he was out of sight did anyone speak. Thankfully, it wasn't me who had to point out the obvious. As much as I loved Malak, he needed some tough truths handed to him right now. Or he was going to watch this whole thing fall apart.

"You understand that if you get between Zy and Revan

again, he won't choose you this time, right?" Hayt asked Malak.

Malak frowned at him.

"Seeing Revan again is already tearing him apart and if that demon is going to be in this house for any length of time – which I'm assuming he will be since you're not going to agree to let Anuka stay somewhere else, right? – they will talk. And they will likely get back together. You're going to need to get your jealousy under control and accept that."

"Revan fucked this up to begin with," Malak said, crossing his arms. He didn't speak loudly and his gaze darted down the hall to where Zyphon had disappeared. "Zy has never been the same."

"I'm sorry you see it that way," Kingsley said, "since it's obvious to absolutely everyone else that this is *your* fault. Every issue we have right now falls on your shoulders, prince. Maybe you need a little humility so you can accept your failures instead of stroking your pride with false injuries and accomplishments."

The demon that Malak was flashed before us. A vision of the monster salos. Basically a big ball of fire, teeth, and claws.

Malak turned away and stomped down a different hall. It was probably good that he didn't go after Zyphon. I was confident that would end badly right now. As much as Kingsley is a pain in the ass and tactless, he's not wrong. At least not this time.

He looked at me, raising a brow. I shrugged. Yes, I'd go after Malak eventually. It was always me who went after Malak. But right now, we really had more important things to figure out. I wasn't so sure Zyphon was in the right headspace to truly come up with an idea that would be helpful.

"The magic is everywhere," Hayt said. "Maybe we need to take turns-"

Kingsley and I shook our heads.

"Bael is right," Kingsley said. "As much as Malak and I don't always get along or see eye to eye, I want him to succeed. Not just because being stuck under the rule of one of his brothers would be an absolute nightmare, but because he is a good prince. He takes care of this circle and his people with pride and care. That it's breaking down weighs on him more and more because he knows he's letting his demons down with his inability to tame the wild magic. He deserves his queen. And any of us trying to tag along with her unless she's interested in it will only hinder that progress. If anything, when they bring her to the wide world, Nuke will see that Malak isn't a bad guy because his people love him."

"I hope you're right," I said.

"I'm right. Right now, we need to get back to tracking the Pride Rings and burying them back underground where they belong. Since the queen is sleeping, there's literally nothing we can do right now anyway."

"And find a way to anticipate where the pridefalls are most likely to show up," Hayt added.

The exhaustion in his voice spoke to how tirelessly we've been working on those two tasks alone. Something is breaking the barrier around our ring, letting other sins in and infecting our prideful demons, making them fall from their pride and submit to another sin. Usually lust, not so surprisingly.

We knew what was breaking down the barrier. It was the wild magic. We've been somewhat avoiding discussing it because there's nothing we can do about it until the rightful queen takes her place in Pride. The things we have tried failed. Instead of focusing our energy on that when we know we can't win, we concentrate on the things we can control.

"Hayt and I will go back to the maps and track movement, deploying the task forces as needed. You tend to Malak, yeah?" Kingsley said.

I nodded, getting to my feet and stretching my back. Nuke wasn't wrong. It's been a long day and I could use a nap, too. Instead, I went in search of Malak.

It would be too easy to find him in his room, but I headed there first anyway. The suite was empty though I walked through every room just to be sure. On a whim, I headed into the bathroom and found Malak standing in the shower, his face turned up to the falling water as he let it run over him.

The bathroom was so filled with steam that it was a dense fog.

He did have a lot of pressure on him. I swear, the man has gotten shorter since we started looking for his queen. Since the breaking of Pride from the wild magic. So much weight on his shoulders that he never let anyone else help him carry. It was both his ego, convinced he could handle it all without assistance, and that he was the prince. He was *supposed to* be able to rule his circle with ease.

And with magic just out of his reach.

I stripped, tossing my clothes to the floor and stepped into the shower with him. Malak turned his face towards me, looking at me with all the pressure he was under filling his eyes. I stepped into him, and he wrapped his arms around me.

For just a second, a brief moment, he let his weight lean against me. Let me feel how heavy he was. How the burden of his station pulled him down.

But then he stood, and it was as if the roles were reversed. He held me as if I were stressed and needing support.

"You okay?" he asked.

I smiled, turning my face into his chest. He was only a few inches taller than me, but I generally curled in so I could be much smaller. I liked the protective cocoon he trapped me in.

His words made me sigh. "Yes. Are you?"

He released a breath, his arms tightening around me. "You know, I can taste victory, it's so close. Yet, I feel like there are so many damn obstacles in front of me that I'll never see the ending."

"One hurdle at a time," I said. "Nuke is going to be spending her time learning about Pride. We don't need to be involved in that. We can choose to accept those demons as a positive addition. They educate her while we concentrate on cleaning up the Pride Rings and eliminating the pridefalls before they cause too much damage as we have been."

"Which hurdle is our first?" he asked.

"I think the one that is most readily in your control to see through. Talk to Zy and swallow your pride for that conversation. Make a decision that puts him first instead of you."

Malak didn't answer me. I wasn't sure he was going to do that. In fact, I was pretty positive he wasn't going to. Not yet anyway. He would. I was sure of it. Because he loved Zy and he knew how deeply his actions had fucked up so much of our relationships, even when they had nothing to do with us.

I only mentioned it now so it was on his mind. He'd need time to ease into the idea. To accept it. And to find the words that would give Zy the outcome he deserved while still keeping his image.

Damn prideful demons.

"How did she manage to find him?" Malak asked, shaking his head with frustration.

Serendipity. That's how. Thousands upon thousands of demons in Pride, and Nuke finds the one that would tear us apart if Malak didn't atone for his past actions. And not because of anything Revan would do.

Things could have gone south really quickly when Malak had forced Zy to make a choice. They didn't because Revan did exactly as Zyphon asked of him. I was there. I watched the way the animation in Revan's face shut down until it was nothing but cold and demonic. Almost that of the demon he held inside him. He didn't argue. Didn't ask Zy to reconsider. Instead, he stood there for a solid two minutes, silent, and waiting for Zy to make a different decision.

When he didn't, Revan left and didn't return. We hadn't seen him since.

I often thought that if he said anything at all that day, things would be wildly different right now. But Revan was a better man than we gave him credit for. He walked away from the demon he loved so that the prince could keep those he needed close.

"Just happenstance," I said.

Malak shook his head. His hands trailing over my wet body, almost absently, as his mind worked endlessly on task after task. A running list of things he needed to do. His unending catalog of responsibilities.

It wasn't until I pressed my hips more firmly into his that he responded in a different manner.

His hands closed over my hips, fingers digging into my

skin. He was trying to stay withdrawn, trying to make sense of the upset that he was now faced with.

I pressed our hips together again, grinding my cock against his.

"Are you trying to distract me?" he asked, a coy smile on his face. He wasn't fooling me. His thoughts were still far away.

"Is it working?" I teased, my hand snaking around his back and pulling him into me.

"I'm never distracted by you," he said, finally returning the kisses I'd been offering for several minutes.

His hands moved up to my hair, bringing my face to his, and kissed me. He kissed me again. And again, and again.

I relaxed into him.

His kisses were slow as he took the time to taste me before backing me against the tile wall of the shower, pressing his entire body into mine. I closed my eyes and felt the weight of him, the heat of his skin, the warmth of his lips, the pressure of his touch, his need for me.

His fingers gripped tighter at my hair, pulling my face closer to his, as he demanded the taste of me. His other hand worked lower, trailing down my slick skin until it found my cock.

I moaned softly when his hand gripped me, his fingers wrapping around my shaft.

His lips never left mine.

He stroked me, his lips kissing away the sounds he coaxed out of me.

We were still kissing when he turned me around and pushed me up against the wall. My body was already slick with water, the steam all around us. He held me, his arms on either side of mine, his body pressed tightly against mine.

I shivered in his embrace.

His hand moved down my body and grabbed my ass, squeezing it firmly in his hand. I moaned into our kisses.

He thrust his hips against me, his cock rubbing against my ass.

I gripped his hair as he ground against me, his lips moving down to my neck where he sank his teeth into my skin.

I shivered, the pain quickly turning to pleasure. He bit my neck again before kissing the marks he left. His mouth worked its way down, from behind my ear, to my chest, and then down to my shoulder.

He turned me around, still standing between my legs, his hand moving to the back of my neck and pulling me in for another kiss.

"I love you," he said, his lips brushing across mine as he spoke.

He slowly kissed me again, his hands moving up and down my back, smoothing over my skin.

"I love you," he said again, his lips trailing down from my lips, to my neck, then to my chest. Waiting for me to respond.

I smiled. "Love you, too, Malak." He made the admissions often but usually when we were alone. He didn't hide it but some things he liked kept privately declared but publicly known.

His hand moved lower, his finger trailing across my skin, down my stomach, and finding my cock.

He gripped me again, his thumb rubbing over the crown. I moaned into our kiss. Then moaned again when he moved his mouth lower, his lips wrapping around the head of my dick.

My hips jerked, his mouth sucking me, his tongue

lapping at my cock, as I worked my hands through his hair. I gripped his hair tightly, pulling it, as I gave into the pleasure he was giving me. Malak was actually a very generous man. He preferred to give more than receive most days.

He ran his tongue up my cock, sucking me into his mouth, his tongue soft and wet against my shaft. He sucked me in, harder, deeper, as he lightly placed his teeth against me.

I groaned, my hand now gripping the back of his head, forcing him to take me deeper. I held his head as his mouth bobbed up and down my cock. The slick sound of his mouth sucking me filled the steamy air around us.

"Malak…" I moaned.

His mouth bobbed faster and faster, his tongue pressing firmly against me, his lips tightening ever so slightly.

I groaned, my hips thrusting into him.

His hand moved around and grabbed my ass, squeezing it as he sucked me harder and harder. His wet mouth, his tongue pressed firmly against me as he toyed and teased my cock, his fingers massaging my ass.

I moaned as he worked me. My climax building until it was ready to burst.

Then his mouth was gone and his hips moved against me once more. He was ready for my climax.

I smiled into his lips, gripping his hair, pulling him closer to me as I kissed him.

His mouth moved to my chest, his teeth biting into my skin. All the while, he continued to rub his dick against mine. Just the way I liked it.

"Malak," I moaned, my hips jerking.

He bit me again, his teeth sinking into my skin, and the pain mixing with the pleasure as he broke skin.

My cock exploded, my cum erupting all over him. He kept his hand wrapped around me, squeezing me tightly as he made sure to help me lose every drop.

I closed my eyes, the pleasure overtaking me.

"Feel better?" I asked, his lips moving down my body, to my stomach.

He chuckled. "Yes. You?"

"Always feels good with you."

Malak grinned. Pride filling his eyes as he stared at me. "Yes."

CHAPTER SEVEN
ANUKA

Voices went in and out as I woke from an amazing nap. I didn't understand them nor were they familiar. I kind of wanted to remain curled on this cloud and just listen to the deep tones as they soothed something inside me.

Only when I heard my name did I open my eyes. For a heart-stopping minute, I didn't recognize my surroundings or the man on the bed with me. Everything in me froze before memories surged forth and I breathed a sigh of relief.

Though it was short-lived relief. That I was waking up in this dream bedroom, on the cloud nine bed with three demons I didn't truly know, after being murdered and consequently trapped in Hell solidified that this was my life now.

Sighing, I eased into sitting.

I thought it would be Revan on the bed with me. He just seemed more the type to crawl into bed with a stranger. But it was Rhyl who lounged against the headboard and watched me. Per usual, a smile lingered on his lips.

Since he was here and decidedly not talking, that meant it had to be Eko and Revan somewhere else in the room.

"Feeling better?" Rhyl asked me.

I nodded, smiling and closing my eyes again. "Can I choose to ignore everything that's happening and just stay in bed?"

He chuckled.

A moment later the bed dipped. I opened my eyes as Revan dramatically fell on top of me. I laughed through an 'oof' while he situated himself to stare down at me with a flirty smile. "If you're staying in bed, we're going to join you. Right, Eko?"

"Yes," Eko answered from across the room. "Rhyl doesn't get all the fun."

Rhyl's smile widened as if we had been up to something other than me sleeping. I flushed, despite knowing differently.

"Okay, so what do we do first?" I asked. "Where can I find this magic?"

Revan brushed my hair from my face, his fingers lingering in my hair. I watched as he studied everything about me. My hair; the way it moved, its exact shade. My horns, my eyes. The shape of my face. My lips. He concentrated on my lips for a long time.

"The magic is everywhere. But I think maybe we need to get you acquainted with Pride. Give you a chance to feel the magic and see what it is you're trying to save," Revan answered.

"You sound fond of being here," I noted.

He nodded. "This might be Hell but it's a good place to be. Maybe not for the souls who led a sinful life, but for demons, Pride is a great place."

"With a good ruler. I've heard stories from the other circles," Rhyl added frowning.

I decided to ignore his subtle praise for Malak and concentrate on anything else. I wasn't in the mood to talk about my murderer.

Revan continued to almost pet me as we talked, his fingers constantly trailing delicately over my skin. It was so gentle and tender, made intimate by the way he lay on top of me, pinning me within the blankets, that I flushed under his attention.

"Pride is made up primarily by waterways. There are bridges that connect complexes. Some parks and darker areas where the barrier surrounding Pride is breaking down. There are also a lot of different types of species in Pride that we should get you familiar with. And you can meet some of the demons who live here."

"Does that mean I get a tour?" I asked, oddly excited about the idea.

Revan's eyes turned to mine as his smile climbed. "Yes. We're going to give you a tour."

I grinned. "Great. I need a shower."

His smile turned mischievous. "Want some help?"

"Another time," I told him. I probably wasn't even joking about that.

My thoughts stuttered as he brushed my lips with his before rolling off me. I caught my breath. For a second, I didn't move. Then I pushed myself from the bed and scurried to the bathroom.

Despite what my sister assumed, I had a healthy sex life. My love life was a different story, but one that was empty by choice. I wasn't interested.

But my life was suddenly very different than it had been. The rules had changed. And the people in it were my kind of people. I could feel their unwavering confidence with every breath. Their self-esteem was, at minimum, arrogant. And while that might not be attractive to a lot of people, to me that meant they were sure of themselves. Of who they are, and what they stood for. Their intelligence and capabilities.

There was nothing more attractive to me than someone who knew exactly their worth and wasn't afraid to be that person. Pride was my kind of place filled with my kind of people. I wasn't sure if these demons were objectively model-worthy, but their confidence made them perfect. I could turn any of them into modeling megastars.

Again, I didn't take long in the bathroom. I would take advantage of that luxury eventually but right now, I needed to focus on the important things so I could get back to my family and business. I didn't break my back becoming the top dog in model recruiting to lose it to a psychopath demon who needed a queen so he can get his shit together.

There was a door in the bathroom that led to the closet, and I sorted through drawers and the items hanging until I found something presentable. I guess if I was going to have a complaint it would be that these were not in style at all. I was a little offended by my options. How was a queen supposed to be seen in this garb?

It wasn't until I came out that I realized all three men had showered and changed while I was asleep. Eko's hair was still damp. And Revan was no longer in a dress. I was almost sad to see it go.

With my compact in my pocket once more, I headed for the door. "I'm ready. Let's get this tour started."

The men followed but I paused in leading the way as we stepped into the hall. I didn't know so much as to whether we should take a left or right.

Revan ran his hand along my back as he passed me, taking a left. Rhyl gripped my hand as he and Eko took up either side of me and we followed.

"For reference, that's the hall we came from when Hayt brought us to your room," Revan said, pointing down a hall we passed. A minute later, another set of giant doors loomed over us as we passed. They were so intimidating in size alone, that I stared. "And that's Malak's rooms. The others generally stay in there too, though their private rooms are down a hall past yours in the opposite direction."

"I take it you spent a lot of time here," I said as we passed Malak's door.

Revan nodded. "Like I said, Zyphon and I were together for a while."

Again, I tried to determine how he felt about it, but his voice sounded neutral. As if it was just another room we passed and not something that meant something to him. I suspected that his neutrality was actually hiding how he really felt about it.

"Are you okay being back here?" I asked.

He flashed me a smile over his shoulder. "Yes. Not a big deal, Nuke. Life moves on."

I nodded as he led us down a set of stairs that seemed to continue downward forever. I glanced at Eko and the look he gave me said that Revan hadn't' been precisely truthful. I was guessing it was a bigger deal than he was letting on. But I wasn't going to push it. If he didn't want to tell me, then that was his choice.

Just as I was reminding myself that we were going to have to climb these stairs to the top again, they ended underground in one of the tunnels that ran under Malak's house. There was a stone path along the side and tied to it were more than a dozen small boats, ranging in size from the ability to carry three people to twenty.

Revan led us to one of the boats that was somewhere between the two extremes in number of passengers. He tapped one of the curving ends a couple of times as he stepped in and the next thing I realized was that one of the strange-looking demons with wings and fins that was primarily a milky white in color took up the enormous oar.

I blinked at his sudden appearance before turning my attention to the boat as Eko stepped in. And then we were off.

The tunnel led us to the back of Malak's house into a wide open pool between the buildings surrounding it. In the middle were floats manned by mermaids.

I felt like I'd left Hell and entered a fairy tale.

"This is Waasser Market. All the goods are produced by the asmodai," Revan said.

"What's an asmodai?" I asked as we got closer.

"The demons who are part fish. Humans call them mermaids, but I assure you, they're not meant for fairy tales."

I nodded and the boat steered down the middle. I watched it all in amazement as we passed stalls of food and textiles. Bright colors and the sound of negotiation on every tongue.

The mermaids, or asmodai, were both in the water and perched on the sides of these stalls, their long tails flicking in the water. I stared, probably rudely, at their enchanting beauty. But as one smiled at me on our way by, I was greeted with sharp teeth and a flash of bright fire in their eyes.

Not meant for fairy tales, indeed.

We pulled up alongside a stall and Eko purchased a

whole array of foods that he loaded into the middle of the boat and the ferryman led us away. I sampled the nearest bowl to me, almost moaning with how good it tasted. But even as good as the food was promising to be, I was still too enthralled with the world around me to pay attention to the food more than to make sure it went in my mouth and not down my chest.

We passed under a bridge and in front of us was a true island with grass and even a few trees. There were flowers and laughter.

"This is Lladdfa. The Park of Terror."

Suddenly the laughter no longer sounded joyous. Instead, they were haunting screams of pain. I shuddered as the boat took a left and followed the waterway between the high buildings. I spent more time studying them than actually watching where we were going.

Revan pointed out a school, something I'd compare to a college. And then the boat took another sharp left, and we were headed through more waterways as I worked my way through the various foods placed before me.

There were two more schools on our tour, one of which was within a swampy area. The buildings and water were being swallowed by what looked like dead trees. In a mangrove, almost, with tree roots that dug deep into the water but rose up, creating natural arches.

In the middle of the swampy area were the armory, one of the other schools, and some ruins that had once been buildings.

"It seems that the magic is breaking down the city quickly at this end of Pride," Revan said as we glided past the ruins. "I'm guessing because it's furthest away from Malak."

We wove through the trees and buildings until the

swamp gave way to dark fog instead. Fog that gave this section of the city a haunted feel. "We've determined that the breakdown starts with fog and moves into the swamp, just based on damage and the charge in the air. Do you feel it?"

I closed my eyes but opened them again as voices met my ears. There was a market in this foggy area and people there. As I began closing my eyes again, the chatter turned to screams and I jumped.

All three of the demons with me lunged from the boat onto the stone path along the outside of the market.

"Wait," I called, surging to my feet and jumping after them. It didn't occur to me until after my feet left the boat that I might not make it.

I did. Crouched on the ground for just a second to catch my breath, I looked up to find Eko was waiting for me. I jerked to my feet and sprinted to him.

The thing I found as we rounded the corner was not one of the regular demons I'd seen thus far. It looked almost like a wraith. No legs or feet, just long flowing robes that made up their body. There was no face except a mouth with red lips. From its shoulders and head were long spikes.

The blood running down its chest following its sternum and pooling at its diaphragm was a bright pink.

"What the fuck is that?" I asked, horrified.

"A pridefall," Eko said.

There were common townsfolk there, trying to get out of its way. And there were more terrifying demons there. I didn't see any of mine but based on the change in shape, I assumed they were ones that looked like actual demons now. Tails, teeth, wings. Teeth. Did I mention teeth? Oh, and the claws!

I paused when I saw Kingsley step forward with a lethal

looking blade and swung it at the demon. It screeched, lunging at Kingsley.

Maybe it was because I recognized him. He was someone I knew in a sea of people I didn't. But when the thing threw itself at Kingsley, I sprang forward.

I was only distracted for a moment as a purple furry thing circled me, brushing its long fluffy tail against my legs. But at seeing that thing try to dig its claws into Kingsley, I threw my hands forward, as if I could stop the thing with nothing but my shout.

Fire shot from my hands, bright purple streaks of dancing flames. They slammed into the side of the pridefall, and it was tossed like a ragdoll into the side of a building. I followed it, mindless, afraid that it would get up.

Falling to my knees at its side, I meant to kill it. But somehow, when I placed my hand on it – which was glowing with a snaking river of this strange fire through my skin – the pridefall didn't die. It convulsed and the monster before me fell away. Melting into a shape I recognized as one of the citizens of Pride.

And then the screaming pain in my body had all my attention and I almost screamed myself. I was a live wire and everything in me hurt like I'd been electrocuted by high voltage. Every nerve. Every cell. Even my thoughts.

Pain worse than the death I was recently served.

CHAPTER EIGHT
ANUKA

"Nuke."

I tried to focus on the voice, but I was shaking as the pain began to fade.

"Nuke, baby. Open your eyes. Look at me, sweet girl."

Laughter bubbled from my chest. Sweet girl. No one has ever called me sweet. The absurdity of that made me open my eyes to find four faces hovering over me. I was once again on my back.

My body still stung but it was fading quickly now. Only the memory and phantom feel of it remained.

"Oh, thank fuck," Revan said as he reached for me. His touch was gentle as he slowly helped me sit up. Then that touch got a little less tender as he pulled me to his chest. "Are you okay?"

"I think you like me," I teased.

He snorted. "Yeah, looks like it. Answer me. Are you okay?"

I nodded. "Whatever I just did, that hurt like a fucking bitch."

"That's the first time a pridefall was stopped without

ending its life," Kingsley said, kneeling next to me. There was hesitation as he reached for me, his hand hovering for a second before he ran it through my hair. "Usually, we have no choice but to kill them. We've been trying for years to subdue them by any other means."

I glanced at the man on the ground. There were others gathered around him, helping him sit up as Revan had done to me. He looked dazed. Confused. Lost. But he nodded and answered questions.

He was one of the milky-looking demons with wings and fins mixed into the same appendages. I hadn't learned what they were called yet.

"You've had to kill them?" I asked.

Kingsley nodded, sighing. "Yes. It's the aspect of the wild magic that's taking the worst toll on Malak. These demons aren't the monsters they're being turned into. They're innocent. But nothing we've tried reverses the pridefall once it sets in. And I cannot tell you the ridiculous number of things we've tried. Some of which were completely absurd and comical. Some far-fetched and stupid. But if there was even the slightest ray of a chance that it could reverse the pridefall, Malak was determined to try it. To save them from a death they didn't deserve."

I shivered and looked away, turning my face into Revan's chest as he soothingly rubbed my back.

"Why are you here?" I asked. "Shouldn't you be sympathizing with His Majesty?"

Kingsley snorted. "Honey, I rarely sympathize with Malak. In fact, he threatens to kick me out daily because I tell him a truth he doesn't like."

"And he still hasn't," Revan said, shaking his head. "Some things never change."

Kingsley smiled. "No. That won't change. Stroking

Malak's pride has gotten us nowhere quickly. Time for some tough loving."

"Is that demon going to turn into a monster again?" I asked, turning the conversation away from Malak.

"Probably not. I brought some of the task force with me and they'll monitor. And to answer your question, I was here checking in with a vendor on some tile we sourced. We try to purchase from this market since it's suffering the most being caught in the throes of wild magic."

Revan helped me to my feet and led me back through the market. It opened through a broken arch to a drop-off on the water where our boat awaited.

"We're not done with our tour yet but want a lift?" Revan asked Kingsley.

"If Nuke doesn't mind me tagging along, sure."

I glanced at him and nodded as Revan handed me off to Rhyl in the boat. I hadn't realized my feet weren't on the ground until I was passed from Revan's arms to Rhyl's. He kept me in his arms as he sat. Eko placed one of the baskets of food in my lap, encouraging me to eat.

"You're remarkable caregivers," I noted. Teasingly but it was the truth, too.

Rhyl smiled the quiet amused look that he tended to share with Eko. None of them answered me, though.

We continued our tour through the creepy fog and the boat paused as we watched a storm in the distance. Something like a cyclone and thunderstorm rolled into one. The boat rocked threateningly on the waves that reached us.

"Is that normal?"

"A new normal," Kingsley answered. "It's a pridemage storm. Basically, a storm made from the wild pride magic."

I sighed and popped one of the little dough balls into

my mouth. I was anticipating sweet, but it turned savory as it melted, leaving perfectly seasoned meat and vegetables in my mouth.

The boat steered back toward the brighter part of the city. The streaks of purple that moved along the bank were enchanting. Glowing flowers. Flashes of purple wisps and smoke. It wasn't until I saw eyes as they darted off that I sat up to take note. I wasn't seeing parts of buildings. I was seeing something.

I pointed it out a moment before it disappeared.

"A watcher, probably," Revan said. "A demonic animal. They're responsible for moving magic through the world, trying to keep it in balance. They're solely responsible for keeping the magic from gathering too strongly in one area and destroying the circle entirely."

"They've done a remarkable job considering that the magic is wildly out of control right now," Kingsley said. "It wouldn't take much for that back region of Pride to completely collapse at this point."

"How do they move the magic?" I asked.

"They bring it within themselves and distribute it where it's weakest."

I spotted the eyes, bright purple like the way my hand had glowed. "I think it gave me magic back at the market," I said. "I think it brushed against me."

"Ah," Kingsley said, grinning. "You've made a friend, then. They're pretty solitary. It's been a long time since we heard of a watcher familiarizing with a demon."

Narrowing my eyes, I looked at him. "I'm not a demon."

He didn't argue but he clearly disagreed. I turned back to the eyes and finally caught a glimpse of what a watcher looked like.

"It's a fox?"

"No but I suppose that's the shape they take."

I was distracted from listening to him when the watcher sat at the edge of one of the city squares to watch me, and a plume of tails fanned out behind it. My eyes widened as I leaned forward.

"Wow." Many tails. There's a name for that.

"You've found an old one," Revan said. "The more tails they have, the older and more powerful they are. And the glowing pattern in their fur denotes their level of magic holding."

The one that watched me was filled with patterns so intricate it was mesmerizing. And then it vanished into a little ball of purple fire that drifted through the air. It circled the boat a couple times before dropping in front of me, once more a fox with seven tails. Seven!

"Hi," said, immediately holding my hand out. There was no hesitation when it pushed its nose into my palm and let me rub its head. "You're the most amazing thing I've ever seen."

It leaned against my leg, placing its beautiful face in my lap, and began purring. Not quite like a cat but there was that familiar rumble and vibration.

"I swear, this makes up for the electrocution," I said as I buried my fingers in his fur.

"Electrocution?"

I nodded. "When that magic burst out of me, it felt like I had so much voltage going through me that I was going to burst into flames."

They didn't answer. Or maybe they did, and I was too distracted by my new foxy friend.

They brought my attention back to the tour when we stopped at a temple. Unsurprisingly, there were waterways through the temple. I watched the glowing walls, depicting

Malak and a freaky-ass demon thing in alternating statues. It didn't take long to figure out that they were one and the same. One was the man version. The other was his true demonic self.

"Is Malak prayed to?" I asked frowning.

Their laughter made me smile. It was Kingsley who answered.

"No, not at all."

"Maybe some do," Eko countered.

Kingsley nodded. "Fair but it's not a regular occurrence or expected practice. This place is one of respect. Somewhere the prideful can go for reflection and peace. Where they can *speak* to their ruler without actually talking to him. I suppose in a way, you can consider it prayer, but it's more of a form of meditation. A place where they can seek guidance from Malak when really, they find the answers in themselves. Somewhere that they can show appreciation for how Malak rules Pride and the souls that end up here."

"I see." I wasn't sure I did, though. Not a deity but maybe a... prophet? A spiritual guide?

What I could see was that there were tons of little pockets within this temple and some of them had someone inside, sitting in various positions and with a wide range of emotions on their faces. Some looked at peace, while others were definitely lost and struggling.

I stilled when I saw a hint of purple smoke lingering around one. And then eyes appeared. The shape coalesced to that of a tiger, its stripes a smokey purple that drifted into the air. But there was nothing more. Where there were no smokey stripes, was just clear air.

"What is that?" I asked, pointing as it faded.

"A murmur," Revan answered. "A smoke demon.

Keeping the pride among demons in balance so that the most prideful balance out those who are just on the snobby end of the spectrum."

The smoke lingered before dissipating. "The animals here are gorgeous."

"They are," Kingsley agreed.

"What kind of demon are you?" I asked.

He smirked. "Nybbus. I play with dreams and nightmares."

I raised a brow, instantly thinking of the horror movie franchise that focused on this. It gave me nightmares for years.

"It's not all frightening. I can show you," Kingsley offered.

"Oh yeah?" The skepticism in my voice was almost sarcastic.

He nodded, turning to the ferryman. "Bring us to Remolí, please."

The boat turned in the water and we were ferried down a waterway that got louder the further we moved. And then we were parking within a strange bridge structure. Kingsley stepped out, offering me his hands. I hesitated for a minute before giving in to my curiosity and let him pull me onto the bridge complex.

The far side had a stone pad with an altar of fire. We were on a curved bridge connected to the circular bridge that fixed the whole complex together. And within the circular portion was a whirlpool.

Kingsley kept my hand and led me onto the round overpass to a set of stairs that led into the whirlpool.

"You're trying to kill me again, aren't you?" I asked.

He chuckled. "No. This is a dream pool. I'm not the only nybbus here. Sometimes we need a bigger channel to let loose some more energy than our personal pools can offer."

I watched as he pulled off his clothes down to a pair of tight briefs that left absolutely nothing to the imagination. By the way his soft dick was shaped, and his balls were displayed, I imagined his underwear had some kind of ball pocket to cradle them. And that dick? The outline was exceptional.

I turned away, pulling off my clothes down to my underwear as well. I've made a life out of judging people's bodies. Of course, that's where my mind went.

That's the story I was going with.

Kingsley didn't call me out on examining his goods. He waited for me at the top of the stairs until I joined him, and we walked into the water. It was warm and though the current was strong, the pull around the pool was gentle.

"How about we look into something pleasant, hm?" he asked.

I nodded. Certainly not interested in a nightmare.

Lily pads that had no business being in a whirlpool popped up and the water around us turned dark before splashes of purples and blues showed up. All around us a night forest grew with a waterfall trickling into the pool we were in. A bridge of thick roots swung over us and I stared up into the canopy of a dark sky.

Plants popped into existence. Bright mushrooms, large and humming with their own tune. Feathery flowers grew along the side of the footbridge, tinkling in the breeze. Ferns that looked like long fingers grew up on the banks, touching the water and sending little glowing streaks through it that danced before fading.

"What is this?" I asked, awed as I watched a glowing pink caterpillar float through the air.

"Someone's dream," Kingsley answered.

"I'm not sure it's strictly demonic watching pretty dreams," I pointed out, spotting an animal prowling the edge of the pool we were in.

"I can change the dreams, too," he said. "How about a floating walkway?"

Before I could answer, out of nowhere planks flipped into existence, one at a time. A quiet *plink, plink* followed each that came to life. And every half a dozen feet, a lantern with soft yellow lights flickered on.

The pool faded away and we were standing in the middle of the path. On either side, the forest floor was covered in little dots of blue lights, like stars. It made the forest surrounding us shimmer with a soft light.

"What do you want to see?" Kingsley asked.

"The moon," I said.

A couple dozen feet away, a bright glow lit the area as it pushed at the ground. And the next thing I knew, it was like I was watching the sky rise on the horizon, only it was right in front of me. Pulling itself from the ground.

No longer were we on the path but in a pastel night field and the moon, a soft pink, was rising from the earth. The dark spots and shapes were enchanting to watch. A willowy tree in the distance danced in a cool breeze.

I shivered and Kingsley pulled me closer, wrapping his arm around me. He brought his hand around, distracting me from the rising moon, as he handed me a flower. The six petals were pointed, rubbery glass that sparkled like gemstones. Its colors were those deep, captivating tones as well.

The moon continued to rise into the sky and with it, trees began towering over us. Crystals shot from the ground as if they were flowers growing. And then there were mushrooms, different than the ones that had been here to begin with. These were growing glass domes.

I startled when one of the domes broke loose and drifted into the air. "Bubbles," I said, laughing as I reached for it. I touched one and it perched on my finger before releasing to float into the sky.

I followed it for a minute before looking at Kingsley. He was still holding me to him, but he was watching me, not the dream around us. A blush touched my cheeks with the way he observed me. A smile as if he were enjoying seeing my reactions to the dreams around us. Relishing in my wonder.

He brushed my hair from my face where the strands got caught in the wind. And then we were back in the whirlpool, being swept gently around with the current, the dream having faded away.

CHAPTER NINE
ANUKA

"That was magical," I said as my eyes tried to come into focus. "I'm almost disappointed by the mundane beauty of Pride."

He chuckled. "It can be a lot of fun," Kingsley agreed. "It's equally as fun terrifying a serial rapist by manipulating their nightmares."

I shuddered.

Kingsley still held me to his chest and for a minute, we were swept gently around the whirlpool as if we were on a lazy river. With a quirk of his smile, he reached a hand out and caught the railing, swinging us around until my back lightly hit stairs.

It took me several awkward moments to arrange myself to pull out of the water and climb the stairs, but I managed to not look like a total freak.

He didn't dress when we reached the bridge again but picked up both piles of our clothing and took my hand, leading me back to the boat where the other three waited. We were met with smiles, but I didn't miss the way all the demons' eyes grazed up and down my body. As if they were hands caressing me, I could almost feel their heated gazes.

A boat of the pale demons with fin wings glided by, watching me with curiosity.

"Okay, what are they?" I asked, causing all four demons to look where I was. "Their race," I clarified, blanching when I remembered our ferryman was one of them.

"Kimaris," Revan answered, reaching up to help me step into the boat. "The only part of the populace that can live in the water and on land."

"Land being relative," I said, watching the buildings begin to sweep by us once more. My little fox watcher was still in the boat, and he snuggled against my side once I settled.

"Correct. They're more or less just floating platforms with anchors holding the buildings in place," Kingsley said.

"One more stop before we head back," Revan said.

"Where's that?" Hopefully one of the markets so I could get some decent clothing.

"Tanndwr. It's the underwater city center."

I glanced at him, wondering how he was going to bring me underwater. But it wasn't long before we crossed the dark waters of the Avenue of Souls and were dumped right into the open water basin in front of the prince's towering home.

It wasn't really all that gaudy. I was just being bitter. I loved the tall peaks and gothic features. It was really something to look at. And all the dark purple that glinted in the sunlight.

How long have I been awake? I feel like it's been two days. Maybe my nap was longer than I thought. It made sense considering all my demons had showered and changed.

Not *my* demons. That had been a slip.

"Look down," Revan said.

I leaned over the side and my eyes went wide. Not only could I see the asmodai clearly, but I could see all the way to the bottom of the waterways. And there was an entire city down there.

It spread in all directions, just like the city on the water, and it was filled with activity and people. Although most of them were the mermaid asmodai, there was a good portion of the milky white kimaris, too. And dragons. I pointed, amazed.

"Look at that!"

I felt their chuckles just as much as I heard them.

"It's a laraje. They primarily live in the water since their function is to keep it clean by filtering it through their wings. But every now and then you'll see one fly," Kingsley said.

"They're amazing." One of the laraje drifted to the surface, turning over like a whale might, and floated just under the boat we were in. I leaned over, stretching my hand into the water to skim along its flank.

I was nearly giddy when I pulled back after it was out of reach. It wasn't hard to imagine that the joy I felt radiating off my face when I looked at the demons with me was reminiscent of a child's. And their indulgent smiles said they appreciated my excitement.

"Want to swim with them?" Rhyl asked.

"Can I? Is that allowed?"

He laughed, pulling his shirt over his head. That he distracted me from the thrill of the beings in the water was a true statement to how stunning this man was. I blinked several times before I could focus on him looking at me.

"Yes, it's allowed. But even if it wasn't, you're the

queen. You can do what you want," he answered as he climbed onto the side to slip into the water.

"I'm not the queen," I said, leaning over. He raised his hands up to help me in and again, like a child, I let myself fall off the side instead of putting any effort into getting into the water more gracefully.

"You're the queen," he argued as he pulled me against him. My breath caught as I looked up into his gorgeous face. I swallowed, my hands tightening on his shoulders just to feel him. How strong and hot his skin was.

Time felt like it was slipping by as I stared into Rhyl's gorgeous face. It wasn't lost on me that I found these demons hot. Breathtaking. There was something almost unsettling about it. They were *demons*. With what logic were they supposed to be this stunning?!

They are the sinful and damned and fuck me if I wanted to make sure my soul went to Hell just so I could be surrounded by them.

The water broke next to us, and I got my first up close look at one of the asmodai. I was going to run out of adjectives quickly. This man with deep blue hair and sapphire eyes made me instantly drool. Not exaggerating. I swallowed it down like I'd just taken a sip of water.

He studied me for a second before looking at Rhyl.

"What brings you here?" the asmodai asked.

"Showing the queen around, Danaan. Meet Nuke," Rhyl said.

Danaan looked at me more consideringly. There was a half a second when he stared at the fiery horns on my head. A smile ticked up his lips and he smirked. "Much better than the last... all of them."

Rhyl nodded. "You'll like her. She's unimpressed with everything that is Malak."

Danaan grinned widely. "I'm in love."

He was teasing and I knew that but somehow, I momentarily forgot who I was and reverted back to a shy schoolgirl and blushed madly before I got myself under control.

He turned his attention back to Rhyl. "We're getting ready to play a game of Nakker. Care to join?"

Rhyl looked at me, smiling. "Rules are easy. A lot like volleyball but played in the water. No nets. There are other details you won't need to concern yourself with. Interested?"

I nodded, shrugging. "I'm a decent swimmer but not sure I'll be great at this."

The way Danaan smiled at me told me that I had clearly missed something. "Actually, how are you at holding your breath, queen?"

Choosing to ignore the title, I shrugged. "I've never timed myself and it's not a skill I tried to hone."

His grin was wicked. "Climb on my back, little bomb. I'll give you a ride you'll not soon forget."

I bit my tongue to point out that those types of rides don't have me on men's backs. Generally speaking, the goods are located on their front. But maybe an asmodai was built differently. Hell, maybe some demons had dicks on their backs! What did I know?! I haven't gotten to the point where I needed an anatomy lesson yet.

Rhyl nodded and released me, for which I was almost bummed about. I could make him a star. It would be a walk in the park. Maybe I could convince him of that once I got Pride in line.

Danaan pulled me to him, and I flushed again as my hands reflexively went to his chest. Smooth like scales, silky and wet. His smirk climbed as he rounded me behind him and grabbed my thigh, bringing it to his ribs until I cooperated and climbed on his back.

Once he had me situated how he wanted me, hoisted up high on his back with an arm wrapped around his forehead so I could keep the other free, he swam away from Rhyl. I glanced back in time to see him climbing onto another asmodai's back in the same position I was in.

"The object of the game is simple. We keep the ball from hitting the water on our side while trying to shoot it in such a way that the opposite team misses," Danaan explained.

"What does that have to do with holding my breath?"

He glanced at me over his shoulder, a mischievous grin on his sinfully perfect lips. "I swim fastest underwater. Have you ever seen a dolphin leap from the water, queen?"

I nodded and had an image of what we were going to do. Maybe I ought to ask for goggles, so my vision was never obscured.

"I'll get us in a good position. All you have to do is hit the ball away, in whatever direction we're facing. Alright?"

"This sounds like it's easier said than done," I pointed out as I tried to adjust my grip appropriately.

He chuckled. "It's just a game. Want to try a couple dives and leaps before we begin?"

I nodded.

Danaan bounced above the surface another foot. His hands tightened on my legs before we sank beneath the water. It was remarkably clear and didn't sting my eyes like salt or chlorine did. And it was even clearer now.

The world I had but a moment to admire suddenly blurred by me as Danaan took off in the water like he had an engine attached to him. The next thing I knew, we were flying through the air.

I found myself laughing, reaching both hands up as if I were trying to touch the clouds. For a moment, it felt like we were flying. And then my stomach was in my throat as we fell back to the water. His hands tightened on me again and I let myself slide down his back a little so I could wrap my arms around him a moment before we went under.

The majestic beauty of the city under the water – that we were in fact nowhere near – was so captivating that I nearly forgot I was holding my breath until Danaan surged into the air again. I laughed madly as the air whipped around, yanking my hair in a wild array as if it were a cape.

This time when we went under the water, he slowed his swim. When we breached the surface again, he looked back at me with a smile. "Ready to play, queen?"

"Yep, though I think I'll be too distracted by how fun this is to be any good at actually hitting the ball," I confessed.

He grinned. "I'll be happy to let you ride me on the pretext of playing Nakker."

Again, he was teasing but was I imagining that there was also an offer in there? Or was he just absently flirting?

Danaan remained still in the water until we were in the starting position. A yell went up a moment later and Danaan bounced in the water before bringing me under. He whipped around and I marveled at everything we passed. The other asmodai, just carrying on. A laraje as it watched us.

And then we were breaking the surface and leaping into the air. I sucked in a breath as I stared wildly around. For a moment, the round thing coming at me had me cringing away, disoriented in my surroundings. It came back quickly, and I stretched in an awkward angle to get my hand under it and punch it into the air.

The ball was light like a balloon though so though I hit it with good force, my aim was shitty and it went a little wonky. Danaan laughed as we hit the water again. I felt like a beached whale as I floundered, trying to keep my breath in.

We rose long enough to get a proper breath and then he had us zooming through the water once more. We dodged another asmodai in the game as he spiraled around us, winking at me as I caught his eye. And then we were out of the water again.

This time, I hit the ball with more purpose, and it wasn't an awkward fumble towards the water but an almost elegant arc into the air. I grinned proudly as we slammed back into the water.

I had no idea who won or if anyone was actually keeping score, but we played for what felt like hours, until holding my breath became too much of a chore. Danaan always seemed to know when I was at my limit and needed to breathe, never letting me get to the point where I was close to drowning.

He returned me to the side of the boat where my demons and Kingsley were waiting. Rhyl was still in the water, grinning at me when I slid from Danaan's back. He caught me, pulling me against his chest and running a hand through my hair as he spoke to the asmodai.

"Have fun?" Rhyl asked.

I nodded.

"How about another ride?"

Danaan had swam away so I looked at him with a raised brow. "What do you have in mind?"

Rhyl smirked, lifting my body against his, his lips hovering over mine. I could feel the heat from them as I stared into his dark eyes. Then he turned me, and I came face to face with the enormous side of a laraje.

"This is Murkak. He monitors the water around Malak's estate. He's a sweet boy."

I glanced over my shoulder at Rhyl, and he grinned.

"He is."

Laughing, I nodded again. "Yes. I want to ride a dragon!"

Rhyl helped me climb on, showing me how to hook my legs around the shoulder joints. When he backed away, I grabbed for him. "Come with me?"

The smile that slowly grew up his face made me flush. This time, it wasn't unexpected. I recognized that sensual smile and was pleased that it was directed at me.

Rhyl climbed on behind me, tucking himself close. As Murkak rose into the air, Rhyl's hand slowly drew up my stomach and between my breasts until he could hook it over my shoulder. He leaned forward, his chest hard into my back. I didn't miss the bulge that pressed against my ass either.

But then all sexy thoughts fled as I stared at the city of Pride below. The way it glistened and sparkled in the sun. How serene and beautiful it was. The crystalline blue waters and the luxurious purples mixed in with earthy stone.

"Wow," I breathed.

I was startled as a bird flew alongside us. Like everything else in Pride, it was enchanting shades of purple. It was large, with several long tails that ended in a leaf-like fan of fur.

"Fenix," Rhyl told me. "They command the storms."

As if his words had been a suggestion, purple lightning

streaked across the clear sky. The fenix's bright purple eye watched me, as if enjoying my awe.

And I was in awe. This place, this Hell that Malak murdered me into, was absolutely breathtaking. There are worse places to spend eternity, I was sure.

CHAPTER TEN
ANUKA

The city wasn't just purple. We weren't in unicorn vomit world. The waters were a crystal blue that glittered under the bright sun. Even from the height I was flying through the sky, I could see how clear the waters were. Though I couldn't make out the city under the water in detail, I could still see hints of it where the city of Pride made larger lanes of water.

The buildings themselves were actually made of stone. Normal sandstone, limestone, and granite. But the roofs and decorative features were all deep hues of purple. Even the bridges that spanned over the water lanes, connecting some of the building squares, were made of stone with touches of purple.

Finally, the sun was setting and as dusk came on, lights lit around the city, giving it an even more magical feel. And if you can believe it, the lights that lit the sides of the buildings also had a purple tint to them.

But as darkness settled, it really emphasized the western end of the city, where the fog and swamp had overcome everything. There were two points of bright magic in the air – one over Malak's house, where it shined and crackled like a magical beacon. And the other over the part of Pride that was falling to the wild magic. But the purple magic that filled the air was dark and ominous there. Threatening.

"This is remarkable," I said as the laraje named Murkak lowered to the water, gently sweeping along its surface as if he were a floaty. "I've never seen a place more enchanting. Are you sure we're in Hell?"

Rhyl chuckled. "Yes. I've visited other places. While they have their appeal – likely more so to the demons who live there – there's no place more vividly gorgeous than Pride."

I was tempted to suggest that perhaps someone had gotten their wires crossed. This couldn't be Hell. There was too much splendor to it. I was sure it might be blasphemy to suggest, but I was sure there were more angelic, heavenly qualities to Pride than hellish or demonic.

Aside from the pridefalls, that is.

Although the animals weren't roaming the streets, there was a clear hint of them everywhere. The smoke demon murmurs, more laraje would breach the water like whales, sometimes we'd see a fenix soar through the sky, and rarely I'd spot the fiery hint of a watcher as it moved through the city.

And the people were equally as mesmerizing. Primarily, there were the greater demons, shax, and kimaris on the land. But the waters were filled with asmodai and kimaris as well. It was an active hub of every species.

It wasn't until Murkak paused next to the boat with our kimaris ferryman, Revan, Eko, and Kingsley lounging in it that I found I'd been leaning back in Rhyl's embrace as I took in the city around me. I'd known these men for such little time and yet, it felt like I've known them my entire life.

Maybe that's not it. I didn't know them. But my body and mind's innate feeling of comfort with them was something. This entire day I'd forgotten that I was with virtual strangers. They didn't feel like strangers at all and yet, there was still the flush and bashfulness of someone new.

Someone new and sexy and giving me all the feels.

But not just someone. Several someones. I was trying to ignore that there were three men that appeared interested in me. Perhaps even more unusual was that there didn't seem to be any kind of rivalry or challenge between them in their attraction to me.

Maybe I was reading too much into their attraction. This was pride. Not lust. Maybe my own vanity was showing in thinking that I was appealing to them.

Eko helped me back in and the ferryman started guiding us back toward Malak's house. My little foxy friend reappeared from the purple flame that hung at the bow of the ferry. His seven tails swished as he settled next to me.

"Do watchers have names?" I asked as the ferry slowed within the lit waterway beneath the building and we started to climb out.

"Yes. But it's up to him to tell you," Kingsley said as he reached for my hand.

The watcher jumped gracefully from the boat to the sidewalk with us, swirling around my calves. I could feel the magic spark within his fur.

"I didn't think they spoke," I said, running my fingers through the tips of the watcher's tails as we started to the stairs. I glared at them, irritated that we were going to have to climb them all again.

"They're animals. They don't speak," Kingsley said, amused. "But he's a demon. He can still tell you his name if he wishes."

"I'm so glad you cleared that up."

He chuckled.

I was pretty sure with the long day I've already been through that trudging up the stairs was going to take an hour. But I swear, they must have shortened in our absence. It was no time before we were on the landing that emptied into the extra wide hall and we were heading toward Malak's towering doors.

"Does his demon get eight feet tall?" I asked as we passed.

"Taller," Kingsley answered, and I looked at him with surprise. I was being sarcastic. "Malak is a salos. They're massive when fully exposed."

"I see. and is there an encyclopedia of demons I can study?"

"There is. I'll have it sent to your room." He paused and looked at Revan. "Or Rev can grab it from the library."

Revan nodded. "Yep. I'll pick it up later. Unless you're interested in reading tonight."

I shook my head. "All that fresh air has me needing another nap."

He smirked, draping an arm over my shoulders. "I thought so."

Kingsley paused outside Malak's door and looked at me. I continued to walk but I afforded him a smile. "Thanks for the ride in the dream pool."

With a grin, he nodded. "Good night, Queen. I'll see you tomorrow."

I nodded and turned away. Nope. I wasn't going to allow myself to feel anything for one of Malak's men. It might have been the prince himself who murdered me, but it sounded as if they all somehow had a hand in it.

My room was just as glorious as when I left. With a sigh, I headed straight for the bathroom. Stripping out of my clothes as I walked, I afforded myself the lapse in memory that I wasn't alone. I flushed but then felt myself add an extra sway to my hips as I shut the door behind me.

With all the time I spent in the water today, you'd think I wouldn't find the need in me to want to take a bath. But that tub was screaming my name.

Gray wood panels on the lower half of the walls. The top was painted a dark plum purple. The floor was marble, the furnishings and ceiling white with black fixtures. And there was a crystal chandelier hanging from the ceiling over the tub.

And the tub was a large, deep soaker that I couldn't wait to get in.

With a sigh, I turned on the hot water before poking around through the drawers and cabinets to find some aromatherapy. It didn't take me long and I chose soothing lavender and lilac. Lavender was known to soothe but lilac was my favorite scent. I'd lick it if I could. Hell, I'd wear a lilac bush if that were an option.

Once satisfied, I climbed in and groaned in pleasure. Such hot water. Sitting straight without slouching, the water reached just above my chest, leaving the tops of my shoulders and above bare.

I sighed, taking a deep breath of the soothing scents and closed my eyes to let the thoughts drift away. I didn't want to think right now. Because as beautiful as Pride was, I'd been stolen from my life. What my mother and sister must be thinking. And Malcolm. What would he do?

What would the world think when they found my

phone abandoned in a museum bathroom and I had simply vanished? Was there blood left behind?

No. I had just said I wasn't going to think about it. I was going to enjoy my bath and let the stress of what was behind all this enchanting beauty wash away.

I really enjoyed the depths of the tub and the scents that filled my lungs. Decluttering my mind and helping my muscles relax. I must have been in there a while.

The door quietly clicked open and I cracked my eyes. Maybe I should have been irritated or offended that one of the demons thought they could just come in the bathroom while I was using it. But I didn't feel that way as I stared at Eko. He remained just inside the door, staring at me with heated eyes and a light smile.

I probably should have told him to leave. Instead, I found myself asking, "You want to join me?"

His smile ticked up, making me shiver. Eko nodded and stepped into the room, dropping articles of clothing as he moved toward me. He paused a moment when he was fully naked to let me admire him. And I did. Then he joined me, stepping into the deep tub and sitting across from me.

We stared at each other for several minutes. Then he reached his hand out, offering it to me. What the Hell? Why not?

Placing my hand in his, he pulled me across the tub until I was straddling his lap. I wasn't at all surprised to feel the stone-hard cock now pressed against my stomach. I smiled and wrapped my arms around his neck, kissing him softly.

A low, satisfied rumble vibrated in his chest and I moaned softly at the sound. Then his large hands slid to cup my ass, lifting me up and setting me down on his lap. I gasped at the feel of him, hard and so very large.

Eko leaned against the wall of the tub and then slid his hand under my hair, cupping my neck. He kissed me again as he began to push his cock into my pussy.

I moaned at the feel of his hardness pressing into me, at the way he held me so tightly and kissed me so passionately. I was surprised to feel my own desire.

A soft growl rumbled from Eko before he pulled me forward, pressing his lips to mine again. He thrust his tongue into my mouth, tangling with mine as he slowly pumped his hips.

I gasped as he rubbed against me, sending fiery trails of desire through my body.

My hands slid over his shoulders and through his hair, wrapping around his neck as I held on to him. My hips found their own rhythm, grinding against him. This wasn't enough.

I wanted more.

Eko let my mouth go, licking and sucking a trail down my neck. He caught my earlobe between his teeth, tugging on it and sending a spike of pleasure through me. My hands clenched his shoulders, trying to hold on. The pleasure was almost painful.

I needed more.

Maybe the demons just knew; because the next thing I realized, we weren't alone in the tub. Revan pressed against my back, his dick sliding along my ass crack. And Rhyl knelt at our sides, staring at me with fire in his eyes.

"Let me in, too?" Revan asked with a deep husky voice in my ear.

My body answered him before I could, wrapping my arms around Eko's shoulders I leaned back against Revan. He growled softly, pressing his lips to my shoulder. Rhyl was there, kissing my neck as he reached around and cupped my breasts.

"Yes," I gasped.

Revan's large hand slid from my shoulder and down my back. He found my ass, cupping it and squeezing gently. I moaned softly, arching into his touch. I needed this. I needed them. Eko's hands slid to my hips, holding me firmly as I rocked back and forth between them. They took care of me.

Revan's hands slid forward, following the curve of my body until they found my pussy. He slid his fingers over my mound, slipping between my folds and sliding into my wetness with Eko's dick. I was so sensitive.

I gasped loudly, pressing against him as he slid his fingers into me. He filled me and slid out again, sliding back in once more. His fingers were so thick. He slid them in and out of my pussy, his cock sliding along my ass crack.

Every stroke of his fingers sent a spark of pleasure throughout my body. I couldn't get enough. Eko's hands slid up my body, as Revan kissed his way down my neck, his free hand sliding down to my breast. He pinched both of my nipples between his fingers, in turn, twisting and pulling on them until I moaned. Rhyl lifted one of my legs, wrapping it around his waist as he leaned forward, kissing and biting my neck. Was he going to try for three dicks in me at once? My pussy was only so big!

I whimpered, my hips bucking against Eko as I gripped his shoulders tightly. His hands slid up my body, cupping my breasts and squeezing them. Then he lifted one of my hands, pressing it against the wall of the tub.

I gasped as his other hand slid down my belly, slipping between my legs. He spread my swollen lips, slipping a finger into my wet pussy. The myriad sensations of their hands all over me and Eko's cock deep inside, their mouths working me, was driving me insane.

My breath came in ragged gasps as I tried to catch it. Eko held me as I rocked between them, my body grinding and bucking. My head fell back against Revan's shoulder. I was going to come.

Revan's mouth dropped open, his breaths heavier against my neck. Then he slid his hand around my body, finding my ass. He pressed against my hole, slipping one finger into me as he twisted his fingers and thrust into my pussy.

I screamed, the pleasure so intense I felt like I was going to faint. My vision swam as my pussy and ass clenched hard around whatever body parts they were sticking into me.

Revan's finger left my ass, quickly replaced by the head of his dick. The way Rhyl had one of my legs wrapped around him meant my pussy was stretched wide, and my ass was squeezed tight. All the more effort it took Revan. And goddamn did everything in me turn to fire.

My body wound tighter and tighter as Revan's cock slid into me slowly and Eko's made the playing of my pussy into a magic dance. Rhyl teased my nipples, pinching them between his teeth and tongue. I was ready to come.

"Not yet," Eko murmured, a smile on his lips.

What was that? I moaned my disapproval but I did what he said, holding onto the pleasure just a little longer. I would have done anything he asked.

He slowed his thrusts, just barely fucking me. Revan slowed as well, keeping his dick inside me but barely moving as he let Eko's rhythm set our pace. I whimpered and pressed back against Revan, grinding against his cock. He was so hard, so delicious.

I couldn't take it. "Please!" I gasped. "Please, I'm so close!"

Revan's breath was hot in my ear as he whispered, "Come for us."

The command sent me over the edge, my body shuddering as I came. I pulsed and clenched around them, their cocks slowly sliding in and out of my pussy and ass. The magic surrounded me, the fire burning bright. Pleasure lashed out from it, carrying along my skin and seeping into my bones.

I was lost in it. I was blissful. And I was perfect.

I didn't know how long my orgasm lasted, but it left me breathless, my whole body quivering with pleasure. But it wasn't over.

"Yes, don't stop!" Rhyl hissed, his teeth sinking into my neck.

Eko smiled, his eyes on mine as he whispered. "Come again for us, my love."

His words were the catalyst I needed, not understanding how they made my body respond when it was already spent. I arched, screaming as pleasure ripped through me again. The waves of my orgasm rippling through my pussy and ass, around Revan and Eko's cocks, as they continued to stroke me. I was so full, so sensitive.

My body bucked against them, writhing and twisting as they stroked me. My breath caught in my throat as my pussy clenched hard around Eko and my ass around Revan. I was trapped between them. The pleasure was so intense I didn't think I could take it.

I shivered in appreciation. I definitely chose the right demons.

We ate breakfast around the table on the balcony

overlooking Tanndwr. There was definitely a hub of activity in the water right there, even if we couldn't see straight down to the underwater city center. Asmodai, kimaris, and laraje were prevalent there more than any other water lane that I could see.

My little fox friend was at my feet, curling three of his tails around my ankle as he lay with his head through the railing, looking down at the activity.

"What are we doing today?" I asked.

"Visiting the market that lines the Avenue of Souls," Revan said. "There's a lot of local textiles being sold there as well as some imports from the other rings."

Yawning, I nodded. "Shopping. What girl doesn't love shopping?"

Revan snorted. I must not have sounded convincing. It's not that I don't enjoy shopping. I mean, sometimes I do. But I'm more of an online shopper. I can browse for ages and have everything shipped right to my door without interacting with anyone. What could be better than that?

"I promise. It's worth going to. And you'll get a better sense of the citizens of Pride, too."

I shook my head. "It's fine. Whatever you think it will take to let me take hold of the magic."

"Learning Pride will be the primary focus to begin with," Rhyl said. "You need to connect with the people and the circle in general if the magic is going to become available to you."

"I'm glad you know about the magic." I dipped my breakfast cookie (yes, that's a thing) in my chocolate milk. I was really hoping I could find a Frappuccino in this place. I wasn't sure how many days I've been here at this point, but I could already feel a withdrawal coming. Was it from sugar? Caffeine? The addictive taste of mocha?

If there wasn't a suitable stand-in, I was going to have to demand someone bring me one. It was going to be a new market.

We headed out after I finished my third cookie. This time we left through the massive front doors and hailed one of the taxis. It was almost no time before the ferryman floated us through the throngs of people floating in the water above Tanndwr. We could almost see the market we were headed to from Malak's house.

It was nice to see that they were purchasing items from a place that needed the stream of people coming and going instead of one from convenience. That we ran into Kingsley on the other side of the city yesterday, deep within the swampy area of a market, said that they were definitely trying to support all parts of the city. Especially those who were struggling within the darker parts.

There were several entry arches at various intervals around the market and the market stood on its own. There weren't any other buildings attached to this bit of 'land' floating on the water. A whole variety of buildings made up thes market, most were round with canopy roofs in various purples. These were permanent structures built into the city block.

And around the cobblestone parks were dozens of vendors. Overhead, to combat the heat of the sun, were wisps of purple fabric to provide some shade.

I found silks and cashmeres, blown glass lamps and intricate wooden carvings. Items made from coconut shells. Exotic spices, wines, and oils. A whole array of handmade candles, incense, and soaps.

And then I found the clothing stalls where my jaw almost hit my knees. "Now, this is the apparel of a queen," I noted.

Revan pulled one of the gowns that I was almost too afraid to touch from a rack and brought it to me. "I don't know. I think I could pull this off better. Though, you have the hips for it."

"And the rack," Eko noted.

I laughed, shaking my head. "I'll tell you what. You get that dress if you can find me something just as exquisite but that I'm not afraid to touch."

"Deal!" he said, turning and bringing the dress to the vendor.

And thus began our fun of poking through the clothing until I was so overloaded with options that Rhyl decided we were just going to send them all to the house and be done with it. Revan got his dress, and I was dying to find out if he was going to wear it.

We were heading into a stall that smelled heavily of coffee straight from the ring of Sloth that was promising that it might have a Frappuccino for me when screaming broke out.

The guys sighed as the crowd began to become jostled as panicked demons tried to get away. Outside the market, the water splashed as the kimaris jumped from the city square into the water to escape.

"Is it another pridefall?" I asked as I tried to peer around the guys who'd somehow blocked me in.

"No," Eko said, his voice dark. "Looks like a Pride Ring."

When the streets had cleared as much as they could through the panic and fear of the populace trying to get away, I felt the heat of fire brush against my face, making me break out into a sweat.

The sight that met my eyes as we made our way to investigate had me looking in horror. Not fear. That hadn't registered yet. But disgust. A group of demons was terrorizing the stands closest to the edge of the water, working their way inward.

Destroying merchandise. Beating the vendors. Burning the stands.

"Who are they?" I asked as we pushed our way through the throngs of people trying to escape their attention. "Are they from other parts of Hell?"

"I wish I could say they were but no," Revan said, frowning. "Let's disband them and then we'll talk."

I kinda wished I had my little foxy friend with me. Maybe he'd give me a bit of magic like he had at the last market. Were markets always targeted?

We weren't the only ones moving in to try and put an end to the terrorism. Several were wearing some kind of uniform. They didn't look like militia but business men. With wings and weapons.

There were others who joined in, too. A whole handful of citizens of all species attempted to help. The kimaris and asmodai were sending water plumes over the walls of the market toward the fire, dousing it.

But the men who were here to cause problems were plentiful, easily outnumbering those who were here to put them down. And as Revan said, I recognized kimaris and shax demons, alongside those of the stronger variety who paraded around like men. Only right now, they didn't look like men but devils.

I found I was nearly screaming in fear as one of the nasty ones turned our way. Not because I was afraid, but because he'd sent a nasty stream of fiery magic straight at Rhyl.

CHAPTER ELEVEN
ANUKA

"Rhyl!" I cried, darting towards him. Fear blossomed in me as time slowed down.

I'd only just met these men. I was barely getting to know them. I couldn't lose them yet. How would I survive if one of them was killed in front of me?

A part of me realized I was being ridiculous. *I just met them. I knew nothing about them.* And still, I was confident that it would end me if something happened to them.

The fire that came at Rhyl was spiraling red and black. For a time, it looked like it slowed as I stared in abject horror. Bit by bit, centimeter by centimeter, it moved closer and closer. I blinked, turning my attention to Rhyl. He wasn't concerned as he looked up. Blue fire (it wasn't purple!) sparked from inside him, glowing through his eyes as a helmet-like bone mask slid over his face and horns branched out from his head.

But his unconcern as the fiery blast sped towards him had me screaming.

Without knowing what I was doing, I internally begged for the same magic my watcher gifted me yesterday.

Please, I begged. *Please let me use some magic to save him.*

Last time, there were streaks of purple fire moving through my veins, moving like a river over my skin. It was different this time. My entire arm from my bicep down turned an almost ethereal purple. Like sparkling glass. Purple fire danced at my fingertips with black plumes of smoke.

Chills covered my body as time sped up and I looked at the man attacking mine. No one will ever take someone that belongs to me. Not in life or death.

I was moving through space as if there were no resistance. As if I could move at the speed of light. In an instant I was suddenly in the demon's face, my glowing hand around his neck.

He screamed, his body bursting into flames from my purple wrath. When he turned to ash, I'd gathered the attention of everyone. Anger surged through me and a dress of fire ringed my body, purple and bright. I might have thought it beautiful at any other time. But right now, all I wanted to do was destroy those who thought they could attack my men. Attack a marketplace.

I screamed, and with it went a torrent of fire that left my body in a half-circle arc in front of me. Everyone it touched vaporized with a terrorized scream. It was enough that after the first wave, the rest of the stupid men went running. Tripping over each other and shoving one another backward to clear their own way as they tried to escape.

Though part of me wanted to destroy them all, instead, I let a few go. A handful. So they could spread the word.

Anuka was taking no prisoners. You mess with my city, I am going to destroy you.

When they were out of my sight, I called the magic back, pulling it inside me so it would stop its destructive path. Only then did I feel the awful pain coursing through me.

I screamed, falling to the cobblestone promenade. I shook as the live current tried to skin me alive. There were no sounds, nothing but the rush of the magic coursing through my veins like a million volts of electricity.

Did I pass out? There's a real possibility. Either I did or I didn't but either way, I was gasping when the magic faded away and once more, I found myself on my back looking up into the faces of my three demons.

Yes, I said it. They're mine. Fuck the world if they think that's going to change.

"Ouch," I mumbled.

Rhyl had me draped in his arms. I was boneless. Stretched across him like a cat.

He sighed, gently pulling me into a more comfortable position, though I wasn't sure that it was. Everything in me hurt.

"Silly queen," he murmured, pressing my face to his chest and holding me like a child. "I had that under control."

"You didn't look like it," I slurred, inwardly flinching at how ridiculous I sounded. I supposed my tongue was seared from the heat of the electric magic, too. "You just watched it come at you."

"Sweet girl," Eko murmured, pressing his lips to my head.

I snorted, closing my eyes. "You guys keep saying that but I'm sure you have no idea that I'm anything but."

"You're sweet," Revan said, his voice shifting location. I squinted my eyes open to see that Rhyl had gotten to his feet. "Everything can be sweet depending on your taste."

I laughed quietly, resting my head and letting the rest of the sting of magic shed away from my body.

Maybe I dozed because the next thing I realized was that I was surrounded by faces, most of which I had no interest in seeing. And I wasn't in my room but somewhere I didn't recognize.

I began to push myself up but Eko's hand on my shoulder stayed me. "Rest, queen."

Glowering at Malak in particular, I leaned back.

"Sorry, honey," Revan said. "They caught us coming back with you passed out in Rhyl's arms."

"And the story followed," Hayt said, grinning.

I sighed, choosing to ignore them. I managed to do so as I contemplated my next move. Thanks to my little watcher demon, who was now curled up at my side on the couch I was laying on, I had the ability to touch magic. Surely that would help me.

The men talked around me and unless someone spoke directly to me, I tuned them out as best I could. Only when the room went silent did I turn. I expected to find one of my demons if not all three. Instead, it was my murderer.

At least he wasn't looking so arrogant right now. Instead, he was frowning as he watched me. Sighing, I pulled myself up, flinching when my muscles protested.

"Why did they leave?" I asked, shifting so I was sitting properly.

"They have various tasks that they take care of," Malak answered.

"Not my men." But then I wondered if they did.

"All prideful have tasks that they perform for the city. It's part of being a responsible citizen." After a pause, he added, "They're not your men."

I smirked at the note of jealousy in his voice. "They are,

actually." Not that I'd cleared that with them. But if for no other reason than to harass Malak, I was pretty sure they'd agree with me. "But if you'd like to be useful for a change, maybe you can tell me why my body hurts so damn much when I touch the borrowed magic that my watcher loaned me."

Malak raised a brow, his dark eyes dropping to the fire demon in my lap before meeting mine again. "That's not borrowed magic. It's pride magic. It calls to the queen just as it does to me. The difference is, you're not cursed and can touch it."

I snorted, shaking my head. "You think being dragged here is not a curse?"

The way his jaw ticked made me grin. "Being my queen is not a curse. The curse is specifically for the sons of Satan."

"Explain," I demanded.

It was clear that Malak didn't take demands often. There was a moment I thought he was going to refuse me on principle alone. Instead, he repeated a somewhat lyrical prose with the dullest tone I could imagine.

> "For the Sons of Satan,
> A curse most tedious.
> For you are selfish, arrogant,
> And all around too devious.
>
> No power nor throne,
> No leader of Hell,
> Without the fated ones,
> You shall be but a shell.
>
> Oh, Sons of Satan,

You're in for a treat,
For once you find the fated,
The curse can be beat."

I nearly sputtered in laughter which only irritated Malak further. "Okay, so let me get this straight. You've been choosing random girls when your curse specifically states that it needs the 'fated one' to break it. Yet, you thought you could just choose some random ninny and mold her into a puppet queen, and voìla! You're ruling Hell."

I could tell I hit a nerve. His eyes narrowed as he crossed his arms, staring at me hard. Apparently, he really did think that.

Rolling my eyes, I attempted to get to my feet, but my muscles ached like I'd run a marathon. Which is not something I'd ever choose to do willingly.

"I was told how you vaporized the Pride Ring," Malak said.

"Yes, well. I thought they were going to hurt someone. What is a Pride Ring anyway?" My guys were going to tell me but then all Hell broke loose.

Was I trying to be punny?

"They're gangs, so to speak. Kind of like fight clubs in the human world. They operate underground and no one talks about them. Last time I heard, there were a dozen or so, though since the magic in Pride is getting wilder by the day, I think they've multiplied."

"What's their goal?"

He smirked. "You'll appreciate it, most likely. To depose me."

"And then who runs pride if not you?" Depending on the answer, I might join with the Pride Rings.

Malak shook his head. "No one, Nuke. It takes the magic of one of Satan's sons to rule the rings of Hell. And if I'm not here and one of my descendants isn't capable, then pride falls. The magic expands and spills into the Depths and further, contaminating the other rings."

"Why not have a descendant then?"

He raised a brow. "I don't have any offspring. It's the queen's job to provide me with them."

I rolled my eyes. "Fat chance, Malak. I didn't sign up for this."

"Yet you're trying to control the magic."

"I'm not. Not yet, anyway. But yes, I am trying to get your magic under control. The only way I can get home is if this place is in one piece. That's what you said, right?"

His frown deepened. I thought the part of that he'd concentrate on was me leaving. Instead, he chose to discuss the magic. "From what I heard, you sought out the magic and it responded."

"I called for the magic my watcher loaned me," I corrected.

He shook his head. "Demons don't have magic, so to speak. We call it magic but it's energy, the power that propels the magic that the watchers disperse. And the only magic that's going to affect you the way it does and considering the strength in which it responds to you, you're already touching the magic of pride."

I took a minute to consider this. A smile played on my lips as I appreciated already having a handle on the magic. That was good news, right? That meant I was already almost there.

As if he knew what I was thinking, Malak shook his head. "No. You're misunderstanding, Anuka. The curse is only broken when I can control the magic, too. Not just you. That's not the way the curse works."

Sighing in exasperation, I tried a different route. "Then we're going to have to come to some agreements. Quite frankly, I don't give a fuck who you are and what you want. You're a dick for murdering me and thrusting me into a position I have no interest in. Not to mention, one that comes with all sorts of lofty expectations on your part that are *not* going to happen. Namely, I will not be *your* queen. I will *not* provide you offspring, nor will I ever be in your bed. So, unless you can think of a way around all that and still get the ending outcome you desire, then I suppose we're at an impasse. And if that's the case, I'll happily leave your ostentatious and flamboyant house to live among the peasants."

I expected him to interrupt me many times over. Instead, Malak listened as I told him off.

"I have six brothers," Malak said, surprising me with this turn in conversation. "Sorin is the prince of lust; Adrian of greed, Lorcan of wrath, Lucien of envy, Bee of gluttony, and Tharul of sloth. When we were younger, we were always competitive though not nearly as cutthroat. As we aged, it became more and more apparent that there was one throne. One seat of rule. That meant, there could only be one true devil. And we all began to vie for that position.

"I admit that it got a bit nasty and ugly. Quite frankly, I knew our father was at his wit's end as he tried time and time again to make us get along. But when we continued to argue and fight over who was going to take his throne, Dad decided that he'd had enough. He cursed us, stripping our ability to access the magic afforded us within our circles, and then disappeared, leaving us with that vague as fuck curse. We've been racing each other to find the 'fated ones' ever since, none of us wanting the others to be able to take our father's throne."

"Would it really be that awful if one of your brothers took it?"

Malak scowled and turned toward the window as he slipped his hands into his pockets. From this angle, my mind immediately started sizing him up as to whether he was good enough to make a model of. Right now, he was nearly there. Much closer than he had been when I woke up in this godforsaken place.

"Can you imagine a lazy fuck who likely couldn't be bothered to make sure that the demons in Hell had enough to eat on the throne? Or someone so damn concerned with what everyone else has, he's not paying close enough attention to Hell to make sure the souls are running through smoothly? Better yet, some jackass who just wants more. More, more, more all the time. He's likely to burn the world down just so his influx of souls could keep up with his greed." He looked at me over his shoulder. "Do any of them sound worthy of running Hell?"

"When you put it like that..."

Malak turned away again. "Yes, I've gone about this wrong. Pride is mine. It's my circle; my city. I have spent endless days and nights, countless hours making sure my demons are happy and taken care of. Do you really think I was going to look for someone to be my queen who would come in here with a bunch of lofty ideas as how to 'improve' what is already perfect?"

"You know, Malak," I said, getting to my feet. Finally, I didn't feel like I was dying anymore. "I've spent a lot of time working with arrogant people. Those who I wanted nothing more than to shape to the mold I needed them to fit into, just so I can strip away every ugly layer and make money off them. I do this with their consent, mind you." I gave him a pointed look and was rewarded with the touch of a smile on his lips as he continued to stare out the window. "I learned a long time ago that an ego is a fragile thing. Stroking one's pride is beautiful when it raises them up and makes them the best they are. But I've also taken a lot of pains and energy to make sure that, while they're sure of themselves in every aspect of their being, they keep their minds humble. They keep their personalities modest. They understand and practice the importance of loyalty. And they keep a positive cosmic energy by being generous when they can. There's a fine line that when you cross, pride can be just as detrimental to your goals as it does to further them. By the sounds of it, you've already fallen well into the worst end of being prideful. Maybe you need to find your balance. Figure out what's actually important to you. Being the most important person in your own life is going to get you nowhere and assure that you fail, as it already has."

I didn't wait for an answer as I walked out of the room.

CHAPTER TWELVE
ANUKA

As soon as the door shut behind me, I frowned. I had no idea where I was. Not that I likely would have found my way if I'd left my own rooms, but I didn't appear to be anywhere near them right now.

That was unfortunate. The least they could have done was put me on the same floor.

I took a right and began walking, gazing into open doors and studying my surroundings. The halls were wide enough to be a room all their own. With an enormous, continuous runner going down the center.

Room after room had me mesmerized by the beauty of this place. Breathtaking, enchanting. Even as it was incredibly over the top and flashy.

But one thing was abundantly clear. I was not going to find my way anywhere on my own.

"Eko?" I asked, hearing my voice sound so small in these enormous rooms.

I didn't receive an answer. I guess when Hayt said that all I'd need was to say one of their names in the hallway, that didn't include the demons I brought home.

With a sigh, I turned and crossed my arms. "Hayt."

I wasn't sure what I was expecting. For him to show up out of nowhere? Walk out of a door in thin air in front of me?

He did neither. He came from the direction I'd come from with a smile. I'll give these demons one thing: they were all certainly sure of themselves. Unlike so many human men, they weren't faking it. I could *feel* their arrogance as if it washed off them like body heat. Not the fake it until you make it kind of vanity.

Humans had a habit of pretending to love everything about themselves. Portraying themselves to the world as if they were IT. The whole package. When in reality, there was a plethora of qualities they hate about themselves but have learned to compensate for and capitalize on their better features.

Thus how I made a living.

These demons were different. If they had weaknesses, they didn't know it nor did they show them. I wasn't sure there was anything they disliked about themselves.

"Hello, queen," Hayt said as he stopped in front of me. "What can I do for you?"

"How about that tour you offered?" I don't know why I asked. Probably emptying myself out into a hall that wasn't even remotely familiar and having to rely on someone else for direction did it.

Not that it truly mattered. I wasn't going to remember the layout of this place. It was far larger than was necessary. Even for Malak and his friends.

"My pleasure." He inclined his head in almost a slight bow.

I sighed. "Cut that out. I'm not your queen, regardless of why I was brought here."

Hayt grinned. "Alright. This way, Anuka."

Somehow, my name on his lips was worse than calling me queen. I gritted my teeth but kept pace beside him.

"There's no true rhyme or reason to the upper floors. They're primarily bedrooms, washrooms, and the random den from time to time." He shrugged.

"Then why is this place embarrassingly enormous?"

Hayt smirked. "Because Malak is a monarch. He hosts shit and people and needs space for that."

"Does he?" Was I included as someone he was hosting?

He nodded as he directed us to the stairs. "Yes, though he hasn't since his father disappeared."

I sighed, shaking my head. It all seemed to lead back to that stupid incident. Goddamn devil. It's his fault I'm here, apparently.

"What does he host?" I asked.

"Parties, primarily. But his father would come to visit. His mother. His siblings."

"His brothers?"

Hayt nodded as we stopped on the main floor landing, and he turned to look at me. "They weren't always hateful towards each other. Craving power does that to a person."

I frowned, turning away from him and looking down the hall. Taking my cue, Hayt started walking, leading me through the main corridor that was at least vaguely familiar. It would take years to become familiar with this place.

He bypassed several doors that were wide open, rattling off what the names of the rooms were. They seemed to be called after common demons from Hell. They were all equally as extravagant as the last so I didn't care that we weren't stopping.

The first door Hayt pushed open and led me inside stole

my breath. Perhaps one of the largest dining rooms I'd ever seen. All decked out in the same dark color palette with pops of purple and gold. It was stunning.

"We haven't actually used this room in years," Hayt said, smiling at the table as if he were remembering something in particular. His pause in dialog made me curious, though I didn't ask. "Once, Malak threw spectacular dinner parties. The feasts this room has seen…"

His obvious reminiscing almost had me smiling.

"What kind of demon are you again?" Have I even asked that?

"Izanami," he answered, turning from the room and leading me further down the hall.

"What does that mean?" I asked when he didn't expand on his own.

"Similar to Rhyl but where he sees time in one continuous stream without really differentiating between the past, present, or future, I can witness events. Visit them. It's easiest in the past but sometimes I can manage a glimpse into something that hasn't happened yet."

"Is this written in stone, these things you see?"

He smiled as he pushed open another door and my jaw literally dropped. I've never seen such an amazing room. Filled with dark stone, crystal, and rich tones. Large expanses of shiny floor stretched across the enormous space. As we stepped inside, the giant chandeliers lit and began rising from the floor to hang in their places. Sconces around the room lit.

"Yes, kind of," Hayt said, distracting me. I wasn't sure what he was talking about, having lost the thread of the conversation in my drooling over a room that was stupidly lavish, and yet, *I wanted it*. "The reason why future events are difficult to see is because the future isn't quite set yet. I imagine one of the reasons why Rhyl doesn't keep time is because everything he sees shifts so frequently that he isn't sure which is a suggestion of the future, or which are actual events that will take place."

I hadn't actually talked to Rhyl about his abilities as a demon. We hadn't gotten to that point. Amazing sex? Yes, there was time for that. Learning about the kind of person he is? Well, it's on my list of things to do.

"Are you and Rhyl friends?"

Hayt smirked, running his hand across one of the plush chairs as we wandered through the room. "No. I've had brief encounters with him. Nothing noteworthy. I'm saying Rhyl but I mean the uvall demons in general."

I supposed that made more sense. "And this room?"

"After the feasts that will keep you full for a decade have commenced, we move the party into the ballroom. And we dance until we cannot feel our feet."

He reached for me, and I wasn't sure he was seeing me at all when he pulled me against his chest. I found myself in a pose I hadn't been in before. He paused, long enough as if to say, 'this is how we start – in this position – so take note.' Then there was a slight dip in our stance before he began weaving me around the room.

I've never been ballroom dancing. Clubs aren't even my thing. But there's something magical about being swept around the room like a princess that had even my cold heart pattering in appreciation.

Hayt hummed a melody that was eerie and enchanting. He swept me through the room, and I felt like I was back in one of Kingsley's dreamscapes again. Floating. Little fires blurring by us as we spun and slid and dipped.

He was an attractive man with dark hair and dark eyes. Soft scruff that rubbed my cheek when he got close. A scent that was mind-numbingly delicious. A strong hold and a sure foot. But his focus was elsewhere, even as it was trained on me.

"What are you thinking about?" I asked, almost amused at how breathless my voice was.

Our dance abruptly stopped. At first, I didn't see that our surroundings changed until seven little boys came racing down the length of the room before dropping their body weight and sliding across the immaculately polished floors. Floors that were not the same dark onyx but now a light silver quartz.

"Hey!" one of the little boys shouted, falling back as another ran into his legs sending him tumbling. He laughed wildly. "Sorin – how did you get so far?"

The boy named Sorin giggled as he pulled himself to his feet. "You have to be aerodynamic, Bee. Like this."

He took off again, sprinting across the floor in his socks. When he dove down, he went to his stomach and slid across the floor.

Before I could see if Bee followed his lead, I was distracted by a little boy that looked remarkably like Malak. I recognized his haughty smile as he sat on the ground next to another of the boys, the oldest by the looks of him.

"What is this?" I asked, keeping my voice low so I wouldn't interrupt the scene.

"A past that Malak enjoys thinking about. One that often comes to mind when he enters any ballroom," Hayt answered. "A joyful memory of him and his brothers."

I was surprised to hear that as I turned back. Everything I've heard from Malak makes it sound like he hates his brothers. As though there has always been bad blood between them. But the laughter I was seeing between these seven boys wasn't wicked.

It was children getting along. Siblings having fun together. Creating memories.

Malak laughed, laying back on the floor and watching the ceiling as the younger boys continued to streak across the floor. A smile danced on his lips as he listened. The older brothers instructed the little ones, teaching them how to properly get the right speed and maneuver their bodies for the most effective slide.

The image faded and I was back in Hayt's arms as if I never left. He blinked a few times before smiling. "Sorry, Nuke. I don't always react quickly when I walk through a memory."

"Why that memory?"

He shrugged, his hand dropping from the formal position on my back to rest just over my ass. "Malak has told us about those moments many times. After maybe the fourth instance of him reminiscing, I searched out a couple of the memories. That one is my favorite."

"Why?"

Hayt smiled. "Because he's enjoying his brothers and he's at peace. Despite how it appears, his family is important to him. Which is hard to see since everything is well, a mess. Including their sibling rivalry."

I rolled my eyes and pulled away from him. "I don't understand why his father didn't just man up and name an heir. Or you know, just give it to the oldest."

"Adrian," Hayt said, a smile climbing his face. I wasn't sure he was fully back in the present as he reached for me and pulled me against him again. "Malak would throw a fit if Adrian took the throne. Prince of greed," he chuckled.

"Which of his brothers would he accept?"

Hayt sighed. One of his hands ringed my back but the

other ran slowly over my hip and down my thigh. "Once, he might have been okay with any of his brothers."

"What happened?" Why can't he just finish this conversation? He must anticipate my questions, but he keeps making me prompt him. But then, by the way the smile remained dancing on his sumptuous lips, I was guessing he was doing it intentionally.

"My guess? The princes need their queens to touch their magic. And none of them were focused on it or interested in it. Without their magic, without them being able to get their own sections of Hell under control, they're not capable of ruling any part of Hell. Personally, I think Lucifer kept tempting them with the promise of his throne in an attempt to get them to take this seriously."

"It doesn't seem to have worked," I noted.

He raised his hand, his fingers running suggestively along my jaw. It was both sensual and sweet. Though I still wasn't sure he was seeing me.

"I don't know. Malak's luck is looking up."

I snorted, shaking my head. Part of me thought to pull away again. Instead, I asked, "What are you seeing right now?"

Hayt licked his lips as he tilted his head. "The most beautiful, prideful, badass queen that will make the city proud."

"Oh yeah?" I asked, raising a brow.

Perhaps I was having a dense moment. Because I didn't realize he was talking about me until he added, "The crown will look glorious on your head, Nuke. I can't wait for you to grasp the wild magic by its balls and make it bow to you. That is a vision I will revisit often."

"You really see that?" I asked, my voice low and hesitant.

Hayt nodded. "I've seen it since you told us we all suck and wouldn't even make proper thirst traps. You're our queen, Anuka."

I shivered, shaking my head. I tried to pull away but put zero effort into it. Hayt's hand went to my face, his fingers tangling in my hair as he cupped the side of my head. "I know you know you can do this. Why do you refuse when the magic wants to connect with you?"

"I have a life," I whispered. "You stole me from it."

He tilted his head. I watched as he blinked several times and finally, he focused on me. His smile was soft. I was surprised when he pressed his lips to mine, kissing me in the most delicious way that had me leaning into him. Encouraging him to continue.

Was it strange that I felt he belonged more with me and my three demons than with Malak and those around him? The ease I felt with him, the way he kissed me as if he'd done so a thousand times already. My connection with him was immediate, even if I tried to push it away.

Because he wasn't mine. He was Malak's.

"Silly queen," he murmured against my lips, taking my bottom one between his teeth and making me shiver. "This isn't an ultimatum. It's not this or that. You or them. It's all and everything."

My face scrunched as I tried to decode his riddle. Hayt smiled. "Silly queen," he repeated, his voice dropping lower. "Just let me kiss you and make you forget that you don't want to like me."

I was going to argue. But then, if I had a choice to walk away or keep kissing this man who kissed like a dream, I was going to choose his lips. And I did.

CHAPTER THIRTEEN
HAYT

Catching events of the future wasn't easy. Unlike a uvall, I don't have access to all of time. I only see snippets. Sometimes I can choose which to find. It takes more talent and focus than I generally care to use.

Did I use this ability to find our queen? Not intentionally. I'd searched for several minutes to figure out whether Zyphon's bet would be a useless endeavor or a fruitful one. I just wanted to see if Malak was going to find his queen or not.

What I found was a future that I was pretty sure would please everyone, even if it wasn't one we were planning.

Of course, the future isn't actually written in stone. We say it is but there are decisions that need to be made and if they go the wrong way, the future that's set can shatter. That's not to say that it's all willy nilly. Based on habit, personality, and situation, the future is on a track and though it's unlikely that the train will derail, it's not impossible.

While I hadn't looked into the future to find our specific queen, once I glimpsed her, I knew who she was. Okay, I knew what she looked like. *Now* did I use that cheat to find her and win the bet? Yes and I have no shame in that. I found her so Malak could bring her here and though he made the future a little foggy, it was crisp once more.

Anuka was going to be our queen!

Also, I could kiss her for days. The way her petite tongue moved against mine had me almost devouring her as if I were an animal.

"Hayt!" Malak snapped.

I sighed, pausing with my lips against Anuka's. Her irritation almost had a flavor. Sharp and somewhat bitter. Pressing my lips more firmly to hers for a minute, I tried to assure her wordlessly that he wasn't actually going to keep me away from her. Even if he tried.

Then I took a step back, though I didn't release my queen, and turned my attention to an aggravated Malak. At this point, I couldn't remember him any other way.

"Yes?" I countered.

The disinterest in my tone had him narrowing his eyes. "Unhand my queen."

"No," Nuke said, bringing her body flush to mine. "I don't belong to you, and I can kiss whomever I damn well please."

"Not in my house."

I rolled my eyes. He was definitely being counterproductive.

"That can be fixed." Nuke pulled away from me and I reluctantly let her go. She took a minute to consider me before frowning. "You would probably be a lot of fun, Hayt, and I think we'd get along well. But I'm not interested in your baggage."

Sighing, I nodded, placing my hands in my pockets. "I understand. It's heavy and argumentative."

Nuke grinned. She kissed my cheek before heading for the door without a word otherwise.

"Where are you going?" Malak demanded, taking a few steps in her direction.

Nuke ignored him completely. No falter in her steps. No turn of her head. There wasn't even a pause in her breathing.

"Anuka!"

She walked out the door.

"You know," I said as I watched her go, "you're lucky you didn't just fuck up."

"What-"

"You're such a bullhead that you're going to break the outcome you want before it's even whole."

As I anticipated, Malak let Nuke go in favor of dealing with me. He wasn't always a pain in the ass. He was actually very kind and generous when he wasn't being a fucking plague.

I was convinced that out of all the Satan boys, Malak was the worst. He had that big ego driving him, after all.

He stopped in front of me, his arms crossed over his chest. He stood so close that his forearms brushed against me. Trying to intimidate me. Waste of time on his part. I knew him well enough that there was no part of me that would ever fear him. "Tell me."

I shrugged, leaning into him and grinning. "I've seen the future, Malak. She's not *your* queen. She's *our* queen. And if you stop getting in your own way, you won't fuck that future up."

I'd known when I presented Anuka Hauptman to the boys that Malak was already in love with this woman, even if he didn't know it. It was written all over his face in the way he stared at her image. I didn't need to see the future to know that.

But it was clear as soon as Nuke woke up that the two of them were going to be two battling flames and if we couldn't get them to unite, I was afraid this would spell the end for pride. I shuddered to think of our demons being forced into the other rings.

Malak stared at me for a long time, determining how he was going to handle this revelation. This assurance.

"What do I do?" he asked. I chose to ignore the bitter note in his voice.

"Stop being a dick," I said cheerily and stepped back. He snarled at me, grabbing for my arm and pulling me roughly back toward him. I grinned. "Honestly, Malak. You're such a brute."

"Hayt," he warned.

I sighed dramatically. "You don't need to do anything. Let her come to you. She will. You're the prince. There are things about Pride that only you handle."

He released a frustrated breath. "Fine. And what do I do in the meantime?"

"Just as we've been doing. The magic wants to connect with her, Malak. And you're the only one who knows more than general information on that magic."

He nodded.

I wasn't sure what Revan's fascination with the skirt was, but I found him in the courtyard swinging his hips, so the fabric swished around him. He just wore a skirt and shoes. Nothing else.

The man was gorgeous. No doubt about that. He was

one of those light demons. Light skin. Light hair. Light eyes. And he'd marked his body with a healthy portion of demonic ink, depicting the tortures he dished out.

I leaned against the stone wall and watched him as he continued to swing his hips. He looked up with a smirk, stopping when he spotted me. After looking around, determining that we were alone, he closed the distance. I didn't miss the sigh.

"What's up, Hayt?"

"Nothing," I said, shaking my head. I dropped my eyes to the skirt. "What's with the lack of clothing?"

He laughed. "I'm enjoying my dick swinging. And the breeze is nice, too."

"You were always odd."

His smirk was arrogant, just like the demon he was.

"Did Nuke find you?"

Revan tilted his head. "Was she looking for me?"

"No. Not exactly. Malak pissed her off and I kind of anticipated she was going to try and convince one of you to bring her home."

I enjoyed the grin that spread across his face. Wicked and sensual. "I'll find her but I'm sure she didn't get far."

"I think you should try to keep her here."

He laughed, dropping his attention to the skirt again, and picking up the revolutions of his hips. "Seriously, Hayt. You ought to try this."

"I'll think about it. Tell me about the Pride Ring."

There wasn't an answer for a moment before he looked up, pausing in his rhythmless dance. "She thought Rhyl was going to get hurt and reacted."

"But what did she do?"

He shrugged. "I'm guessing that she's either some strange fire demon, which might explain the watcher since there hasn't been news of a familiar in pride in a long time. Or she touched the wild magic."

"Your guess?" I pressed.

"You know the answer. Why are you asking?"

"What makes you-"

His rolling eyes made me cut my words short.

"Don't play daft. You had a vision of her as your queen and you all hunted her. That's why she's here."

"I'm glad to say that's not at all accurate except that I did glimpse a future where she's our queen. The cause and effect are different, though."

He shrugged, turning his attention back to his skirt. I didn't press the issue again as he went back to swinging his hips. It was as if he couldn't help the smile that touched his lips.

I was about to wipe that smile off.

"Have you spoken to Zyphon?"

The glare he gave me could rival Malak's. "No. I didn't come here for him. I came here for Nuke."

Did he expect I was going to believe that? When he continued to glare at me, I thought that maybe he was trying to convince himself. "Regardless of the reason you came, that doesn't change the question."

This time when he rolled his eyes, it was with such dramatics that I thought they'd get stuck in the back of his head. "He told me to stay away. He made his decision. I'm not going to beg or argue."

"And what if that decision was a mistake?"

He paused, his body stilling. Then he turned away, giving me his back, but didn't move. By the rise and fall of his shoulders, I knew the truth he's been hiding since he stepped foot back into this place.

It wasn't a fling between Revan and Zyphon. They were

nearly paired. Their love ran deep. And all these years later, the pain of being apart was just as raw as the day they split.

Revan was good at hiding it behind careless laughter and smiles. Especially when he had an audience. But when you caught him off guard, he let those solidly constructed walls shake and crack.

"It doesn't matter," Revan said, his voice quiet, though he tried to put some conviction in it. "I'm going in a new direction now."

My brows knit together in confusion. "What does that mean?"

He glanced back at me with a frown before taking a few steps away. "It means I already have two men and a woman I'm involved with. Zyphon made his choice and never took it back."

I watched as he walked away. There was no swish in his hips as he tangled his skirt. Not this time. I sighed, shaking my head.

Malak always makes a mess of things.

Perhaps I could play matchmaker... or should I stay out of it? What had been in the bit of the future I saw?

The only thing I'd paid attention to was the black crown of pride sitting on our lovely Anuka's head. Of course, there were other things amiss. She didn't have wings right now and the event I saw, Nuke clearly had wings. Fiery perfection that matched her horns.

Sexy as all hell.

My smile slipped as I closed my eyes to think about it. She was there. As were we. And yes, those three demons she's chosen were, too.

Zyphon and Revan were on opposite sides of the gathering, appearing as if they were pointedly ignoring each other.

I shook my head, ridding myself of the image. That can't work. Because that much tension within a group like this, especially if we were all going to enjoy our queen together, would be toxic at best.

No. I couldn't let that happen. We needed Nuke. And you know... I kinda liked her.

A smile climbed my lips as I turned. Yes, I liked her just fine. A woman that we all wanted. And not just because she'd be our queen. Because Nuke was a bombshell, and it was addicting.

Time to see who I could recruit to help me patch Revan and Zyphon. I headed back inside, debating on my options. It seemed that whatever the Fates were up to, it put Zy right in my path. Apparently, he should be the one to help get them back on the same page.

I watched him approach as I stood at the side of the hall. He appeared lost in thought, not seeing me until he was right on top of me. Then he paused, giving me a smile that wasn't anywhere near true.

"Where are you going?" I asked.

Zyphon glanced down the hall before looking back at me. A moment of confusion crossed his face before he shook his head. "No idea. Just wandering, I guess."

"Walk with me." I offered him my hand. He raised a brow, an amused smirk on his mouth.

"I know you well enough to know you're up to something and want me in on it." Though his words might suggest he wanted no part of my shenanigans, he placed his hand in mine and allowed me to lead him away.

I didn't actually have anywhere in mind to go but I pulled him along. "I've been thinking."

"Mm. All mischief begins when you think."

Grinning, I turned to the right and down a different

hall. "I think I have Malak and Nuke under control." Zyphon snorted. "That means I can concentrate on other things."

"Yeah?"

"Like you."

He chuckled. "That's sweet, Hayt, but I'm not really in the mood-"

I squeezed his hand as I shook my head. "Not what I meant. You want to selfishly keep your cock to yourself, that's fine." Zyphon laughed. "I'm talking about your broken heart."

His laughter died immediately. There was a sudden halt in his step before he realized he did so, jerking me to a brief stop before we carried on. He couldn't hide the momentary fall in his façade, though he tried.

"I'm-"

"About to lie to me."

His demure smile flashed as he sighed. "It doesn't matter."

"It matters."

"And you'll have me do what?"

"Fix it."

This time he intended to stop, pulling me still next to him. And I knew in that moment that the reason the event I witnessed of our queen and her horny bunch of demons was showing Revan and Zyphon so far apart was that both of them had decided they were not going to speak to each other. They wouldn't seek each other out.

They weren't going to fix what was broken. Instead, they were going to continue to suffer.

"Hayt."

"Trust me, Zy."

He watched me warily.

"Just talk to him. No planned dialog, just seek him out and talk to him."

"And say what?"

I grinned. "I just said no planned conversation."

He scowled, shaking his head. But his hand in mine was trembling. Just slightly.

"A love so deep doesn't come around twice," I said gently. "Maybe you can learn to love another, but you will never replace the love you already have, Zy. And if you let it rot, it will eat at you both."

Minutes went by and like Revan, his chest rose and fell with struggling breaths. "I just- what am I supposed to say?"

"Why not start with 'I messed up.' Or 'I love you and always have'? I think those are two really strong options."

He smiled around the lip he was chewing. "Maybe," he conceded. "I'll think about it."

Already I could feel the future shivering. I smiled, nodding. I just hope that when it shifted, it wasn't going to be pride burning as the magic ate it into extermination.

CHAPTER FOURTEEN
ANUKA

As the days passed, I was increasingly getting 'I don't know' as answers from my demons. And even when I chanced being around one of Malak's demons, though they had more information than mine, I'd reached their limit, too. Most conversations ended this way.

Well, most ended with me frustrated and stomping off. I didn't want to talk to Malak. It was more than that; I was almost willing to fail if it was between that and talking to prince shithead.

Of course, then I'd kick myself and determine that I would find the man with a tail up his ass because I *refused* to fail. My family and my business were completely out of reach until I made that happen.

I still needed a map of this place. I had gotten to the point where I'd go room by room when looking for someone since nothing seemed intuitive and the sheer volume of rooms – the vast majority of which were unused, by the way – was overwhelming.

A map wasn't offered so I was back to hunting little by

little. My mission today? To not try and kill Malak while I learned more about pride, the magic, and how the world works. By world, I mean Hell.

Maybe I'd paid my toll with karma. I didn't waste hours looking for Malak this morning. He was on the second floor in one of the rooms that looked remarkably like an office with massive windows overlooking the city. If I remembered correctly, he was facing Tanndwr though I wondered if he could see the underwater city from up here.

I paused in the open door to study him. He stood in the window with his hands in his pockets frowning. In the distance, I could make out one of the storms. What did my demons call it? A pridemage storm, I think. The details of how the air swirled and brought purple streaks of lightning with it made me frown.

It made Malak frown, too. He sighed heavily before his head turned to the left. At first, I thought he'd found my presence but a moment later, a demon walked out of nothing at his side.

"My Lord," he greeted Malak.

Malak nodded. "Hey, Zo. What shitstorm is happening now?"

"I'm offended that you think I always bring you bad news," Zo said.

"You do. How about you start with something positive, hm?"

Zo smiled, inclining his head. "The rice terraces are producing a new strain of product that is absolutely divine. They'll be harvesting it this afternoon."

Malak smiled. "See? I appreciate knowing that."

"I reported it to Kingsley."

"Yes, as you should. And I'm sure it's on his list of things to tell me. But that meeting hasn't happened." Zo inclined his head again. "Alright. Now you can tell me what you came to."

"Unfortunately, this isn't a happy thing. The fog has moved west, eating the walls of another set of dwellings. The demons have already evacuated and have moved inward."

Malak sighed. "Thank you. I'll take a look."

Zo nodded. He didn't leave, even as Malak turned back to the window, as if he could see what Zo had reported.

"Was there something else?" Malak asked.

"No, my Lord." Still, he remained where he was. I wondered if he was waiting for a formal dismissal. Maybe Malak thought the same thing as he turned back to Zo with a brow raised.

"I understand that there are several demons you trust. Maybe you need to take a break for a while. I can *see* the weight on your shoulders."

Malak smiled lightly and turned back to the window. "Thank you for your concern, Zo. My demons already have full plates, unfortunately. I'm not sure drowning them to lighten my load is the right answer."

"Understood." This time, Zo bowed with a shallow dip of his head before turning away and walking into the air.

I rose my hand to knock on the door, but my hand remained suspended when Malak moved.

He let his head fall back, his hands going to his hair as he grabbed fistfuls. And for the first time since waking up in Hell, I could see the strain and pressure he was under. It wasn't irritation and resentment on his face when faced with something else he needed to attend to, adding more to his agenda. It was concern. Stress. Maybe even a little defeat, hopelessness, and fear.

His hands fell to his sides as he turned and froze when his eyes landed on me. For a minute, we stared silently.

"Do you need something?" he asked, his tone not at all reflecting the emotion I saw in him before. It wasn't there now. The moment of vulnerability when he thought he was alone had passed. Turning once more into his composed, asshole self.

But his voice, though strong, was lower than usual. There was a tiredness in it.

"I have some questions and it seems you're the only one who can answer them," I answered, dropping my hand from where it hovered to knock on the door.

He nodded. "Can it wait? I have something I need to check on."

"What is it?" I asked, curious as to whether or not he'd tell me.

"The fog produced by the wild magic has eaten through the magic I was able to place on the buildings it was brushing up against and has begun its deterioration. I need to see if I can salvage it or if I need to let it go." He glanced at the window over his shoulder for a second. "Or if there's anything I can do at this point," he added. I thought that maybe that was supposed to be an internal thought that he hadn't intended for me to hear.

"Okay," I said. My questions were semantics. Not people losing their homes.

Malak turned back, his gaze landing on me for a minute, before he nodded and headed for the door I stood in. I stepped away to let him pass. Once again, he paused. "Would you like to accompany me? I'm not sure how much of the city you've seen but you can ask whatever it is you'd come here for on the way."

If I was going to be queen, this was something I should see firsthand. I mean, I'd already seen it, but I hadn't seen a family newly uprooted. I had taken the falling buildings as old damage. This was brand new.

"Yes. Thank you." I spun on my heel to follow.

We were silent as we walked through the enormous building. Nothing was going to convince me this wasn't an extravagant show of status. The smallest fraction of the space was actually inhabited and used. And what of the rest?

I was led under the building as my three demons had brought us the other day. Or last week? I lost track of time down here. But I was surprised when Malak led us to one of the small canoes that only fit three people. He helped me climb in before joining me and took up the oars himself.

Maybe it was unflattering to look at him shocked that he was doing the physical labor himself. I didn't take him for that sort of person.

After he'd moved us through the busy throughway over Tanndwr and onto one of the water lanes that led east, he looked up at me. A smile spread over his lips, amused. "What?"

"I didn't know you knew how to operate a canoe," I said.

Malak laughed. "Of course, I do. There's not much in Pride I don't know how to do."

"Really?"

He nodded. "Were you brought through the harvest fields?"

"I didn't know you had fields."

His chuckle made me frown. Only because I didn't like the way my body responded to it. He might not be perfection that I could make into a star, but he was gorgeous. Which I hated. Because he was an ass.

An ass who murdered me.

"There are floating fields throughout the city where our produce and fruits are grown. There are also a whole lot of rice terraces. And then there's the fishing bays that are right outside the city and import all the sea life we need. Otherwise, there are more than a dozen ports where we import and export goods."

I must have stared at him for several minutes as if he were a fly. He chuckled. "What were you shown?"

"Well, our tour ended abruptly when the Pride Ring came out. I suppose that they hadn't gotten to those parts of the city. But I saw Waasser, Tanndwr, that park of terror, the Remolí. Some markets and your temple." I waved a hand in the air.

He nodded. "You saw the beauty of the city. Not the parts that make us prosperous."

"I guess. I also got to ride a dragon."

His grin was indulgent. "It's a lot of fun."

This was a different man than the one I've encountered every other time. I almost asked him if he had a twin.

"We'll take a tour around the barrier beyond the city and visit the working-class after we check out the newest failing building."

I nodded, turning to look at the buildings that towered over us in their sunlit glory. I just couldn't get over how stunning this place was. I couldn't possibly be in Hell. That just wasn't logical. There were flowers hanging out of window baskets, cascading down and fluttering in the breeze like a curtain. Their scent mixed with that of the clean water, and this was a paradise.

"What questions did you have?" Malak asked.

For a moment, I had no idea what he was talking about. I didn't have questions. I was just along for the ride. Returning my attention to him, I watched as he expertly maneuvered the canoe around other boats of various sizes while seemingly using very little effort on his part.

When he looked at me again, I got my shit together. "I've apparently reached the line at which everyone has the answers to. I want to know how the city is run. What kinds of jobs there are, though I suspect you covered a lot of those. I want an explanation on the magic, what it means to be the son who rules Hell." I waved a hand in the air as if saying 'etcetera' and glanced at the first child I'd seen. A toddler kimaris! They were even more strange looking as children.

"All the rings of Hell have their own magic, which can only be controlled by their ruling son of Satan. The magic I use now is all my own and not nearly as strong as what it should be. My father stripped my brothers and I of that ability when he cursed us, and we were forced to forward his agenda by finding our queens so that we can once again have the ability to control the magic. As you can see, when left untamed, the magic gets destructive. It becomes wilder and more unmanageable the longer it goes unhandled."

"And he did this because you and your brothers wouldn't stop fighting?"

His lips quirked up in amusement. I watched as he nodded a greeting at some demons as we passed them. "Yes. It grew beyond sibling rivalry and good-natured bickering. When we really started exchanging throws and insults, and truly fighting about who should be our father's heir, he finally had enough."

"I can't say I don't blame him."

Malak shook his head. "Neither do I. There's a part of us

that knew it was coming. Not this particular punishment but something. We'd crossed the line so long ago, we didn't even know where the line was."

"You don't hate your brothers."

A wan smile touched his lips at about the time the canoe began drifting into the fog. "No. I don't hate them. I never did. But that doesn't mean I think any of them are good enough to rule Hell."

"But you are."

His dark gaze flickered to me, his smile climbing slightly. "Yes."

"Tell me about the magic of pride in particular."

The charged fog had fallen around us. The noise of the city fell away and it became eerily quiet. The only sounds were from the movement of water as we moved through it. I thought I could pick out the building we were heading for. There was something about it, unlike the others. Not only was it only partially surrounded by fog, but it didn't look like it had been broken for long.

And by broken, I meant that there were entire chunks that had fallen away. A hole in the roof. As if it had been abandoned and was falling into disrepair.

"There were people here when this happened?" I asked before he could begin to tell me about the magic.

Malak nodded as he pulled the canoe up and tied us to the side that wasn't falling apart. He climbed out before offering me his hand. I took it and allowed him to pull me onto the stone dock.

"Yes." We studied the exterior from where we stood for a moment before he turned and walked along the perimeter to the door. I followed. "The magic can only be touched by two individuals. Me as the ruler of pride. And my queen. The magic itself is the essence of pride. Of my little circle of

Hell. It wants to connect. It wants to be controlled. I can feel it all around me. Picking and poking and grabbing. And when I can't quite make contact with it-"

He held out his hand and I could visibly see that the magic gathered. Little flickers and sparks. But when he couldn't grasp it, the magic dispersed in a gust. The bit that ricocheted toward the building slammed into the wall, sending a chunk of it tumbling. Malak pulled me out of the way, though it wasn't actually anywhere near me.

"When I can't take hold, it gets frustrated as if it's a living thing. It kind of is but more of an animal than anything with sentient thoughts. It reacts. Becomes mischievous. Caustic. And the longer it goes this way, the more devastating it becomes."

"Like a child calling out for attention."

Malak chuckled. "Yeah, something like that."

We stepped inside and it was almost like a line was drawn down the middle. On the right was where the magic had eaten the building apart. Biting into the supports and having taken chunks of stone from the walls.

On the opposite side, it was a beautiful modern house with classic furnishings and décor. It looked like much of the furniture had been removed and I assumed that meant most of the cabinets and drawers would be empty, as well.

"Demons aren't weak. Especially not those of pride," Malak said. "They held out until it became structurally unsound. Trusting that I could keep the magic away."

Another time, I might have pointed out that he failed them. He didn't keep the magic from eating their house. But I didn't. I recognized that I would have at one point and yet, I had no desire to bite back.

I could physically see that this bothered him. Not the errant magic but his citizens being displaced.

"Where would they go?" I asked.

"Good question." We both turned at the voice in time to see Bael and Zyphon walk in. "That was officially the last spare apartment in the city that we moved this family into. Zy and I took an hour to check out the other buildings close by and at least four more are on their way down."

Malak released a breath, closing his eyes for a moment. I almost felt for him.

Almost.

"Have the third floor of my estate cleared out and temporarily sectioned off into apartments. Have we heard from Mayor Jurd?" Malak asked.

Zyphon nodded. He looked at me first. "Jurd is the mayor of Tanndwr," he told me before addressing Malak. "He will take in as many as he can. But like Pride, Tanndwr is at their limit."

"I figured."

"Why not just build more houses?" I asked.

"There's nowhere left to build except up," Malak said. "Which we're not opposed to but we've put that on hold because there's no use in building more if the magic is just going to tear it down."

"You can't build outwards? Beyond the current city limits?"

Malak shook his head. "The rings don't get any bigger. We grow exponentially for shades – souls of the dead – but not for demons. We're supposed to live in a constant plateau. The old die as frequently as the new are born."

"And that's why I've only seen a single child since I've been here? There is a ton of school space for that little number of children."

"Oh no, there are plenty of children," Bael said,

grinning. "They stay away from the wild magic and tend to stay inside for fear of it."

All I was hearing today was that the magic was a problem that needed to be dealt with right now.

No pressure.

CHAPTER FIFTEEN
ANUKA

Malak rubbed a hand over his face as he turned to look at the falling building. "Bael, want to take Nuke on a tour of the barriers and the harvest fields? I can feel the foundation trembling, so I'd like for all of you to leave the building sooner rather than later."

"And you?" I asked.

He was observing a crack in the ceiling as he answered. "I'm going to check the surrounding buildings. See if there's anything I can do to stall their failings. If not, I'll see if I can convince my people living inside to leave before they're forced to."

"I'll head home and get started on transforming the third floor," Zyphon said.

Malak nodded. "Thank you."

Zyphon didn't answer as he turned away and walked out. Bael frowned after him before turning his attention to me. "Ready?"

I nodded, looking at Malak again.

"You can finish your questions tonight, if you'd like," Malak said, meeting my eyes.

For just a moment, I thought that maybe something almost peaceful passed between us. I nodded. "Okay."

Bael offered his hand, and I allowed him to lead me out of the falling building.

"If it falls-" I started.

"Malak will be fine," Bael said as he helped me into the canoe that I assumed he brought. That begged the question as to how Zyphon left. He wasted no time getting away, either.

I didn't answer as he helped me in the canoe and like Malak, he maneuvered it on his own. No ferryman in sight. I wasn't sure whether or not to be impressed or if the demons I'd brought enjoyed being carted around.

Maybe that had been for me more than anything.

Bael moved us through the water lanes away from the fog until we moved from within the city limits. There was an abrupt halt of buildings and as we moved away from the city, the noise dropped away becoming overrun with the sound of rushing water.

He pointed into the distance. "We're surrounded by waterfalls. The circle of pride is basically in a caldera."

"That seems appropriate somehow," I said.

He chuckled. "Yes. The arrogant can erupt in unrighteous fury."

I smiled as I watched the shapes within the distance. I was too busy trying to make out the shapes of what I was seeing to truly engage in conversation.

Bael moved next to me, pointing in the direction I was looking. "Those are the harvest fields. A series of floating landmasses that move within the inlet."

"What do you grow?" I asked.

"Primarily fruits and vegetables. Each little island contains a single species of food. Fox grapes. Aronia berries.

Asparagus. Mint. Persimmons. One is strictly hickory trees for their nuts."

"That's incredible," I said. "Who operates them?"

"Different demons. Generally those who fall within conceited."

I looked at him confused. "What does that mean?"

He chuckled. "Sorry. Guess that part wasn't explained to you yet." I raised a brow, shaking my head. "All demons have a job here. It differs depending on their level of pride. The lowest levels of pride are snobby, followed by haughty. They generally maintain the rice terraces and fisheries. The middle levels of conceited and arrogant man the harvest fields. And the higher levels of vain and then prideful maintain the docks. And all demons rotate within the realm of maintaining the tortured souls that end up in our ring throughout the year. Weeklong tours."

"What about the asmodai?" I asked.

"They have their own vocations depending on the same scale. They take care of tradable goods, jewels, and textiles. All things that take a whole lot of water."

We were coming up on the floating fields and I stared in wonder. They were beautiful and they smelled amazing.

"How about a fresh smoothie?" Bael asked.

I looked at him skeptically and he grinned.

"I promise, they're worth it."

"Alright."

Bael moved away to propel the canoe between the islands, moving slowly so I could take them all in. The smallest were easily three or four football fields in size. But the bigger ones were enormous fields of vegetables and even a couple that were only trees.

We paused next to a floating dock that looked like a

small market. It was a float-by. We didn't get out of the boat but ordered from the asmodai within.

When the smoothie was handed to me, Bael said, "Everything in this has been freshly picked from the harvest fields."

I sipped it and though it wasn't a frappuccino, the notes of berry that burst on my tongue were glorious. "Wow," I said, greedily taking several more large swallows. "This is amazing."

The asmodai within the floating stand grinned. "Glad you enjoy it, my queen."

"Enjoy it doesn't come close. This is fantastic."

He beamed at me. I turned to find Bael watching me with a smile as he sipped on his. "Want to check out the floats or you want to move on?"

I shrugged. "I want to see it all. Show me everything."

Bael nodded and used his oar to push away from the stall and back into the tangle of islands. With the quiet, peaceful sounds of the water and what felt like natural vegetation, I could almost imagine I was on vacation somewhere. And in the background was the relaxing sound of a waterfall.

We stopped at an island of cranberries. There were large sacks of them bagged up and ready to be taken from the field. Within the field were several demons, primarily shax and a few kimaris. I didn't see any of those who looked like people. None of the nastier demons.

I wasn't sure what I was expecting. Maybe a plantation in the old days of slavery. Hot and miserable. But they didn't look unhappy at all. They were working in pairs, straddling a row of cranberry bushes, talking while they picked. There was laughter and smiles as they looked up at Bael and I.

"Everything good here?" Bael asked.

One of the shax stood. This was the closest I'd ever been to one and I could see why Malak had thought that perhaps my soul might have chosen that species of demon. She certainly had that purply fire energy about her. The same kind that clung to my horns.

But she didn't have horns.

She smiled, bowing slightly to Bael. "All is well."

"The harvest?"

"Very, very good. Yielding slightly above expectation. There's only a very small number of bushes in the northernmost rim that we think were touched by the wild magic. We're working on removing them down to their roots, so they don't infect the rest of the crops."

"Good to hear. Thank you, Tass."

She smiled brightly, turning her attention to me. "No problem."

"I'm Nuke," I offered.

"Oh! The queen!"

I flushed at her enthusiasm. Her words hushed everyone around us, causing them to turn. And I didn't miss that outshining their curiosity and interest was hope. It was so thick I could almost feel it.

"Yes, our queen," Bael agreed before I could counter.

"It's so wonderful to meet you. Thank you for visiting our field," Tass said excitedly.

I smiled in return. "It's remarkable. Make sure you have a smoothie. I think they're laced with an addictive."

She laughed. "Oh, I know. The asmodai spoil us for sure."

"Are there any fields that need help from the magic?" Bael asked.

Tass shook her head. "Not yet. I think the last blanket of

defense Malak gave us is doing well. But one of my lovers works within the rice terraces and he says that there's a batch of red rice that's going to have to be thrown. And my neighbor said that some of the monkfish are looking a little... odd. I'm not sure what that means."

"Noted. Thank you. We'll check it out."

She smiled, nodding, and turned back to her work after giving me another beaming smile.

As we walked toward the north, I couldn't help but feel a little more pressure was placed on me. It was one thing knowing that I needed to take control of the magic so that I could leave Hell and return to my family. It was another seeing and hearing about how much the demons of pride were expecting me to save them from the wild magic.

The northern rim was just how Tass had described it. There were a handful of cranberry bushes that were prickly and dark, the berries looking reddish gray. Almost like olives. They were already barricaded off with a kimaris demon digging them out, paying meticulous attention as he shifted through the soil to get every single root.

He looked up when we stopped there and smiled at Bael.

"Doing okay, Poa?" Bael asked.

Poa nodded. "Yes. It's been pretty easy so far. But I think we ought to just burn this section of the island to make sure I get all the roots." He held up a thin stringy branch with a frown. "When you get to the deep roots, they become hair thin and though I'm being careful, I don't want to take any chances."

"I'll let Malak know. That's not a bad precaution to take."

The demon nodded and went back to his work.

As we walked away, I asked, "Do you know everyone?"

Bael grinned. "Possibly. I oversee the workers."

"What do the others do?"

"Whatever Malak needs," he said, shrugging. "Primarily, Zyphon brings us failproof plans for whatever we ask for. We kind of keep him without heavy responsibility because of that. That way, when we need him for something unexpected, he's not tied up. Kingsley is in charge of Malak's estate. Making sure it runs smoothly. Giving Malak a hard time. I'm pretty sure that must be in his job description based on how thoroughly he concentrates on that lately." I laughed as we climbed back into the canoe and Bael moved us through the islands. Though we were headed west, he took his time to let me check out all the fields as we went. "And Hayt deals with the new issues of the Pride Rings and pridefalls. He's created a task force that is quick and usually able to subdue the pridefall before it causes too much damage."

"What does that leave Malak?"

He smiled and propelled us ahead with more speed now that we were out of the fields. "Everything. Talks to the citizens and addresses any of their needs and requests. Is constantly battling the pridemage storms as best he can. Attempting to save the city from falling from the wild magic. Reading every report from every station. Keeping the army in shape."

"Why is there an army?" I asked.

Bael chuckled. "Just in case a greedy, envious, or wrathful brother gets any ideas." At my look of surprise, he laughed. "No, not really. I mean, they're prepared for any kind of battle, but they primarily deal with the shades."

It wasn't long before we came upon what could only be the fisheries. There were incredible waterways that almost looked like a fun park, but they were designed as if by nature. I mean, the twists and turns, not so much, but the greenery and rock for sure.

We parked at the edge and Bael helped me climb out again. There were primarily kimaris here. Very few shax. I was surprised to see some asmodai as well but there was no mistaking them as they popped up from the canals and pools before diving back down again.

"Are there many fish?" I asked.

He nodded. "You have your common salmon, halibut, tilapia, perch, bass, tuna." He waved his hand. "Then there are the less common monkfish, swordfish, orange roughy, catfish, mahi-mahi." We walked along a path that was packed down like it might be within a park, twisting our way through the different pools.

The waterways weren't filled with fish on top of fish, all crammed together like you might see within a traditional fishery. I saw more than I might in nature, but the pools looked like they were there to swim in.

Until we got down to the point where enormous nets were being pulled from the water, filled with fish. I'd never been this close to a fishing boat or anything of the like. It was almost intimidating to see as it was pulled over our heads and into a large container filled with ice.

We bypassed that and stopped a few dozen feet away at a kimaris demon sitting at the edge of the pool, frowning into the water.

"Lyta," Bael said.

The demon named Lyta looked up. He stood with a smile. "Bael. Good to see you. Have you stopped by for the weird sideshow?"

Bael nodded. "What have you got?"

Lyta bent back to the water and stuck his hand in. A minute later, he pulled it out with a fish. That fish not only had two hands, but it was a strange puke-orange color, and its eyes were enormous.

"When Tass said they looked odd, I wasn't sure what to expect," Bael noted.

Lyta nodded. "Yeah, we don't know what to make of it either. Since we're in an inner pool, we're hesitant to blame the wild magic since none of the other fisheries are displaying any strange effects like this. But I'm not sure what else it is if not the magic."

Bael shook his head. "That is an odd occurrence. How many are you finding like this?"

"A lot," Lyta said, frowning as he dropped the fish into the water. "More than half of every hatch."

Sighing, Bael shook his head. "I'll let Malak know. Do what you can for now and we'll see what we can do to come up with a solution or a plan of action."

"Thanks. I'm sure he has an idea." Lyta crouched down to the pool again and it hit me that everyone was relying on Malak. Not on Malak to find someone to fix their problem. But Malak himself.

That was a lot for one man to take all on his own. I knew that it wasn't strictly on his shoulders, though he bore the brunt of it. He had his most trusted with him.

Bael walked me through the pools and showed me the different kinds of fish before we headed back for the canoe. "How does Malak come up with solutions?" I asked as he started propelling us forward again.

"No idea. Usually, we'll have a problem, and he comes up with an ingenious idea that works nine out of ten times." He shook his head, frowning. "I'd like to say it was his magic allowing him to come up with these solutions but it's just him. He's good like that."

"And the one time he doesn't have an idea?"

"It gives him gray hair."

I snorted, laughing. Bael grinned.

"He's always willing to listen to ideas from anyone who has one. Regardless of whether they're a prideful or just a little snobby. When he can't think of something on his own, he puts the problem to us. And if we can't think of an answer, he'll put it out to everyone."

"Why not just do that from the start?"

"Because he doesn't want to burden our citizens with problems. As the ruler of pride, it's his job to take care of them. Not their job to fix what's broken."

I looked out at the waterfall in the distance, watching the mist rise and wondered if I judged Malak too quickly. Unfairly.

Then again, I wasn't ready to forgive him for murdering me. I wasn't that big of a person. I refused to have pity toward my killer.

CHAPTER SIXTEEN
REVAN

I never knew Rhyl or Eko until Anuka. I knew of them, but I didn't know them. I was stupidly pleased they'd known of me, too. Generally speaking, I kept to myself, but I was known around as ready to laugh and have a good time. I never took anything seriously. I never shared my life.

When you do that, you set yourself up for being hurt.

Eko was a badass known for tormenting demons just as readily as he would souls. He was one of those people who you made a wide berth around and didn't look at him. I wasn't sure he was easily offended but since he wasn't one that struck you as conversational, it was simpler to err on the side of I don't want to be tortured.

Oddly enough, I found that he was a cuddler and since we began bedding with Anuka in Malak's estate, I often found myself curled up in his big embrace. It was a nice place to be.

Rhyl was intimidating. There was something in his gaze that all uvall share, telling you that he could be here in the present or seeing the past or future fall around him. He wasn't all here. Ever.

I've heard that was the issue with uvalls. And something that drove a lot of them mad. He wasn't demonic in the 'I'll bite your dick off and feed it to your soul' type of demon. He was one that would drive you insane by dropping everything he saw around you. Echoes of all times until you didn't know what you were seeing or hearing.

I'd never spoken to him before Anuka either. Again, I knew of him. He was a very old demon and one who I'd actually seen drive a shax insane with his time visions. It was terrifying. I made it a point to not get in his way, though I didn't outright avoid him either.

Since bunking with our queen, I found he was thoughtful and kind. Basically, he liked to be left alone.

He's done well to make that happen. I wasn't the only one who steered clear of him.

I wasn't sure where our lady had run off to this morning. I got out of the shower, and she was gone. Neither Rhyl nor Eko had known, either.

"We're not her keepers," Rhyl said, tilting his head to the side as I plopped down next to Eko. He shifted to wrap around me, and I smiled at Rhyl, snuggling in for a morning cuddle. "I didn't think to ask where she was heading."

"Part of being in a relationship is talking," I pointed out.

Rhyl tilted his head to the side and narrowed his eyes at me. "Relationship?"

I rolled my eyes, feeling Eko chuckle behind me. "Crazy demon," I muttered. "Yes. You can't possibly think you're ever going to walk away from our lady, do you?"

The absent expression I received in answer was almost unsettling.

"I've learned that that look means he hadn't considered

that. Now we've likely lost him for a while as he sorts through time," Eko said.

The two of them ended up hanging out more often than not. Maybe not in a friendly, social way, but in whatever we were doing to assist Anuka.

I wasn't sure what we were doing to help her aside from answering questions. Questions that we increasingly didn't have answers to. I frowned. That needed to be fixed.

We all knew a lot about our little circle of Hell. It's pride in where you come from. Pride in where you live, how you live, who you live with. Pride in everything. I didn't feel I was exaggerating that pride was certainly the best circle. I was confident in that even having never visited one of the others.

Despite the dispute among the brothers, imports and exports was a strong, healthy market. And I enjoyed some of the finer delicacies from the other circles. Icicle wine from greed was delectable. And the tea from lust was a trip.

That being said, no one had finer pears or underwater gems than we did. Our rice terraces, produce, and fish were top-notch. We had so many exports that were of the highest quality that there was no way any other ring stood a chance of bettering us.

Anyway, pride is the only place to be. All demons who lived here knew that. And though we took great satisfaction in knowing a lot of our own little slice of Hell, we didn't get down to the nitty-gritty. I didn't know how the rice was harvested. I just knew we grew more than a dozen different varieties and were working on creating new ones all the time. I didn't know about the waterfall or the barrier. I just knew they were there, protecting us. How was I going to help Anuka when I didn't have answers?!

"I think I'm going to the library," I said after a while of

watching Rhyl get lost in his time sight. Rhyl didn't acknowledge me, but Eko nodded.

"Okay."

I shifted so I could look at him. We were close enough within an intimate embrace that we could be lovers. Looking at him, I decided I wasn't necessarily opposed to that. He was sexy as fuck. The way the corner of his lips quirked up as I studied him told me he knew that. I liked that confidence. My kind of demon right there.

But I wasn't into letting my heart be ripped in two again. I could handle Nuke. I was sure that she and I were growing together at the same rate. It was easy to gauge her since she didn't hold anything back. You got exactly what you saw, something I appreciated.

She was a lot like Zyphon in that.

Blinking several times, I banished those thoughts entirely. Nope. No time for that. Right now, it was time to research.

"Want anything while I'm out?" I asked Eko.

"Snack," he said.

I nodded, impulsively leaning in to kiss him quickly. Just a brief peck. With a grin, I stood and headed for the door. Okay, I was just testing the waters. I had told Hayt I was involved with two men and a woman. Just because I hadn't meant that in a physical sense didn't make it untrue, right?

It was a stretch.

The library was on the main floor, with beautiful dark cherry wood, dark metal pieces, and of course, purple accents everywhere. There wasn't much bare wall, but like Anuka's room, the walls were painted a rich plum, dark and beautiful.

It was quiet when I walked in, and I took a few minutes

to see who was about. This library wasn't the only one within the city, but it was the most frequently used by everyone. There was even a river winding through for the asmodai. They weren't built to be out of the water and yet, somehow, they still managed to move with grace.

Though, it was still somewhat amusing to see.

I found a handful of demons scattered throughout and a table within the lost relics section with items spread out as if someone were coming back. The aisles on pride itself were empty, I was happy to see so I took a few minutes to browse and pulled a handful of books to take to a table with me. I could have brought them back to the room, but it was nice to have some peace.

Time slipped by as I lost myself within the pages that outlined in great detail everything there was to know about the magic of pride. It told of the other circles, too, but in lesser specifics. It was actually quite fascinating, and I was a little embarrassed finding that I didn't know nearly as much as I thought I did.

It was also enlightening that Anuka had all the signs of truly becoming our queen. I wasn't sure if I was giddy over that or slightly terrified.

A shadow made me look up and my breath caught in my throat to the point where I almost choked. It had been so long since I'd actually looked at Zyphon that my heart clenched in my chest. I could still feel the phantom touch of his stubble under my fingers. The feel of his hard, taut body along mine.

"Hi," he said.

I couldn't help myself; I raised a brow. Especially since he was holding a large bit of fabric in his hands.

"Hello," I said, ignoring the way my body stiffened. I expected that at some point we'd run into each other. I couldn't actually avoid him forever. Especially not living under the same roof. Even if that roof was enormous. "What's up?"

He tilted his head, a smile touching his lips. Maybe at my fake nonchalance. I wasn't fooling either of us.

"I brought you something," he said, holding up the fabric.

Okay, now I stared at him as if he'd grown a second head. There were so many 'whys' that I wasn't sure where to start. Instead of asking any of them because words were hard right now, I got to my feet and let them mindlessly carry me to him.

When he held up the fabric for me, I took it, careful to not let our fingers touch. I let it fall as I took a step back, holding a hem until its shape became apparent. It took me several minutes until I figured out what I was holding.

An exquisite dress, unlike anything I'd ever seen before.

"It's not the one I was looking for," Zyphon said, shrugging. "But since I was almost stabbed three times while retrieving that, I thought I'd get out while I was still breathing."

I laughed, despite myself. One of my favorite things about Zy was that he was a massively strong oriax demon, but he was lazy as all fuck. So while he generally finds what he's looking for, the adventures in retrieving it are hilarious.

"Where did you go to get this?"

"Babylonia." He shrugged. "Not that I'm overly surprised, but they frowned upon me just walking out of the air and trying to rip this off a woman."

"The easiest way to find a lost thing is to go to a time when it wasn't lost," I repeated. Something he used to tell me all the time.

Zyphon grinned. "Exactly. Still, the colors are weird. Not like what is shown in the image I was studying. There's either another version of it, history got it wrong, or maybe the color changed with time?"

"Why a dress?" I asked.

He shrugged again. "You've been wearing dresses and skirts."

His gaze dropped to the skirt I was currently wearing. I'm not gonna lie. There's something freeing about skirts. I love to swing my hips and feel my dick slap my thighs. There's also the pleasant side effect that when you're wearing nothing under it, the breeze has a way of keeping your junk from sweating. Therefore, no bat wings when your balls stick to your legs with sweat. Fucking brilliant.

These things weren't made for women. They were truly designed for men. We have the dicks that hang. Women belong in pants where there's nothing for that crotch to pinch, wedge, and chafe. Nothing to squish or force you to sit on. Skirts give you all the freedom.

Let's be honest here. Dresses and skirts were invented by dick-havers so that they could get to pussies more easily. You can't convince me I'm wrong.

"You should try it," I said, looking up to him again. He was already watching me with his light eyes that made my heart stutter.

"Sure," he answered.

For a moment, silence fell between us. My next 'why' was why he hunted this for me. But I couldn't bring myself to get the words out. I was too afraid of the answer.

"I'm sorry," Zyphon said. Before my eyes, whatever wall he'd erected fell at my feet. "I love you. I've loved you since we met. And I still love you all this time later. I made a mistake. Please tell me there's a way to fix this."

I was speechless. Honestly, I waited for the day when he'd seek me out to say such a thing. But those days ended a long time ago. Years ago. He never came for me. And I gave up, closing myself down and building a wall around me.

Now here he was. Telling me just as I always dreamed he would. Was I supposed to forgive him? Just like that? Shouldn't I make him work for it at the very least? Do a little groveling?

None of that would actually make me feel better. It didn't matter. I tossed the dress behind me, making sure it landed on the back of a chair, before pulling him to me. I'd meant for a hug, but his mouth found mine instead.

A kiss hasn't felt more desperately filled with emotion in my entire long life. It was filled with apologies and promises, filling me to the brink before I nearly exploded. He clung to me as tightly as I did him.

"I'm sorry," he repeated. "I made a mistake."

"And when he tells you it's him or me next time?" Because that was the true test. It was one thing to apologize, even when you meant it. But unless his loyalties have shifted, too. Unless he's ready to change his priorities-

"You," he said, biting my lip. His fingers dug into my back. "I should have picked you before. Picked the one who would never make me choose."

I nodded. Yes, he should have.

His hand moved to my hair, trying to get a fistful of it but it was too short. He settled on forcing my face back so he could look into my eyes. "I will never choose another being, living or dead, over you again. No matter what the ultimatum is."

His words had already started to heal a bit of the wound within me. I believed him. Right or wrong, I trusted that he meant it.

"I'm sleeping with Nuke," I said. "And I'm not sure what's going on between Eko and me. Probably nothing between me and Rhyl though."

"Okay," he answered, still staring intently into my eyes. "We can work around it all."

"And you?"

He laughed quietly, bowing his head. "No one, Rev."

"Malak?"

Zyphon shook his head. "I've mostly hated him since I made you leave. Sometimes I imagine smothering him in his sleep, just so he's not standing in my way. Of course, the reality that I'm in my own way comes back and I push my treasonous thoughts aside."

I chuckled.

"It's been a fucking liberating treat watching Nuke make him miserable as he falls a little more for her with each passing day."

"I bet," I said, shaking my head.

A smile touched his lips as he leaned his head against mine. "I don't expect you to forgive me immediately or trust me right away. I'm prepared to work for it. As long as I know there's something I'm working towards."

Nodding, I kissed him. Even when the kiss stopped being a kiss and our lips just remained pressed together, I didn't move. "Yes," I whispered. Feeling the way my heart protested at the idea of letting myself be vulnerable again. But Zy has always been my demon. How could I live without him?

CHAPTER SEVENTEEN
ANUKA

I could see the rice terraces from quite a way off. They were stunning works of art as they tapered downward. It was like looking at abstract art with the thin bits of stone cutting into the shallow valleys of rice at different angles, making wedges and swatches in a magical pattern.

"I've never been to rice paddies," I said, leaning over the side of the boat. It tipped a little, but Bael managed to keep me out of the water. "They're remarkable."

"We're pretty proud of them."

There were people everywhere, wrapping bundles of grassy green stems and pulling them out. But they only tossed them behind them and moved on.

"That doesn't look like rice," I noted.

Bael chuckled. "There are a few more steps. They're not actually harvesting right now."

He pulled the canoe up to the side and anchored us in. Then he began taking his shoes off. "Best not to try shoes. The ground is mostly soggy and even where it's dry packed earth, the chances of getting muddy and dirty are high."

I followed his lead and discarded my shoes, rolling my

pant legs up my calves. Then we climbed out and started walking the thin strips between the terraces. He began pointing out the different kinds of rice. Arborio, jasmine, basmati, viacone nano, carnaroli, and different colors, too. Including the red rice which we were heading for.

Bael paused, his face scrunching. "I anticipate that we're getting close to the infected grains," he said.

At his words, I smelled it, too. Rot and something that smelled suspiciously like an infection. That sick, acrid scent. Eww.

"That's gross."

Bael nodded, taking my hand and pulling me along. It grew stronger the closer we got until I finally pulled my shirt over my nose. It wasn't enough but it was something. A little bit of a screen between my nose and the stench.

Hayt was already there. He handed us both a bandana to wrap around our faces.

"This is not normal, right?" I asked.

Both demons shook their head, as did many kimaris demons that were there, likewise wearing bandanas. It didn't keep out the nastiness, but it was better than the thin layer of my shirt.

"We don't actually see anything wrong with the crops," one of the women said, her attention on Bael. I was guessing she already told Hayt. "But this is the epicenter of the diseased crops."

"How many terraces are affected?" Bael asked.

"As far as I can tell, only this one. But since the scent is pretty consuming for quite a distance, it's hard to say for sure."

Bael sighed.

"Why haven't they been pulled up and discarded yet?" I asked. When the woman looked like I hit her, I quickly added, "I know nothing about rice production. I'm genuinely curious."

"It's alright, Rate," Bael said, smiling kindly at the demon I somehow terrified. "She's new to the City of Pride, and doesn't know how to work in the fields."

Rate looked at me, her eyes lingered on my horns for a minute before widening. She dropped to her knees in a bow. "I'm so sorry, my queen. I did not mean to offend."

I looked at Bael and he shook his head, grinning. "Rate, get up. She isn't offended. Just asked you a question that you should answer."

She reluctantly got to her feet, looking at me with trepidation. After another minute passed in which Rate steadied herself and regained her breath, she answered me. "Because we can't actually find anything wrong with the crops. It seems a waste to just throw out perfectly good crops."

I frowned. Clearly, I didn't understand. But I'd wait to ask further once we left the timid demon.

Hayt must have seen my confusion though. "If the crops aren't actually what's causing the offending stench, then we don't need to get rid of them. Right now, we just suspect there's something in this bed that's causing the issue since the odor is originating from here, best they can tell."

"But if it's the water or even the soil, it will need to be cleared out and addressed, right?" I asked.

"Oh yes," Rate said. "We are sanitizing a bed in the west paddies right now. We think that a bit of wild magic got in." She shrugged.

"What happened?"

She sighed. "I don't know. The crops turned a strange color and it seemed safest to get rid of them." She tilted her head and looked off in the direction I presumed the field was. "They didn't smell bad, though."

"This one is on the inside, too," I noted. "Just like at the fisheries."

Bael nodded. "I was just thinking that. Odd." After a minute, he turned to me. "I'm going to hang out here for a bit. See if I can't help them come to a definitive conclusion. Why not hang with Hayt for a while."

I nodded. "Sure."

Hayt smiled, a look that had his expression going far off for a moment before returning to me. "Come on, beautiful. Let's check out the barriers."

I placed my hand in his when he offered, and he led me in a different direction than where we came from. Once we were far enough away to where I didn't feel like I was gagging, I took a deep breath.

The boat that Hayt led me to was more of a kayak than a canoe. We were sitting within the boat, but it was shallow, and our legs were primarily straight in front of us.

"It's the horns, isn't it? That's how everyone recognizes me," I said.

Hayt chuckled. "Yes. They've heard stories about the beautiful demon with horns that can command magic. She is our future queen and will free the City of Pride from the destructive touch of the wild magic."

"No pressure."

I could feel his smile behind me. "You're already partially there, honey girl. It's reaching for you and you're responding."

"Then what's the problem? Why can't I put all this shit to an end?" When he didn't respond right away, I glanced over my shoulder. He was watching me.

"You know the answer."

I scowled. He was right. I knew the answer. The magic doesn't just need me to touch it. It needs Malak, the ruler of pride. Without me, he cannot wield it. And with me, I didn't like him enough to make him king or whatever title he was going for here. I didn't like him at all most days.

"This seems like an impossible task."

"Only if you allow it to be," he said.

Since I wasn't keen on his answer, I chose not to respond. Instead, I watched the mist as we got closer to the waterfall. An endless waterfall that surrounded the entire water City of Pride.

It wasn't the most relaxing sound since you just knew by the noise of it that the water moved with speed and force. And yet, there was something remarkable about it that I just kept wanting to get closer.

Then again, the closer we got in this little kayak, the more nervous I became.

"Hayt?"

"Yes, beautiful?"

I smirked. "Are you not afraid that the current will pull us over?"

"I am not."

That was it. No further explanation. Frowning, I looked over my shoulder to level him with a glare. He laughed.

"The water that runs down the falls is beneath the surface."

In other words, somehow Hell was defying physics. Not sure how I felt about that. What if the wild magic reversed the physics into something else entirely?

It wasn't until we were right at the edge, where the water fell into oblivion, that I saw the lip. A thin line of stone that seemed to float on the surface. Hayt secured the kayak and climbed out. He pulled me to my feet a moment later and turned to walk along the narrow path.

We didn't walk far before we came upon some stairs, and we traveled down. They were carved into the side of what felt like a mountain. I remembered Bael said this circle was basically sitting in a caldera. So did that mean we were inside a volcano? What were the odds that the volcano was still active?

I was surprised to find that there were a bunch of people working. And these people looked like people. Which meant they were strong demons. Not the common citizens of pride. But these demons looked different. They were a hybrid form of man and devil. Horns, tails, wings, spikes, claws, hooves... so many different appendages that had me nearly gawking.

At the base of the stairs, we were greeted by a demon. "Hayt," he said, grinning wickedly. "How's it going, mate?"

Hayt smiled in return. "Wonderful. How's the hole?"

"Malak's patches are working. It's just time consuming, which is partially our own fault since we're being meticulous."

"Good to hear. Can we have a look?"

The demon nodded. "This way."

Following his spine was a row of nasty spikes, needle-like but super thick. I shivered before wondering how he lay on his back. Hell, how did he sit?

He led us to a ledge that looked like a sheer drop where a dozen demons were gathered close. It looked like they were weaving air with silver thread. Wait, not air. The mist of the waterfall. It was as fascinating as it was confounding.

"The barrier is visible because of the rushing water," Hayt explained. "See where it looks like there's a hole in the fog?"

How I missed it before he suggested it was anyone's guess. It couldn't be missed. It was screaming at me. A gaping hole that, once again, defied physics. I nodded.

"They're using pride pressed into a string to sew it back together," Hayt said, and I looked at him with a brow raised. He grinned. "It's a thing. I promise."

I shook my head, astounded.

"You're doing a great job, Yivy. Keep it up. Let us know if there are any mishaps."

Yivy nodded, grinning widely. "Will do."

Hayt took my hand and pulled me along, passing more demons as we went. They were just as fascinating as the barrier itself. When Hayt pulled me from the path along the wall into what felt like the side of a mountain, I paid more attention to where we were going.

Once again, this place was filled with people. And, unsurprisingly, a river where asmodai swam. I didn't ask where we were going as he led me deeper inside. We finally stopped within a large cavern that looked like a food court.

"Okay, on the menu is rolls. Sushi. Are you interested?" he asked.

I shrugged. "Not the biggest fan of raw fish but everything else that comes in a sushi roll I'm down with."

"Done." He ordered several different things that I wasn't following and guided me along the counter as the demon behind it – an asmodai – loaded a tray. When we reached the end with a platter that could feed six, Hayt led me away.

There were little alcoves with windows that overlook the falling water below. Again, how that worked with gravity and the way of mountains and water, I wasn't going to ask. It was cool as fuck though.

Hayt sat close, wrapping an arm around my shoulders.

He chose one of the rolls and offered it to me, bringing it to my mouth. I indulged him and took a bite, letting my lips brush his fingers. He traced my lower lip with his thumb before licking his fingers and popping one of the rolls into his mouth.

It was good. I didn't ask what was in it in case he decided to try me on fish. If you don't know what you're eating, sometimes you can trick yourself into trying new things. And so far, this was really good.

Hayt made eating an erotic affair as he fed me rolls of rice and veggies. Sometimes, instead of taking his own bite, he nibbled on my neck or ear. Kissed me heatedly between mouthfuls. We were halfway through the platter when he gave up all pretense of eating the food and concentrated on licking and sucking my neck.

Was I aware that we were quite clearly in view of the rest of the demons in the cavern? Mostly, yes. I could hear the chatter. The sounds of a restaurant. The footsteps of those coming and going.

But I was having a hard time forming words as to why this was inappropriate right now because Hayt's hand slowly trailed the inside of my thigh. And naughty me, I spread my legs to oblige him.

Like the demon he was, his touch was sinful, making everything in me heat up like fire. I swallowed as he pressed his lips to my neck. Pushing my shirt out of the way and kissing my bare shoulder.

"So soft," he purred. "So perfect." His fingers brushed my pussy, sending a jolt through me as if my panties weren't there. "So beautiful."

"Hayt," I moaned.

"Shh," he whispered against my skin. "You're quiet. We're quiet."

He kissed his way down my neck. I could almost feel his lips on my breast, but his fingers slid inside me, making it impossible to think. I tried to keep quiet, but I was so wet I couldn't breathe.

"I love how wet you are for me," Hayt said, his fingers sliding in and out of me, making my eyes roll back. He finally kissed my breast, and I pushed my body down onto him, helpless to his touch. "I knew you'd be this way," Hayt said, his voice deep and rough. "I've thought about you since our first meeting."

I was going to come right then but I had a feeling he wasn't ready for this to be over. Hell, neither was I. Gripping his thick hair, I pulled his mouth back to mine.

"You put me under your spell," I accused.

"This isn't a spell," he vowed. "This is us. This is what happens when two people are so connected they can't even think properly."

I rolled my eyes at the corniness even though I knew exactly what he meant. My panties were soaked, my body on fire. I leaned in, kissing him as he moved his hand up my back.

He unclasped my bra with a single flick of his fingers and it fell open. He took a moment to explore each breast, rolling my nipples between his fingers, before ripping my shirt open, leaving my chest bared. Before I could blink, he was licking my breast and then the other.

I made the mistake of opening my eyes and many faces were looking in our direction. I flushed at being watched.

I shivered and he growled, "I'm going to devour you," he whispered, his words sending a thrill through me. "Always so wet."

Hearing the approval in his voice made me even wetter. I swear, I must have sprung a leak.

He grunted, his eyes darkening as he found my clit, making me gasp at the pleasure. My body trembled as he began to rub me through my delicate panties while still working his fingers deep inside me. My whole body felt alive, as if electricity were surging through every vein.

"I can't get enough of you," he whispered, his lips gently kissing my neck.

My back arched as he touched me. He gave me a wicked smile, humming and pushing further into me, stroking my G-spot.

"Hayt," I whimpered, trying to twist away from him. To roll off him and hide how easily he worked my body. This was almost embarrassing.

"Don't." He grasped my thigh and pushed my leg down, spreading me wider. "You're amazing, Nuke. I want to feel every wet inch."

When I met his eyes, they were so dark he looked almost scary.

"I was right," he said, his voice a low rasp. "You're everything I knew you'd be. A goddess."

I whimpered as he kissed my neck and his fingers pushed deeper, hitting all of the right places. "Oh, God, Hayt."

I was going to come, and I hated that my body was such a traitor, but I couldn't help it. He was driving me crazy.

"Do you feel me inside you?" he asked, moving my thigh up and spreading my legs even wider. "Do you know what you do to me?"

I gave a shaky nod, my whole body on fire, my own breathing coming in pants, and I knew it was only a matter of time until I came. His fingers were relentless, teasing me, driving me out of my mind.

"That's right," he said, his voice rough. "You're the most

amazing woman I've ever met. Your body is perfect and I want to worship it. To taste it. To touch you."

A shiver of anticipation went through me and Hayt smiled, sending a fresh round of shivers through my body.

"I want to fill you up," he said, sending my heart racing. "I want to feel you come all over me. I want you to scream my name, love."

Oh, God.

I bit my lip as he pulled me up and bent me over the table. I blushed hotly as he pulled my pants down, revealing my ass to the room.

When I realized I couldn't see a thing, couldn't see the room around me as they watched, I tried to turn over but he held me in place, his fingers teasing the edge of my panties.

"Don't move," Hayt ordered. "Stay as you are." He then shredded my panties, and I gasped as he spread my legs.

"Wider," he growled, his fingers sliding into me again, making my whole body tremble.

"Hayt," I whimpered.

"Perfect," he murmured, his fingers gliding into my folds. "So wet. So tight."

"Oh, God," I moaned, my knees shaking, my body on fire.

"I love this," he growled, his fingers slipping inside and finding my G-spot again. He rubbed me gently, teasing me, his fingers sliding in and out of me. "I love tasting you. It makes me hard every time." As if in emphasis, his hand left my body and a moment later, I heard the unmistakable sound of him licking his fingers clean.

The first lick of his tongue made me cry out, my body jerking in surprise. When had he even moved?

"Hayt," I gasped, my hands fisting in my hair. "Oh, my God."

He growled and the sound made my pussy clench. His tongue lapped at me, once, twice, then he went deeper, finding all of my sensitive spots, making me cry out in ecstasy.

I tried to remember that we were in a public place. All I wanted to do was moan, to beg him to keep going, to give him what he wanted. But I couldn't do that. So instead I tried to hold my mouth shut, biting my lip as I moved my hips back, creating a rhythm with him.

"That's right, baby," Hayt murmured against my skin. "Work my tongue."

He grabbed my ass, his teeth grazing my thigh, urging me on.

"Hayt," I moaned, clenching my walls around his tongue. "Fuck, Hayt, I'm going to come."

It was almost embarrassing how fast he made me come. My orgasm slammed into me, taking me by surprise and I cried out, my body jerking as he growled and dove into me, licking me faster. I felt like my whole body was convulsing, like I was coming undone.

He growled and the next thing I knew, it was his thick dick sliding into my swollen pussy. I cried out, pushing my hips back, begging him to take me, to fuck me until I was limp.

He pumped into me, my body still trembling, my clit still aching.

"You feel so fucking good," he groaned, his hand sliding around my hips, teasing my clit.

I cried out as he rubbed me, my body almost too sensitive. Then yelped as he pushed in deeper, hitting my G-spot.

"Nuke," he moaned, his hand rubbing my ass as if he were waiting to slap it. Prepping me to take it.

He was huge, filling me in a way that had me crying out, burying my face in the table, trying to muffle my voice. The table scratched my stomach as he thrust into me, his thick cock pounding in and out. He was being rough and it was so damn good.

"Hayt," I moaned, my body straining as I pressed back into him. I didn't care that people were watching anymore. I wanted them to watch. To see how a master handled a pussy.

"So sweet," Hayt cooed, his hand landing hard on my ass. The sound of flesh on flesh echoed through the room, mingling with my moans. I cried out, my pussy clenching around his dick, my next orgasm slamming into me like a freight train. He roared, his hands grabbing my hips, pulling me onto his cock as he thrust into me, stretching me around his thick shaft.

I groaned as my body shook.

"That's right," he growled, his hand landing again, the sound reverberating in the room, feeding into the lingering effects of my orgasm. Or was it a new one? Just as powerful as the last one, my pussy spasming and clenching around him, my whole body shaking.

Another slap, this time on the other side, and a fresh wave of pleasure assaulted me. I cried out again, this time my voice carrying through the room, echoing off the walls. My skin was on fire, my body trembling as Hayt pounded me, as his cock stretched me, as his hand landed again and again, as my pussy clenched and spasmed around him.

His words were dirty, told me what he thought of me, and I cried out, my body shaking with his words.

"So good," he murmured, his hand landing in the same spot again. "So tight. So fucking hot."

I couldn't believe how easily he made me come.

But then I felt his leaking down my leg. It didn't stop him from driving into me over and over again, like he'd just begun.

"So good," he purred. "I think we'll just keep going."

I wasn't sure I'd live through it.

CHAPTER EIGHTEEN
ANUKA

Maybe I was getting too comfortable. The first few times I left Malak's ostentatious estate, something ridiculous had happened and I'd been electrocuted by magic. But the last time I went when I had an entire day of educational experiences on my tour beyond the city boundaries had ended pleasantly.

Even if there was that moment of inappropriate public fucking right in the middle of the day. There were voyeurs but no one said anything.

I remained within the enormous house for a few days, joining Revan as we hung out in the library researching the magic. Even on this Malak wasn't as helpful as I thought he was going to be. He didn't know the answers, either.

Most things were just innate to him. He did. Without thought, he just did.

As much as I'd like to say that he was being a pain in the ass intentionally, I could tell he was trying to think of ways to explain what I was asking. How do you feel the magic? How do you call on it intentionally when it's not a time of crisis? What does it feel like? Why is it so sharp to me when I use it?

He wanted to give me answers, but he couldn't think of them. He just didn't know. I was at least confident he was being honest because without a queen, he was a useless man. Unable to take care of his own shit.

But now I knew he wanted to.

Anyway, after the first few times going out and something ridiculous had happened, I thought that was just going to be the way of it. But then I got to tour the outermost reaches in peace. That was probably why it was different. The population was dispersed.

Today we were going to the one place I hadn't been yet. The docks where they import and export goods. It wasn't just a little production, either. My demons were coming and so were Malak, Hayt, and Bael.

We took a larger boat, one that could seat twelve, and this time a ferryman brought us. I thought I'd never get tired of seeing the city as we passed between buildings. It was such a surreal place to be. Although I knew the buildings didn't float, it felt like they did.

And all the friendly faces. Yes, they were all demons, but they were more personable than people you pass in New York City. And I wasn't afraid of being mugged, stalked, or assaulted. There was a heavy feeling of safety surrounding the entire city.

The buildings were still right on the water, even to the edge of the city. And extending beyond were various wooden bridges with little huts on them where a whole array of canisters were being unloaded. There were boxes and crates, baskets and chests. Bags of silk and ones made of canvas. There was so much to look at, I wasn't sure where to concentrate.

The further we walked, I found that the enormous ships at the end of the docks with massive white sails were impossible to miss, yet somehow, I hadn't spotted them until we were right there.

"I know we haven't actually left Hell or pride, but I feel like I'm in a completely different place." It actually smelled like seawater here. I hadn't noticed but the air wasn't salty or briny within the city. It smelled clear and fresh, laced heavily with flowers and herbs hanging from windows.

"It's a different ocean," Hayt said. "This one connects all the rings through different portals. Makes trading easier."

I could almost tell just by looking at the ships which belonged to which ring. The pretty, sensual rig with deep pinks and sparkle had to belong to lust. And the dark one that looked remarkably like a warship was probably wrath.

And then there were fleets of those being loaded that belonged to pride. And maybe I'm biased, but they were the most striking of all with the whitewashed wood and dark purple sails.

I knew I hadn't been in any other circle, but I couldn't fathom any of the other ones looking this magical. I mean, maybe greed was something to look at. When I think of greed, I think of gold and riches. Maybe I'm way off but I could see that.

We broke away from Malak and his demons and visited some of those I knew belonged to pride. They were going through the inventory of what came in, making sure what goes out was of equal value.

It was entertaining to watch, only because the number of objects that came out was fascinating. I felt like a kid on Christmas, watching packages being opened and amazed at the treasure revealed. I was pretty sure I was oohing and aahing, too.

I sampled some treats as we made our way through the various docks. Chocolates and truffles and spices and fruits. Everything was exotic, even if it was just mundane foods I'd eaten back home. I also found baked goods and enjoyed an exquisite cookie.

I must have met my quota of peaceful outings. I turned at the screams, spinning on my heels and searching for the source. I wasn't sure which I would find.

It was a Pride Ring marching in like a group of Satanists in blood-colored hooded cloaks with long pikes of fire. They touched them to stalls as they went, sending the structures into bursts of flames.

I started sprinting towards them, internally calling for my watcher to find me. I needed my demon. I needed to borrow more magic. I couldn't let them burn down the docks.

Behind me, my demons called for me, but my vision had focused on one thing in particular: Hayt as he shifted from his man to something altogether not human. Muscles and a tail with massive horns on his head and a halo of fire surrounding him.

Next to him was the demon I was sure was Malak. There was nothing even remotely human about him. He was barely bipedal. His body was somewhat skeletal and covered in what I associated with lava. His black skin cracked with a fire that burned within. But his head was a kind of animal with a scrunched face, a wide jaw that housed a whole lot of terrifying teeth, and wicked horns that reminded me of a bull's.

Bael stood off to the side, watching with a frown. I almost paused at the lack of concern on Bael's face and the way the Pride Ring hesitated for a moment. But then the ring decided that was a challenge it was going to take and charged, some of their demons breaking out, too.

I was suddenly looking at the scene from above as I flew over the water separating the dock I was on from the one where the Pride Ring was setting everything on fire. I landed with a thud making everyone except Malak turn to look at me. Malak used my surprise presence as a useful distraction and produced a thin whip of fire that he used as if he were lassoing cows. The whip wrapped around the nearest demon many times. When Malak yanked backward, it sliced through the demon every place it wrapped. Not like it made many lacerations. It literally sliced through him like cheese.

Bile rose in my throat as Malak regrouped to grab another. The others took notice then and returned to the fight; only by now, I'd garnered attention. But on my sides came three more demons I assumed were my men. Each a little more terrifying than the last.

Only because of the mob of Pride Ringers, or whatever they're called, were my demons a threat. I enjoyed watching as the demons fought. Fought with such a fierce conviction I felt like I was part of a battle from eons ago. Back when wars were close and more personal. When you could see into the eyes of the enemy you were fighting.

And I did. As I stared into the green eyes of something thinking they had the right to set the docks on fire in protest, I reached out with a fury all my own. These weren't demons of pride. These were assholes who had no business being in my city.

A fire erupted around me, coating my body until I was a walking inferno. I had no weapons. No real sense of how to fight. But all I had to do was get close enough to touch them and they'd disintegrate. Turn to ash. Melt. One even boiled.

I assumed their deaths were based on the types of demons they were. Or perhaps it was the punishment of their souls.

It wasn't long before we'd taken down the entire gang, some being subdued and dragged away in magical chains that glowed purple, and the laraje in the water started shooting up, carrying with them sheets of water raining down over the docks to put out the fires. I wasn't sure if the dragon animals moved in herds or family groups, but a handful of them went over what felt like a choreographed elegant leap, dousing everything in water, before diving back in on the other side.

I turned to look into the water to see what was beneath the surface over here and stared instead at my distorted reflection. No longer did I just have horns covered in a purple fire. I now had the unmistakable suggestion of wings made of the same fire.

"Woah," I said, leaning over to look at myself. Had anything else changed? Oh, well, I was covered in flames, too. The water hadn't put me out.

I turned, intending to ask what kind of demon I was, when I had the misfortune of watching several of the demons on the dock succumb into the monsters of the pridefall.

"Wrath," Eko's demony face said. Was it wrong that he was just as attractive like this? Okay, maybe not totally attractive but there was something enthralling about him in this shape.

My somewhat disturbed thoughts disbanded as we were faced with six pridefall. Six!

"Is it normal that they change in groups?" I asked.

Bael shook his still human head. "No. Not at all. Maybe this is a new evolution in their falling."

Malak seemed to think he had this one under control.

He went straight in, wrapping the nearest one in his fire lasso. His flaming eyes made contact with me, and he spun the pridefall toward me. It teetered on its feet, trying to regain its balance and control of its projection.

Rhyl and Revan caught him before he slammed into me, and I grabbed hold of him before he could rip away. The blood-like fluid that ran down the other one I saw that had been pink was black in this one. Maybe that denoted them as falling into wrath.

That begs the question, how does one fall from prideful to wrathful? What's the cause and effect of this?

The discussion would have to wait. I set my burning hands on the pridefall and watched as the anger and monster fell away. It was less than a minute later that the demon knelt before me. I patted his head and moved around him as Malak flung me another.

The others kept them occupied while Malak and I did this dance for four more. But on the last one, Malak must have gotten a little too arrogant. It felt like that in the way he was almost prancing around. But that deathly lasso missed its target and landed on Hayt.

I watched in one terrifying moment as Hayt shuddered, his red being turned dark and started to fall away.

Screaming, I dove for him without giving thought to what I was doing. I ripped Malak's lasso away and the enormous mass that was Hayt fell into me, sending us both careening to the docks. I wrapped my arms around him, pressing my hand to his chest where his heart was slowing.

"No, no, no," I chanted, tears in my eyes. "Please no. Hayt, come back."

Malak was there a moment later, falling to the docks next to us. I looked at him with such rage that my vision blurred. Maybe that was the tears.

"What is wrong with you?" I screamed. "You had one job. One. Just round up the stupid monsters. That's it. Why did you have to fuck that up, too?"

"Too?" he said in a voice that sent chills down my spine. He was still an enormous demon, after all.

"Yes, too! You fucked up with your brothers. You caused your father to curse you. And that thoughtlessness hasn't just cost you the magic, it's also tearing pride apart. And instead of trying to determine the best course of action from the beginning, you waste more and more time while trying to find a fucking puppet you can control. Meanwhile, your carelessness is causing the wild magic to rip this ring apart! As if that's not enough, you were so haughty and sure of yourself, you misjudged your target and got Hayt."

"It was an accident," Bael said.

"Shut up!" I screamed. "You're always defending him. Always praising him. Get off his dick and open your fucking eyes."

I had enough sense to see that Bael looked at me with wide eyes. I'd hurt him. I could see that.

But I didn't have it in me to repent. Not only was it accurate, if a little harsh right now, but Hayt was dying in my arms.

Bowing my head, I closed my eyes and willed all the fire to me. It was there. I could feel it surround me. Reach out and stroke my hand. My will. My pride.

Not me, I told it. *Hayt. Please, save Hayt.*

I was momentarily surprised when I felt an answer back. *Command me. Use me.*

My eyes snapped open and widened. There was a massive storm around me that obscured everything. Billowing storm clouds, thick fog, massive thunderheads shooting purple lightning through the violet vapor.

I wasn't sure how to use the magic, but it was here for the taking. Swallowing, I closed my eyes and took a breath. There's a reason I was named one of the City's up-and-coming sharks. I knew my worth. I knew my strength. And I wasn't going to let Hayt die.

Something in me reached for the magic and took hold, gripping it with both hands and both feet. I think I even sunk my teeth in it. And I wrapped that shit all around Hayt like a damn cocoon. It surged through us both until I compelled his heart to beat in time with mine. I commanded his lungs to take in air. I forced his mind to come out of death.

Hayt groaned, coughed, and swore. "That was not part of the event I saw," he muttered.

I think I sobbed in relief. And then my body actually felt the fire I was covered in.

CHAPTER NINETEEN
EKO

Nuke was not to be soothed. She was consumed in a firestorm of magic for countless breathless minutes. When it fell away, she was sobbing over Hayt.

I think we all froze, staring in shock. And then Hayt moved to sit up, pulling her into him. I didn't know Hayt any better than any of these demons, but I sighed in relief when he came to.

Sometimes it's difficult to *not* see the souls of those around me. Much like an uvall who cannot turn off their time sight, the ability to see the souls of the living occasionally was stuck in the 'on' position.

And the souls around me were all live wires. Hayt was in pain. With every move, he hurt. His soul was shivering from death as it attempted to keep a hold of the life Nuke gave it.

Nuke's was glowing so brightly I squinted. Alive with anger. Alight with magic. Trembling with fear.

Malak's was just as upset. If a soul was ever a caged animal, Malak's was. It thrashed in horror, humiliation, and desperation. For all that Malak was, he loved his demons deeply. To have killed one unintentionally tore at him fiercely. So much so that I could see his pride waver.

"Let's go home," Hayt said, his voice raspy. Death still clung to him. I could see it. But it didn't have a hold anymore.

He and Nuke pulled each other to their feet. I wasn't sure who was leaning on who. Nor could I tell which of them was leading the other. We followed close, all of us ready to catch them should one of them stumble. It was fortunate that it wasn't a long walk to the boat, and we helped them climb in.

Malak sat on the opposite side as the rest of us. Partly a counter balance since he was still demon right now. And also, because the fire around Nuke flared hotly when he got too close. I didn't know him well, but I could see how upset he was. How he needed to feel Hayt's life restored just as much as Nuke did.

But he kept his distance, staring intently at Hayt's every breath.

Bael sat next to me. His soul felt like a wilted flower. It wasn't shame. But Nuke's words had hurt him deeply. It's not that she had been wrong, precisely. Bael was a bit of a lapdog. Though he meant well. He cared greatly for those around him and did everything in his power to try and keep the peace and make everyone happy.

I was surprised when Hayt and Nuke separated once we got upstairs in Malak's home. Hayt moved stiffly into Malak's room while Nuke walked numbly towards hers. Her wings burned brightly, whisps of fire drifting through the air until they burned out.

She stood in the middle of the room and looked around. We could see how lost she was. How exhausted and angry and frustrated. Around the edges, fear lingered.

Nuke turned and walked into me, burying her face in my chest. I wrapped an arm around her lower back, hiking her up higher in my embrace, and buried my other hand in her hair, massaging her scalp and I made silly cooing sounds.

She remained in my hold for over an hour. We didn't move from that spot nor that hold until Nuke pulled her head to the side and sighed. "How do I turn them off?"

I glanced over her head at Rhyl and Revan, raising a brow. But their confusion mirrored my own.

"Turn what off, sweetheart?" Revan asked.

"My wings."

I grinned, kissing the top of her head.

"It's like the muscle game. You tell a muscle, one at a time, to relax and make it so. You can do that with your wings, too. And your horns, for that matter," Revan told her.

She wasn't relaxing. Perhaps she wasn't playing along with the muscle unwinding game but she remained as tense as she had been since Hayt died.

After a minute, she sighed again, her arms tightening around me. "Bring me to bed, please."

"Happily," I answered, dropping my hand from her head and bringing both to her supple ass. I picked her up, encouraging her legs to wrap around me, her arms circling my neck, and turned for the bed.

Since she was new to her wings, I lay on my back, bringing her with me so she was sprawled across my chest.

And there we remained for three days. Okay, not in the exact position and we moved throughout the room. But that's it. We moved around the room and didn't leave.

Hayt came by frequently, hanging out for a while before returning to whatever he was doing. Zyphon stopped by just as frequently. He'd check on Nuke and then he and Revan would step outside the door for a few minutes. Revan would return but Zyphon left. Kingsley also came by daily.

Nuke was happy to see them all. However, she refused to see Malak when he'd attempt to talk to her. Likewise, she put an end to whatever conversation turned towards Malak when someone brought him up.

Bael stayed away. I wondered if Nuke understood how much her words had stung.

On the fourth day, Rhyl, Revan, and I stood in the door to the balcony watching Nuke. She stared at the city with a vaguely neutral expression. There was thought there. A struggle. But no intent. Or purpose.

Revan glanced at Rhyl and me before he moved to her. Rhyl and I followed, keeping close so Nuke knew we were with her always. Revan crouched in front of her, drawing her attention to him.

"Talk to us," he said.

"That cloud looks like a limp cock lying against a thigh. Still impressive, though."

I blinked several times before looking at the sky. It didn't take me long to locate the cloud in question. Cloud man was packing. There was an extraordinary sac, too.

Bringing my attention back to Nuke, the other two did at the same time. And then Revan burst out laughing. "You're the best woman I've ever met," he said, shaking his head.

A smile touched Nuke's lips. The breeze picked up, making her hair move behind her in a curtain. It was a fascinating color. Deep red with a hint of purple mixed in. The purple meant it wasn't quite auburn or burgundy. It was a stunning color.

"Really, Nuke," Revan said, tracing his fingers lightly over her jaw. "What are you thinking?"

"I'm debating how important it is to me to succeed because I'd really love to just let Malak fail."

I closed my eyes. Maybe we needed to be doing a better job of encouraging her. Of teaching her. We said we'd help her and so far, the only productive thing we've done is give her a tour of the city.

"But in reality, I've never failed at anything. That's never been an option for me. But even if I learn to control the magic, it's always going to be just out of reach of tame because there's no fucking way I will ever be Malak's queen. He doesn't deserve this city."

"Maybe you're concentrating on the wrong thing," Rhyl said. His hand circled my wrist for a moment before he knelt at her side. Her attention was drawn to him. "In order to achieve what you want, you need to be queen."

Nuke narrowed her eyes, scowling at him.

Rhyl smiled lightly, kissing her arm where it rested on the chair. "And what if you're not his queen but our queen?"

This time, her brow rose as she considered him. "Are you a lost son of Satan?"

He grinned, shaking his head. "You're not wrong that in order to be queen, you need Malak. But forget all that." He gestured to the city. "They need a queen strong enough to put the magic in line. They need a queen to care about them and fix what is broken. You are that queen, Anuka."

She sighed, turning her attention back toward the city.

"Sweet girl, you can't stay in here forever," Revan said.

"You can leave when you want to. You're not required to stay here," she countered.

"Mm," Revan hummed as he leaned in and kissed her.

Despite herself, Nuke smiled against his lips. "I'm not saying that because I want to leave. I'm saying it because there's a world out here that needs a queen. I know this wasn't a role you chose. You didn't ask for it and don't particularly want it. But you're here and you're glorious, with more strength and compassion than anyone else. You can be the Queen of Pride if you choose to."

He kissed her cheek then her nose and stood.

Nuke didn't leave the balcony for the rest of the day. We joined her with food and sometimes for a cuddle. I also enjoyed pleasing her on the balcony, not missing that Malak was on his further down the building. Not that I was ever a slouch, but I made sure her orgasms were good and loud knowing he was watching.

The next morning, Nuke determined she was going to the library and then she'd be back with a plan. Since she didn't expand, we didn't know what this plan included. Or what it was even about.

We'd always made it a point that one of us stayed behind in the room when Nuke left. There'd always been someone here when she sought us out.

"I think maybe we need a plan," Revan said after she'd been gone for a while. "She can't be queen without Malak. And though I'm sure she can do a fucking lot with that magic, she's never going to be able to control it all. Not the way Malak will be able to."

"I'm not sure she's ready to forgive him for killing Hayt," I pointed out. "It's a little too close to home remembering that he also murdered her."

"It's more than that. His carelessness and arrogance put someone she cared about in direct danger. That's not a miscalculation Anuka makes nor forgives," Rhyl said. "We have never asked about her life, but I'd be willing to bet that she's not come from a cushy childhood. She's witnessed the actions that Malak displayed which is why she's always been damn sure never to make those same mistakes."

"You haven't confirmed that, have you?" I asked, raising a brow.

Rhyl smirked. "Concentrating on a life and watching the stream of it is arduous. Generally speaking, I just let it run while I attempt to remain in the present."

"That sounds exhausting," Revan said.

Rhyl nodded. "It's easier to infer from events that I've seen than actually follow a specific life. And really, I'd be willing to bet I'm right. I'd also wager the careless, arrogant person in her life had been her father. She's only ever shown concern for her sister and mother."

"I think we're going to have to let Nuke find the direction that suits her. Malak had been climbing into her good graces, but I think he fell further into her pits of hatred than he started out in," I said. "Pushing her would be detrimental to all of us."

"I never wanted to push her," Revan said. "That hadn't been my intent yesterday. She'd been so silent that I was concerned. And as fun as you two are, I think we could all do with a change of scenery. It's not healthy to remain cooped up in here."

"Why not go find Zyphon?" I asked.

He grinned in return. "He'll swing by when he's done his rounds. I think he's also trying to find a way for Malak to pick up the pieces and so far, they're all striking out."

"I'm going to take one for the team, then," I said, getting to my feet. "I'm going to find Malak. See if I can get anything productive from him."

"Good luck," Rhyl said, shaking his head. He leaned

back on the couch, yawning. With Revan and me leaving, that left him here in case Nuke came back and needed someone.

"You want to go instead?"

"Not a chance." He waved his hand. "I'm going to nap. I kind of enjoy playing the role of a cat."

Chuckling, I headed for the door.

Malak's room was close even if it felt like you were walking a mile of hall to get there. I doubted he was there but thought I'd check. There was no answer on his door, so I went hunting for him.

I found him sitting at a table in the kitchen of all places. There was a mug of tea in his hand as he absently stared out the window. He took no note of me in the room, so I got myself some tea before joining him. It took me sitting at the table across from him for Malak to notice I was there.

"Eko," he greeted. He was tired. His soul was tired. There was the weight of defeat that was almost fully embracing him.

"Prince," I returned.

His quiet snort of humorless laughter had his eyes dropping to his tea. He considered it as if he hadn't known it was there. I watched as he brought the mug to his lips and took a sip. And then he stared distractedly at the tea as if it would tell him his future.

I was fairly certain it wasn't that kind of tea.

"What are you going to do?" I asked.

"About what?" His voice was just as tired as his soul. Everything, all the pressure and stress, was catching up to him. Accidentally killing Hayt had brought it all to a boiling point.

"You need to get the magic under control. And you need

your queen to do so. What are you going to do to get to that point?" I asked.

Malak shook his head. "You'd know better than I what I should do. She won't speak to me. Not that I think she should. It happened exactly as she said it did. I was too arrogant in what I was doing and didn't control my throw when the pridefall moved, snagging Hayt instead."

"I think that Nuke needs to be left alone and that this is going to take longer than it would have if the recent incident didn't happen. She's already seen what good you're doing in the city. That you are the caretaker of all of pride. Nuke has heard and seen that your citizens speak fondly of you, look up to you, and rely on you. And that you don't disappoint them."

"So what are you suggesting?"

"Find some humility for her. But don't seek her out for a while, either." I paused, thinking about her telling us that she was seriously contemplating doing nothing in order to let Malak fail again. "In fact, don't seek her out at all."

Malak rubbed his face and nodded. "Fine," he said, sighing. "Whatever plan of action gets me the ability to control the magic, so it stops tearing apart my city and displacing my demons, I'll do."

If only Anuka could hear those words from him and knew exactly what it was he was willing to give up to achieve that goal. But right now, I'm not sure she'd care at all.

CHAPTER TWENTY
ANUKA

I spent many days in the library, trying to learn whatever I could about the magic and other ways to control it that didn't involve Malak. There was an entire section of 'lost relics' within the library. I could have probably spent years there and not gotten bored with all the things I found.

Not found. But learned about. They were all still missing.

Maybe there was a crystal ball. Or a ring. Maybe even a scepter. Stories of all of these things were there. Many, many were lost. And each of them controlled magic in one way or another. But I wasn't sure that any of them would control the magic of pride.

Then I thought, maybe I don't need a lost thing but something that's, well, here. Maybe not in pride but in Hell. Or fuck, in the world somewhere. That seemed too much of a stretch though. Magic didn't exist in the human world. Besides, I couldn't get to it if it did. I was stuck in Hell until I was queen.

Leaning back in the chair, I closed my eyes. Maybe there

wasn't just one thing I needed. But perhaps I could find something to address many different parts. The rice. The fish. The fog and swamp. The pridefalls?

Maybe I didn't need to control the magic. In a sense, I already could. Not freely but in times of duress.

The little fox watcher climbed onto my lap and looked up at me. I smiled, wrapping my arms around him and smiling. Sweet little kit.

I could feel the magic like static electricity in his fur. It didn't shock but it was there. Charged.

"What do you think?" I asked him. "Somehow, you are the key, right?"

He didn't answer. Of course, he didn't. Even in hell, animals didn't speak.

"Nuka." I looked up at the voice to find Revan and Zyphon approaching me. I've always squashed the use of 'Nuka' in the past. It was either Anuka or Nuke. But if I was letting 'sweet girl' fly, then I supposed 'Nuka' would be fine as well. As long as it was one of my demons and not some rando.

"What have you been doing here for three days?" Revan asked as they took seats across from me. Zyphon pulled one of the books around to peek inside.

"Looking for a solution to the magic."

"What did you find?" Zyphon asked.

"Frustration."

They both laughed.

Sighing, I said, "I thought maybe I just needed one thing. Something that I could use to draw the magic and make it simpler to control. Then I thought that was asking for too much so maybe I needed separate things for separate jobs. But now as I say it out loud, I'm looking for a bandage and not an answer."

"Bandages are temporary, yes," Zyphon said. "But a temporary patch that can hold better than what's in place while you search for the more permanent solution isn't a bad thing."

"It's not counterproductive?" I asked.

He shook his head. "Of all the counterproductive things going on right now, this is the least of them."

"Does that mean you're encouraging me to find something?"

"Depends what it is. What do you have in mind specifically?"

I closed my eyes to consider the many, many issues in the world right now. I suspected the Pride Rings weren't actually caused by the errant magic like the pridefalls. So were the pridefalls more of a concern than the way the magic eats at the city?

I pulled out my list of issues. The ones I knew about anyway and scanned down them. "Maybe the answer isn't so complicated in some of these cases." I looked up at the demons. "The pridefalls are one of my bigger concerns since they're arguably innocent demons succumbing to another sin. If we can save them from death, that would be optimal. The way I'm figuring this is that their level of pride is falling, making room for something else to take a deeper root. Am I right so far?"

They both nodded.

"You also have murmurs that dispense pride where it needs to be. Is there a way to communicate with them and give them a task?"

"I like where you're going with this," Zyphon said, grinning. "Using what we already have naturally. I can have a message sent to-" He paused for a minute to consider this.

"I think Eko might be best equipped since he messes

with souls and such," Revan suggested. "I'm sure he'd be willing to help."

Zyphon nodded, accepting that idea. "Good. I like this plan. I'll keep Hayt apprised so he knows what's going on."

"Okay, good. Next would be the swamp and fog that's eating the city. That seems like a rather high priority. And I don't know how to combat that. Oh! I was thinking about the issue in the rice fields. What if we get a laraje to check out the water? I know it's incredibly shallow but surely not all laraje are giant?"

Zyphon grinned widely. "I'll have a message sent to Mayor Jurd to have him send some laraje into the outer waters."

"Maybe they can check out the fisheries, too. See what's going on with the monkfish?"

He nodded. "Sounds good, Nuke. I'll make it happen."

"It seems like the hole in the barrier is being repaired so although I added that to my list, I bumped the priority down since it's being addressed." I scribbled on my piece of paper what we'd talked about so far. "Okay, so I think the biggest issue is really the way the magic is eating at the city. And I'm tapped out of ideas. I need a magical remedy."

I scratched the watcher's head as it dozed on my lap, quietly purring against me. My sweet little furball with seven tails and glowing paths of magic in his fur.

"Ah," Zyphon said as he got to his feet. He disappeared within the shelves for a minute before coming back with a book. He set it on the table and flipped through it until he found what he was looking for. Then he turned it to face me. "The staves of diablo. There are nine of them that were lost to time. They're powered by sinful lure stones."

"Which conveniently are purple," I noted, enjoying that I was surrounded by my favorite color.

Zyphon grinned. "Yes. They act both as a beacon for magic and a barrier, depending on how the stone is placed."

"If it repels in a ring, we're going to have to circle the entire city. Is nine enough for that?" Revan asked.

"Maybe not the entire city. Malak's innate magic keeps everything close away. This is just a theory, but I think that's why the fog magic has stalled in moving closer inward," Zyphon said.

"I'm impressed that his reach is so far," Revan said, shaking his head. "A little further and this wouldn't be necessary."

"Not true. The magic would find another way to terrorize. And it will when we cut off this route. It'll be slow to push the magic away, but I think it'll work. It's going to be trial and error."

"So... this sounds like a great first plan but how are we going to find these lost staves? I know I was looking in lost relics, but I figured if something present would work, it already would be in use," I said.

"Fortunately for us, we have an oriax," Revan said, grinning at Zyphon.

I'd clearly missed their reunion, but I could see how happy they were now. I wouldn't have thought Revan wasn't happy before but the change in him now was obvious. It reminded me that I didn't know these men. These demons.

"Remind me what an oriax does," I said.

"I find things. Usually after some unfortunate misadventure since I've never been interested in mastering the skills I was born with, but I tend to come out with what I want eventually."

"And a few new scars and nightmares," Revan added, teasingly.

"That sounds fun. How does this work?"

"Maybe you can send your watcher after the stones we need to power the staves once Zy finds them," Revan suggested. "And get Eko on the murmur thing while Zyphon sets up his summoning circle. I'll grab you from your room and you can join us for some fun."

I grinned, getting to my feet. For the first time in a week, I felt like I had a purpose that was achievable. With the book in my hand and carrying my foxy friend with me, I followed the men out. We parted ways in the hall, and I headed back to my room.

Eko was there playing on a tablet. He looked up with a sexy smile.

"How do you feel about a task?" I asked.

He sat up, setting the tablet down. "Anything for you, my queen."

Feeling in a good mood, I smiled sweetly. "We'll test that later. For now, I'm hoping you can somehow communicate with the murmurs and set them on a purpose of increasing pride where it's weakest. We're hoping this will help us combat the pridefall appearances."

Eko got to his feet and nodded. He stepped in close, placing both his hands on the sides of my face, and kissed me so thoroughly that my toes curled. *"Anything* you want," he repeated in a deep, husky voice. "But I'll see what I can do about this for now."

"Thank you," I whispered, hearing how silly my voice sounded right now.

He left the room as Rhyl entered. He smiled. "Good to see you looking to be pleased."

I nodded. He probably meant aroused. I was there. "I think I have the beginnings of a few plans that we're going to try." I spent the next few minutes outlining what Zyphon, Revan, and I had come up with. "What do you think?"

"Sounds promising." When I narrowed my eyes, he grinned. "I mean it. This really does sound promising."

"I think Zy is busy right now with his summoning circle construction. Would you mind tracking down Hayt and relaying what we came up with for the laraje?"

"Sure. And I think I have an idea on how to secure the staves of diablo where they would best serve the purpose and we can see if it's going to work as intended while we're at it."

I kissed him, pressing myself along his long, hard body. His hands landed on my hips as he 'mmm'd' against my mouth. "I'm glad Eko left you in a good mood that I get to enjoy."

"Hurry up and enjoy her then. We have a retrieval date to get to," Revan said from the doorway.

Rhyl sighed dramatically. "Just take her away. I'm not a fan of 'hurry up' when it comes to pleasing my girl."

I flushed as I pulled from his arms. He winked and I walked by him, allowing myself the pleasure of running my hand across the hard planes of his chest. Is there anything like a well sculpted chest? I didn't think so.

The room Revan led me to was down a whole lot of stairs. I thought we were headed for the boats in the underwater tunnels, but apparently these endless stairs led into stone hallways lit with torches that reminded me of a dungeon.

In fact, the room Revan led me to was definitely a dungeon room. There were shackles on the wall and everything.

When Zyphon caught me eying them, he told me, "Once, Malak used to have souls tortured in the basement. He enjoyed their screams."

I raised a brow. I supposed they were demons. This couldn't be that much of a surprise, right?

Turning my attention inward, I found a drawn circle as cliché demonic as it could be. That being said, I've never seen one in person and the detail was exquisite. There was a dark beauty to it. I say dark because I was sure that it was drawn in blood and also, I could feel the demonic essence radiating from it.

"Now what?" I asked.

Zyphon stepped inside and held out his hands to us both. Revan and I each took one and he pulled us inside. It was like walking through a bubble membrane. I even felt a pop.

"Now, I try to scour the world across time and spot one of them," Zyphon said.

"I suppose it's too much to ask that they were all lost together," I said.

Revan laughed.

"Yes. Almost nothing is that easy," Zyphon said.

We spent a long time watching the static of the world go by around us. It twisted in a whirlwind of nonsense and confusion to the point where my head was spinning, and I was cross-eyed. Not only that, but I was also basically useless here. I was not able to make out even a single comprehensible image.

"There," Zyphon said, grabbing both our hands and leaping.

I screeched as my feet left the ground and we were airborne. I yelped again as we began to fall.

"Grab it," Zyphon said, pointing below us.

We were falling in a cavern with rushing water. There were cracks in the rocky side that let in bright light. It was blinding if you looked anywhere near it.

Revan kicked his feet against a wall and sent himself careening towards the stave. His hands circled around it. He came to an abrupt, jerky halt where he was suspended above us before abruptly coming loose and falling once again.

"Now you can get us out?" I yelled over the sound of rushing water that was getting closer.

"Not unless I can touch you both," he said. "If I don't have my hand on you, you're stuck here."

"Uh, let's avoid that," I suggested.

He laughed as Revan turned himself and streamlined his way to us. But Zyphon didn't get a chance to reach out as we hit the running water. I was plunged under into the freezing cold and swept away on a waterslide ride of epic proportions. It might have been fun if I knew where we were going to be dumped.

As it turned out, the waterfall emptied out the side of a mountain and, once again, I was freefalling through the air, too breathless to scream.

A hand closed around the neck of my shirt, and we were yanked from that moment. My feet hit the ground inside the summoning circle, and I looked around myself in alarm.

Both men were behind me, grinning. Revan held the stave in his hands. We were all sopping wet.

"That was both terrifying and a lot of fun," I said, shivering.

Zyphon laughed. "If I was better at this, I could just reach in and grab it. It wouldn't be an all-body experience."

"Meh. I always loved the adventure," Revan said.

Zyphon smiled, pulling him to his chest and kissing him. I watched with a smile.

Finding the staves was fun, adventurous, and somewhat terrifying, but also sexy. Yes, it was an afternoon well spent.

CHAPTER TWENTY-ONE
KINGSLEY

In the week since Nuke got the staves of diablo installed, they've had to be moved outward twice as the magic retreated. I've caught Malak staring from the balcony into the distance, pride shining in his fiery eyes.

His demon was always right on the surface. His horns, though smaller, hadn't retreated since the mishap that resulted in him killing Hayt. I didn't have to be there to see the turmoil it had created within the household. The tension was thick, even with Nuke maintaining as much space between them as possible.

Though that was unfavorable to the current predicament of getting Malak access to the magic, it hadn't stopped Nuke from doing just as she said she was going to: getting the magic under control without him.

Granted, she'd also said she'd do so without us and I have seen on numerous occasions Zyphon and Hayt helping her. I wasn't overly surprised. She's spent quite a bit of time with both and has developed a relationship with each of them.

The amount of success Nuke has shown in the last week

has been stupidly impressive. Putting the murmurs on the distribution of pride to counteract the pridefalls was brilliant and so inanely simple, we should have thought of it. Getting the laraje to sift through the waters of the fisheries and rice terraces – amazing. They didn't fix the monkfish issue, but they managed to clean up more bacteria within the rice paddies than we knew were there.

I almost wanted to put her on the issue of the hole in the barrier. Yes, Malak's solution of sewing it back up was working but was it permanent? Would that last forever, or would the barrier always be weak right there?

The true testimony was the magic on the western side of Pride. The staves have pushed the magic back more than a dozen feet in a week. That might not sound like a lot but considering how much of the city it had eaten away, it was impressive.

We weren't ready to retake those city blocks yet, though. Like the barrier, we weren't sure it would last.

If there was a negative, it was that the pridemage storms were increasing. The trouble with them was that they didn't remain on the surface. They tore apart Tanndwr as well.

"King."

I looked up as Bael and Zyphon walked in, both smiling. Bael wasn't often seen smiling these days. Not since Hayt's death. I gathered that it had little to do with the actual event and something more specifically tied in with Nuke. He's avoided her like she was a gluttony demon.

I shuddered at the thought.

They sat around the table with me as I considered the map of the third floor. I had four families secured into four suites and had a few more being prepared. You never knew what was going to happen. In the eventuality that the staves stopped working, I wanted to make sure we had room for more of our demons should the need arise.

In all honesty, it was time to look at expanding the City of Pride by a ring. One more band of dwellings so that our people were happy and didn't have to live right on top of each other.

"Hi," I said, eventually managing to pull my attention away. "How's it going?"

Zyphon shook his head. Not long ago, we couldn't get him to smile. Now the smile never left. Since he's reconciled with Revan, he's also kept his distance from our dear prince. Something that was making Malak even more angsty.

The man was becoming a romance novel. Stuck in a bunch of silly love triangles and filled with angst.

"Good," Bael said. "While Nuke's plans are succeeding, they've also managed to put off the Pride Rings."

"I'm not convinced that one has anything to do with the other," Zyphon added.

I shook my head. Neither was I. The Pride Rings had their own agenda. Primarily, dethroning Malak. While I found it comical, it was even more preposterous thinking that any random demon could run pride. Considering *only* a son of Satan could control the pride magic, what did they think they were going to do better?

"Maybe they don't want a patriarchy," I muttered. "Maybe they want to begin a democracy."

"What?" Zyphon asked and I realized I spoke out loud.

Chuckling, I shook my head. "Sorry. My thoughts side tracked to the Pride Rings' motivation."

Bael rolled his eyes. "They're hilarious if they think they can rule pride without Malak."

I shrugged. Malak was a good ruler. He was

compassionate and strong. But in the week that Nuke has been here and intentionally worked towards bettering the wrongs in pride, she's been wildly more successful.

It didn't change the fact that we needed Anuka *and* Malak to truly right this place.

"How are the storms?" I asked, moving us from the subject of Malak. I was too internally conflicted regarding him at the moment to be objective. Considering I wasn't sure what the outcome needed to be anymore, I thought it best to keep my thoughts to myself.

"Getting stronger but so far, they're staying in the outer water," Zyphon said. "Nuke is already brainstorming ideas for them. Her goal is to have a counter before they become an issue."

I almost wished I'd found her. She sure was something.

"They're made of magic. There must be something else lost that you can bring her."

Zyphon shrugged. "Maybe. We're not ignoring that possibility. But we haven't found the right thing, either. Magic made into a storm can be a tricky thing to handle. We don't want to cause it to get worse."

"The real issue right now is internal," Zyphon said. This was why they came to me. I sat back, crossing my arms while I listened, already anticipating where this was going.

For what felt like eons, we've been waiting for a queen. Waiting for Malak to be able to take the throne, rule over Hell when his father is ready to step aside and manipulate the magic as if it were his own breath.

At some point, something inside me shifted. I still thought that Malak was the best option for taking Lucifer's place, but I no longer thought he was the best demon for the job of running pride. Quite frankly, his pride was a hinder more than a help.

"Malak and Anuka," Zyphon said, and I nodded absently.

"You don't care about that outcome, do you?" Bael asked, calling me out.

I shrugged, hoping we could brush by it. But since this was what they intended to speak to me about, I wasn't going to be able to ignore this conversation for long. Might as well just dive in.

Sighing, I sat forward. "No. I support Anuka, wholeheartedly. But quite frankly, she's right. Malak has focused on everything unimportant when looking for a queen. And since her arrival, she's been more successful in righting pride than he has since Satan cut off his access to the magic. I'm not sure he's fit to be the ruler."

"Ouch," Bael said, frowning.

"You really want to tell me I'm wrong?"

He opened his mouth to counter, but an odd thing happened. A flush covered his cheeks and he looked away, not speaking. Not defending Malak, right or wrong. I raised a brow, insanely curious.

Zyphon patted his hand before looking at me. There wasn't any indication that he had any insight as to what just happened, but he also didn't address it either.

"Bottom line is pretty simple, and we have no options," Zyphon said. "Malak is Satan's son. Therefore, he's the only one capable of controlling the magic in its entirety. Regardless of whether or not Nuke can grasp it, something she's incredibly close to, it's not completely managed unless we have both rulers in place."

"So, like it or not, getting Malak and Nuke on the same page is the goal," I said, sighing.

I wasn't disappointed. Malak wasn't a bad guy. Far from

it. And our job as his friends was to make him better. I could commit to that.

"Alright. What's our assignment?" I asked.

Bael smiled, though it was almost shy. I was dying to know what this was about. Seriously, what had happened here?!

"We think Malak is subdued enough that he's not going to hinder his own progress." He paused, frowning. He didn't need to say what we were all thinking. 'Not again, anyway.' "We need to concentrate on warming Nuke up to him without pushing her."

A siren blared in the air loud enough that I cringed. I jumped to my feet, my chair falling over behind me. Zyphon and Bael did the same as we looked at each other.

"What does that mean?" Bael yelled over the noise.

It had been so long since I heard it, I couldn't remember. Zyphon turned to the window and although I couldn't hear him over the ear-splitting alarm, the amazement mixed with dread on his face was easily distinguishable.

Bael and I moved to his side and felt his awed panic. I'd never seen a pridemage storm so large. It was big enough that even in the distance where it continued to pick up steam and grow, it was enormous - so large that it could swallow three entire city blocks.

And wouldn't you know, it was heading for the city.

Zyphon turned and raced from the room, Bael and I on his heels. We ran into Nuke as she darted to the main doors and threw them open. Silly woman. Didn't she know that we needed to lock down right now, not open up?

"What do we do?" she cried out, watching helplessly as it inched closer and closer to the outermost buildings.

"Nothing we can do now," Bael said, taking a step back. "What do you do to prevent or disperse a tornado?"

The destitute expression she turned on him said she was not at all impressed with that answer.

And then the noise that the storm made as it tore into the side of a building while running straight through another overrode even the alarm. Debris flew overhead, shooting out of the wind like missiles. Falling like hail the size of basketballs.

Zyphon yanked her out of the way as a sliver of window the length of my arm came whistling through the air, cutting through the space where she'd been standing and embedding into the stone behind me.

We needed to get inside. I pulled at Bael, dragging him backward as Zyphon did the same to Nuke. With the giant doors shut, we continued deeper into the house, going down stairs until we were almost in the bowels.

Nuke immediately went to the window that was only barely above the rising sea as it churned and slammed against the house. We didn't have a straight on view of the storm, but we could see the damage it was causing.

"I'm going to need more rooms available," I noted.

"Rooms?!" Bael said. "We're going to need an entire three floors."

"If the estate remains standing," I deadpanned.

As if my words had been the command, debris began slamming into the building, making it shake and tremble.

"Why isn't Malak's magic preventing damage?" Nuke demanded as she stared outside.

"Because Malak doesn't have magic right now, queen," I told her. "Only you can touch the magic."

There was a moment of silence before she turned to

look at me. "Yes, I can. How do I stop the storm with magic?"

"That's not what I mean," I said.

Zyphon pulled her around. "Yes! Call on your little foxy friend and let's go." He dragged her through the door as Bael called after them, taking up the chase when they ignored him.

Throwing my hands in the air, I ran to catch up.

The watcher was already sprinting at her side as Zyphon pulled his phone to his ear. What a time for a phone call. He made an abrupt turn and started jogging up the stairs. I was sure it was adrenaline making us take the five flights without pause at this speed.

We stopped as Zyphon threw open the massive doors to the balcony that was an entire enormous room outside, overlooking Waasser market. Just as he pulled her outside, her demons came around the corner.

She looked at them with a quick, wide grin before giving her attention to Zyphon.

With no barriers between us and the storm, it was a constant game of dodgeball. And between its noise and the alarm, I couldn't hear myself think nevermind what they were saying.

In order to know what was going on, I got closer. Right on top of them.

"See if your watcher can connect with others and draw the magic from the storm. I'm not up on the prideful animals, but if they can communicate with a few fenix to try and dismantle the storm, that would be great," Zyphon yelled over the noise.

Eko pulled Anuka and Rhyl down in time to avoid a hurdling terracotta pot that smashed against the wall. By the time we stood up, the watcher was already gone, and Revan was holding out his hands.

Lying on his palms were a handful of dark purple stones.

Zyphon kissed him sloppily before shoving one into each of Anuka's hands and turning her toward the incoming pridemage storm. To say I never wanted to be this close to this much magic didn't cover what I was feeling right now.

"Focus," Zyphon said. "Feel the magic that's so close, reaching out to you." Wings of purple fire unfurled from her back and Zyphon grinned. "That's it, sweetheart. Just like that. And now it's just a matter of shaping the magic to your will. Start small. Make us a magical shield that prevents anything from touching us."

I wasn't sure it worked until a random belt came whizzing through the air and stopped dead.

"Yes!" Revan said. "That's it, queen! Look at you!"

"Good girl," Eko praised, grinning at her as if she were the only one in existence.

Rhyl didn't speak but he looked at her with all the hunger of a lust demon.

"Now expand it. Little by little. Don't get overzealous. Start with the balcony and then move the bubble outward."

It was easy enough to follow Anuka's progress. Projectiles paused suddenly in the air before being tossed aside. And the area that they stopped in moved further and further away, expanding in all directions.

Just as she'd covered all of the estate and had moved out to Waasser market, the first fenix flew into the storm. Another followed and then a third. It wasn't long before streaks of purple fire danced in the air as they converged on the storm from the water and buildings.

"This is wild," Bael said, grinning in admiration. If he wasn't in love with Anuka before, he was now.

Fuck, we all were. I was ready to drop to the ground and lick her feet.

I spotted Malak then, standing just inside the door as he watched her with fire burning in his eyes. Pride didn't even cover his expression. Worship. Our great prince was ready to worship Nuke as if she were a goddess.

Hell, I was now convinced she was.

CHAPTER TWENTY-TWO
ANUKA

I think part of my hesitation in touching the magic was not wanting to feel the electrocution that followed. The pain of it was excruciating.

But faced with going through that, knowing it didn't last, and watching this storm tear its way through the city... I chose the pain.

There was something different about it this time. I could feel it running through me as if it were my blood. There was no resistance, only eagerness to do as I commanded it. Begging me to give it direction. It was hungry to obey.

As if the magic was a living thing acting out to get the attention it craved, it easily did as I wanted.

While I pushed the bubble outward, I could see little spots of purple light within. Not the lightning that burst from the storm, striking and setting fires as it ripped holes in buildings, but the fire that was the watchers. The purple streaks that were the fenixes.

Slowly, the storm began to break apart. To slow and lessen. And when it finally dissolved entirely, I collapsed backward as if the weight of the magic I'd been commanding became too much and I fell under it.

Zyphon caught me, looking down at me with a beaming smile. He rubbed my hair from my face and kissed my forehead. "Perfect," he purred.

I sighed and closed my eyes, waiting for the shock of the magic. But it didn't come. At least, not in the capacity I anticipated. There was a sting, but it felt more like an aftershock instead of touching a live wire that was strong enough to keep a dinosaur in place.

Exhaustion tapped at me as I was jostled. I briefly squinted my eyes open in time to see Eko picking me up with a gratified smile. I jumped when my watcher fell into my arms and snuggled close. And then I closed my eyes.

Expecting sleep to take me, I lay awake in my bed for a long time as I listened to my demons talk. Listened to the reports come in of damage and who was being moved into Malak's house. I didn't think they'd so much made my room their new headquarters, but all the demons were keeping close.

I smiled, sighing. The bed dipped and I opened my eyes as Revan curled at my back. "You're amazing," he murmured in my ear. "Do you have any idea how many lives you saved?"

Though his words were praise, I flinched. How many lives had been lost before we managed to come up with a working plan?

"Easy, my sweet girl," he said, kissing the shell of my ear. "I know where your mind went. We're looking into it, but it'll be a while before we hear a hard and fast number. Rest assured that it would be much more if you hadn't intervened."

"Is it normal to have storms that big?" I asked, trying to

force my mind from the dampening truth that some had died.

"No," he answered.

"The storms typically remain small and in the outer water," Bael said as he came closer to the bed. "I can't remember if we've ever seen one this big."

"What caused it?"

"I suspect it's because we're pushing back the magic on the eastern side of the city and it's gathering in other ways," Zyphon said from where he sat at the end of the bed.

I sighed. "Can't win."

"You can and you did," Bael argued. He crouched to his knees to face me. This was the first time we've spoken since the incident that caused Hayt his life. "Anuka, the amount of good you've done in pride in so short a time is nothing less than astounding. That storm was strong enough to be able to rip through the entire city and you stopped it. You did that. All on your own. The number of lives you saved is astronomical."

"But some died," I whispered.

"Maybe. Probably. But don't diminish the lives you saved with the ones we lost. You kept pride standing."

I recognized the truth in his words, but it didn't change the burden of knowing that I failed those who hadn't been so lucky.

———

By the time I crawled out of bed the next day, there was already construction happening on the buildings that the storm had torn through. Three had been demolished. Three more had been damaged to the point where it made more sense to tear them down. A handful of others had structural issues that needed addressing before they could be fixed further.

The amount that had less damage were in the double digits and I'm not talking ten or eleven.

Eight had died. The alarm had called attention to the threat, enabling most people to get out of the path of the storm. The eight that died had been caught in the winds, unable to free themselves.

Stories were coming in of those who had been able to escape once I started moving the shield outward. And when the fenixes and watchers started siphoning their perspective energy from the storm, even more were able to break free of its hold on them.

Yes, it was good news all around.

Except those who died.

"We have the fenixes and watchers on patrol for gathering storm cells," Eko told me. He lifted my face to meet his gaze, his gentle touch under my chin. "Stop beating yourself up. You defeated the storm, Anuka. Without you, it would have leveled pride."

I sighed, nodding. "Letting go of loss is hard for me."

"Do you want to talk about it?"

I smiled, leaning into him so he'd pull me into his lap. Eko was an expert cuddler. "No. But I'll try to stop digging my heels in and celebrate that more lives were saved than lost."

"There's something bigger to celebrate." When I nudged him so he'd continue, he chuckled. "You made the magic your bitch, woman. You have no idea how amazing it was to see. You were a fucking powerhouse."

"You were hot as fuck," Revan added as he walked in the room. "You're always hot as fuck but I think I almost came just watching you."

I laughed, shaking my head as he crawled onto Eko's lap with me. Sandwiching me between them.

"You okay?" he asked after a minute.

I nodded. "Yeah. I'll be okay. I'm already feeling better."

"Good." He grinned. "We're heading to the Avenue of Souls and sentencing the sinful. Want to watch?"

"I get to see you judge people's lives?"

He smiled. "Yep."

I nodded. "Yeah. Let's do that." I was going to enjoy judging people. It has always been one of my favorite pastimes. Even better that we got to do it on a boat.

The boat in question wasn't huge. It sat maybe six but there were only four of us. They didn't bring a ferryman this time but Revan maneuvered us to the darker waters of the Avenue of Souls.

All around the city, the waterways could easily fit three or so boats in the width. But the Avenue of Souls, aside from being a much murkier, darker water, was three or four times as wide. We'd crossed it briefly on my tour of Pride, but we hadn't taken time to examine it.

Now that we were close, it looked like just under the surface were floating bodies. Faces that stared out blindly, devoid of life. But there wasn't just a single layer. They were deep. When one was displaced, there were many, many more behind them.

"This is disturbing," I said. Once, I was pretty sure my stomach would have roiled in protest but I was surprised that my only real response was shuddering and pulling away so I didn't have to see over the side of the boat.

I stared in startlement again. The demon that sat in place of my beautiful Revan was... creepy. He was mummy-like, with a pike, a lantern that glowed an eerie green, and a scroll. Strangely enough, it looked like he was wearing a crown. As if he were royalty of some kind.

He looked at me with eyes that matched the glow of his lantern. It was then that I noticed he had no mouth. The strange fabric (it wasn't really fabric but looked like ashen dried skin!) loosely covered where his mouth would be. The more unsettling part was that I could see a hollow of nothing where the fabric skin didn't quite meet. Not bones. Just nothing.

Oh, and massive dark wings rose out of his back. They were kind of pretty. And the faint green glow also emanated from between the wrapping that covered his body.

Revan turned his head and let his scroll fall open. I watched in fascination as he held up the lantern and one of the bodies rose from the water. This time, bile rose in my throat to see its gray form. In the light of the lantern, the body twisted in painful, unnatural angles until a shadow was pulled from it. The body fell away, vanishing into dust before it hit the water again.

From the scroll rose letters that I didn't recognize, spelling words.

"They're her sins," Eko told me as I watched them line up in the air before the floating soul. "He's calling them forth to pass judgment."

There was something magical about the way they drifted into the air. Beautiful as they glowed a haunting green.

When Revan looked up, he pulled his pike back and cast it through the air at the soul. It went through it like, well, air. There was a moment where it remained suspended. But when Revan brought his hand down, the pike was there once more and the soul streaked through the air with a screech that I felt in my bones.

"That was mesmeric and also incredibly disconcerting," I said.

Eko and Rhyl chuckled.

"Where do they come from? How do they get here?" I followed the dark water of the Avenue of Souls into the open water surrounding the city. I didn't remember it looking dark out there and I was pretty sure I nearly circled the whole city the other day when we were visiting the fields.

"From the Depths of Hell," Rhyl said. "They get disbursed from there to the various circles to deal with."

"Yes, but *how* do they get here?"

"Doorways. Portals. Whatever you want to call them."

"I've also noticed that this is very unhellish here. So, where are the souls that get punished?"

"Ah," Eko said, grinning. "When Revan needs a break, we can take a look. I'm surprised you weren't shown to the Punishment Caves."

"They sound like a wonderful destination," I noted, making him smirk.

Revan took a break after another hour but he didn't change back into a glorious man. As Rhyl moved the boat, following it down the avenue, I absently wondered if they could choose to keep aspects of themselves when they return to a man shape. For instance and specifically, I would love for Revan to keep his wings a while. I kinda wanted to hang on to-

My thoughts disbanded when the boat felt like we fell down a hole. My breath caught as my heart lodged in my throat. Before I had a chance to scream, our surroundings had changed completely. I stared with wide eyes at what felt like a more stereotypical scene of Hell.

And there were screams, too!

Ahead of me was a line of men hunched over with enormous boulders on their backs. They trudged along while demons used whips to keep them moving. The weights were too heavy for them to lift their heads.

"When one's pride makes them think they're bigger than everyone else, we make sure they feel the weight of their misconceptions," Rhyl said as he watched them with a smile.

Something overhead screeched and a scream followed. A man – soul? – went hurdling overhead and slammed into the stone. It remained there long enough that I thought maybe there were spikes or something that it was now embedded on, keeping him there. But then he fell, sliding down the wall like a deadweight. The sickening sound of his body slamming and crunching almost made me gag.

"And those who had been more concerned with their own self-worth, letting it get in the way of their judgment where others suffered grievously."

I'm not sure how that punishment works. How is that a counter to the sin? But then, maybe it wasn't necessarily about matching the crime. It was severity meets the equivalent in brutality.

For eternity.

"Out of curiosity," I said, distracted by seeing a woman tied to the stone on her knees, crying in agony whenever a drop from the ceiling landed on her. "What would my punishment have been had I died naturally and brought here?"

My three demons looked at me, the two that were men raised brows. My frightening Judgement Day just stared.

"You wouldn't have gone to Hell in this capacity," Rhyl said.

"Are you so sure? I've made my life's purpose deeply rooted in pride," I argued.

"Yes, you have. But everything you do balances out," Rhyl said.

"You're incredibly generous and unwaveringly loyal. Cutthroat but completely fair and honest. Trustworthy," Eko said.

"How do you even know that?" I challenged.

Revan held up his scroll.

"Revan told me," Eko said, smirking. "He's got a gift for it, you know."

I laughed, shaking my head. My breath caught as my laughter died down when Revan stood in front of me. I shivered as he stared at me and when his terrifying clawed skeletal finger touched my heart, I could *feel* his smile.

"Thanks," I said. I was half tempted to kiss his cheek, but he still frightened me a little like this. Besides, I felt like I was sucking up to the judger of souls if I did that.

We went back to judging souls. While Revan was hard at work, Rhyl, Eko, and I lay in the bottom of the boat, watching the streaks of soul flit through the sky when Revan passed judgment. They began to look like shooting stars as the day wore into evening and then melted into night.

It stopped being disturbing and became almost magical.

CHAPTER TWENTY-THREE
ANUKA

I had just settled into bed, snuggling down into the cloud-like luxury when Rhyl asked, "You ready?"

"You must be asking if I'm ready for bed since I'm already changed," I said.

He smiled and my stomach flipped. It's funny. Until you meet a man that has that effect on you, you can't help yourself when you scoff at people who say it. Yet here I am. With a growing number of men who make me all woozy and shit.

He chuckled. "No. We're going to the roof to watch the fenixes."

"What are they doing that requires us to watch?" I mean, the promise of watching multiple of them was almost enough to get me out of bed anyway. They were remarkable creatures, and I certainly wanted a closer look.

"It's their yearly mating."

I paused as I sat up and looked at him with skepticism. "You want to watch birds fuck?" Wait, did birds fuck? That was not a subject I was up on.

He laughed. "No, Nuka. It's their mating display. They

come from all around pride and gather over the city while they attempt to attract a mate. It's a spectacular show."

A lot of animals in the world have extravagant mating rituals. And there are equally as many that have strange ones as well. People filled a lifetime witnessing and studying them.

Sighing, I crawled out of my comfortable bed and slipped into some house shoes before letting Rhyl lead me out.

I think these rooms were on the middle floor. Maybe like the fifth or so. It was hard to say when we went up various sets of stairs, down halls, and then more stairs. I lost track after a while, especially since some had landings within the flight.

This time we were going up. If I wasn't as stubborn as I am, I'd have asked to be carried. Then again, I was pretty sure even if I hinted at it, Rhyl would pick me up. My demons liked holding me.

Before I could seriously contemplate that, we made it to the landing and Rhyl pushed open the door.

The roof itself wasn't anything you might think of a typical roof. Not even a rich man's roof. It looked like a terrace garden. There were grassy areas (real grass), flower beds, stone paths, marble benches, and ponds. On the roof!

"Damn," I said, shaking my head. "This is insane."

Rhyl smiled. Taking my hand, he led me along a path, twisting and winding our way through different serenity gardens, herb gardens, and a vegetable garden. Hell, there was even a large pool with fish in it.

And then we came upon a little green oasis with trees (again, on the roof!) and lush grass. There were blankets and rugs. Cushions. Softly glowing lanterns.

There were the demons I recognized from Malak's

household and then a whole lot that I didn't. Rhyl brought me to the blanket with Revan, Zyphon, and Eko. I still didn't know the entire story between Zyphon and Revan but the way they looked at each other was the kind of love every person dreams about. Sweet and obviously deep.

As I settled with them, being snuggled in close by all four demons, I spied other roofs within the city laid out in the same fashion. Green havens. And demons on them, preparing for a show like we were.

"We don't have many parks," Zyphon said when he saw me staring. "We make up for that with green rooftops."

"It's smart, tranquil, and very green of you," I said.

He grinned. "Malak will appreciate your praise."

I rolled my eyes. Apparently, this model was his idea. I'm not all that surprised. It sounded like he was a very good ruler, for all his personal faults.

We snacked on finger foods and sipped wonderful berry drinks as the sun continued to go down. It was nearly dark, and I was seriously questioning how we were going to see the fenixes. Just as the sun dipped fully on the horizon, the lights of the city turned off, too, and we were cast in moonlight.

The sky was gorgeous, filled with stars. It very clearly wasn't our sky from – earth? – since there was no Milky Way. The foreignness of it made it even more magical.

My heart skipped when I saw the first streak of purple lightning in the air. I sat up, staring with trepidation. Please, no storm in the dark.

But answering bolts shot through the sky all over the city.

"Oh," I said, still watching as if I were a child seeing a unicorn. This just might be better.

I leaned back again as the lightning began in a rhythm

that followed the movement of specific fenixes. It was their charges that made them visible. The way their wings glittered and sparked, their eyes glowed, their tails trailed arcs of purple fire.

It was remarkable, especially when two of them started flying around each other in what looked like a choreographed dance. Soon it wasn't just around each other, but with each other.

This was better than fireworks. Stunning.

It began to feel like a dream. A fairy tale. Especially as I closed my eyes, and the streaks of lightning began to fade behind my eyelids. Somehow, I drifted asleep as we watched the enchanting mating displays in the sky.

When I woke, it appeared that everyone else had remained on the roof as well. My demons and Zyphon were wrapped tightly around me. Close by were Malak, Hayt, Kingsley, and Bael, all still asleep as the sun began to climb the sky.

I remained where I was for a while, contemplating where Hell was. There's the common assumption that Hell is below us while heaven is above. And if heaven is in the sky, that means Hell is within the ground.

But the sky that's overhead does not fit in with that theory. At best, we must be in a different realm. A different plane of existence.

With a yawn, I carefully disentangled myself from the men around me and quietly picked my way through the sleeping bodies. Most were curled up together on blankets and cushions like I had been. But some were simply sprawled across the grass.

Stopping at the edge of the roof, I peered into the city. I could just make out on the closest buildings' roofs that had others sleeping there as well. There was just starting to be movement. Maybe that was part of the tradition of watching the fenixes.

Far below, I found a sight that was equally pleasing. It appears that even the asmodai surface to watch the fenixes and fall asleep in that state. They were floating on flat boats, their tails hanging off. Some were just floating on the surface of the water. I even spotted a few on the back of a laraje.

I found myself smiling. Of all the spots to be trapped, there could be worse places. I couldn't think of anywhere more beautiful. Or anything that would make it more enchanting.

In the next several minutes, I soon found out that not everyone was just coming out of sleep. And those that were wide awake, were so with a very specific agenda. I'd fallen into their hands as if I'd followed steps to get there.

I separated myself from my demons. Standing alone and away from everyone else on the roof. In the wide open. In all honesty, I couldn't be all that surprised, right?

They scaled the side of the house before leaping into the air on their massive wings. Demons that weren't kimaris but the more dangerous kind. Four of them leapt up over the side.

I stumbled backward as they converged on me. Somewhere behind me, someone called my name. I made the mistake of giving these demons my back as I attempted to turn and run.

Claws grabbed my arms and I screeched in irritation. And then a little in fear as my feet left the roof. I flailed and kicked out, trying to worm my way free.

Maybe they underestimated me or hadn't learned of my wings. But when I needed them, they burst from my back and I broke free.

However, I've never intentionally used them so I probably looked like an idiot as I attempted to fly. I was quite certain that the reason the demons who were attempting to abduct me (yes, I was going to be kidnapped for the second fucking time!), watched with amusement as I moved around in the air like a fish out of water.

But when the commotion had alerted my demons, all bets were off. They came at me in earnest. Adrenaline made me figure out flying a little more and I was able to dodge my attackers several times. As I was beginning to think that maybe I stood a chance, something slammed into my back. Not just a hard force but it dug into my spine, sending shooting pain through me.

I screamed. My screams changed to those of terror as I began dropping from the sky. Somehow, they managed to shut off my wings. How was that even a thing?!

Claws dug into me next, sending more pain through my body as they broke my skin. On the one hand, I was no longer falling to my death. On the other, that didn't mean death wasn't awaiting me.

I tried to keep track of where we were going but perhaps I'd lost consciousness from the pain. It was nearly as excruciating as when I touched the magic. The next thing I knew, we were not in pride any longer. At least, not the city. We were somewhere underground.

I suspected we were in an underground like the torture pits for sinful souls since there didn't seem to be a true underground to Pride. Instead, there was a city that was built out of the water.

Then I remembered that the city was sitting in a massive caldera. So there was a chance we were in the volcano itself.

The demon dropped me on a high ledge. Literally

dropped me. My bones jarred and I groaned as I lay there. For a minute, I did nothing more. Just lay there. Waiting to see what would happen next.

When nothing happened, I slowly picked myself up and looked around. Wherever I was taken, the roof was high above me. I was on a rock tower that almost looked natural and was easily four or five stories from the ground.

From the edge, I could see the demons who had taken me. They remained in their demon forms so I couldn't identify them. Not that it would have mattered. I wouldn't have known them anyway. But maybe they remained like that not to conceal their identity but to stay in their more powerful form.

I could hear their voices as they bounced around the large room. Not clearly and I was sure I was missing words here and there since not everything I heard made sense.

"... lucky he didn't catch up."

"Are you sure he's going to give in? Which queen are we on, anyway? Twenty-three?"

"I think we can double that number."

I raised a brow, almost amused. Malak really had failed quite miserably at finding a queen he could manipulate in an effort to gain access to his magic.

"... miscalculated. She's just a girl."

"No. You saw her wings. This is the right one."

"... been at least three others with wings."

Their bickering and argument carried on for a long time. Once I determined that they'd kidnapped me in an effort to make Malak give up his throne and leave Pride, I realized that they were idiots. But they were idiots who had cut off my access to the magic. Stealing my wings from me.

My horns remained. I touched them for comfort.

Then I determined that I was going to find myself a way

out. There was a deadline looming for Malak to respond to. A deadline that he needed to leave the ring by. We all know that wasn't going to happen and they were delusional for thinking it.

With my body aching, I began examining the ledge I was left on. I walked around the perimeter, determining whether there was an opportune side for attempting to scale down it without dying. Considering I've never rock climbed, there was a good chance I was going to die anyway.

Once I found the area I thought gave me the best possible chance, I waited a while longer to see if they were going to pay me any attention at all. But the whole time I'd been scouting my prison, I'd determined that I was just a tool. Someone they were using and they didn't care whether I lived or died.

For some reason, they were convinced that my abduction would be enough to make Malak leave Pride in defeat but not enough that he'd retaliate or refuse outright. There was so much wrong with their plan that I seriously questioned whether they were pride demons at all. Who had made this stupidly flawed plan and convinced a whole bunch of strong demons that it was going to work?

And their numbers continued to grow. More and more demons meandered in as time ticked on. Not a single one even glanced in my direction.

Taking that as a sign that they truly didn't care what happened to me and that my use to them was fulfilled, I decided that I was going to try my escape attempt. With a deep breath, I lowered myself to the side and very carefully let myself down.

I was barefoot, having lost my house shoes in the flight. Therefore, my grip sucked at best. And it was fucking painful. Both my fingers and my feet hurt like a bitch. A long, dull, throbbing pain that never ceased. My ankles hurt, my calves hurt, my neck hurt, my arms were almost noodles.

How did people do this for enjoyment?!

I almost let go in despair when I found I'd made it down maybe ten feet. At that point, I thought it might be best just to sit on the top and await my fate. But I found climbing up was just not going to happen. I already didn't have that kind of strength in my arms.

Closing my eyes, I concentrated on my breathing. Then I looked around the face of the rock cliff to see what else I had. There were roots here and there. Little ledges where I could rest if I could just get there.

Mentally, I made a new map of where I was going and concentrated on moving one foot at a time. Testing where I was putting my bare feet.

Then the entire cavern shook. Rocks rained down on me and I struggled to hang on. My heart raced as I nearly slipped, and I struggled to catch my breath.

When it shook again, I wasn't so lucky. I slid down the side, barely grabbing onto a root that slid painfully through my hands before I managed to stop my fall. Did I scream? It was hard to tell with all the roaring and chaos going on.

I wasn't at the best angle, but the cavern was suddenly filled with more demons. I'd have thought nothing of it except that there was now a battle going on. A handful of demons were tearing through the greater numbers of my abductors.

And I recognized him easily. Malak was many times bigger than the rest of the demons and his fiery whip lashed out like lightning itself. But every time it hit the wall, the entire cavern shook, and I was one step closer to my death.

This time, I must have screamed as I began to fall. The only thing that stopped me was slamming into a little rock outcropping. I hit it so hard that it knocked the breath out of me. Maybe I also broke some bones. The pain was severe as I lay there trying to breathe.

The battle raged on, and I remained on my back, wishing death would hurry up. I wondered what Revan would sentence me to an eternity of. Seriously, rock climbing would be my idea of true hell.

"Nuke."

I turned my head. When I couldn't see anything and my name was called again with more agitation and worry, I forced myself to roll over until I could see over the side.

Malak was there, staring up at the walls. When his eyes landed on me, there was no mistaking the relief in them.

"Jump," he commanded.

Rolling my eyes, I almost turned back over. "Not a fucking chance," I muttered.

"I'll catch you, Anuka. I'll always catch you when you fall. I'll catch you when you jump if you don't let me jump with you. And I swear, I'll never let anything happen to you again."

His words made me freeze. My breath caught for an entirely different reason this time. He didn't think I was going to trust him now, did he?

But I looked at him as he tried to get closer to me. How I'd missed the river of fire directly below was something I'd have regretted when I got closer to the bottom. All these towering spires of rock now made sense.

He could command fire that he made but apparently not that which flowed within the belly of... pride? Were we still in pride? We had to be since he told me that I wouldn't be able to leave until I was queen. And I was sure I wasn't queen.

"I promise, Anuka," he said when I didn't move. His voice was dark and filled with fire. And the promise he just made.

I stared at him, biting my lip, and was surprised when I decided that I believed him. He was going to catch me. I just had to trust that he would.

It was a struggle to pull myself up but I did. He reached for me as far as he could stretch.

The cavern shook again and enormous chunks of stone fell to the floor like bombs, exploding with debris. I pressed myself against the wall of the tower I was stuck on until it stopped. And then I ran the few steps I had and leapt with every ounce of strength in my aching body.

Once again, I was airborne. But this time, I stared into the fiery eyes of Malak as I let my fate lay solely in his hands.

CHAPTER TWENTY-FOUR
ANUKA

He was an enormous demon. He didn't just catch me like a ball but as soon as I hit his hands, he pulled back to act as a shock absorber and brought me to a stop. Then he pulled me to his chest to cradle me like a football.

I had the strangest feeling of being caught not just physically but ethereally, too. Like something inside me latched on and helped guide me straight into Malak's hands.

As he turned back to the room, I could feel his fury. And then I could feel the magic. It surrounded us, stroking and grabbing excitedly. Malak tipped his head back and roared. I stared with wide eyes as a stream of purple fire in a magic whirlwind accompanied his booming howl, streaming to the ceiling like a volcano bursting.

The magic responded to someone's command that wasn't mine. I could visibly see it as it swept through the room with purpose as if it were a snake. Choosing which demon to devour and which to bypass. There were a lot, and it took several long minutes during which I tucked myself into his hold and closed my eyes.

Everything in me hurt. Everything. Even my thoughts.

Only after a few minutes of silence did I open my eyes to find Malak staring at me. He remained perfectly still but I felt his sigh as I looked at him. Maybe he thought I was dead.

Very gently, he pulled me from his hold with his other enormous hand and carefully set me on my feet. Then he knelt in front of me, shrinking down until he was somewhat more manageable at maybe seven feet.

"Thank you," I said.

His hands moved to me again and slowly placed featherlight touches all over. It took me a minute to decide he was checking me for injuries.

"I think they're all internal and might just be muscle," I told him. "I also think I'll be one giant bruise."

Malak sighed. "I'm sorry. I'm sorry for killing you without your permission. I'm sorry for being a bear. I'm sorry for not protecting you when you needed it."

"I think that last apology isn't necessary. You can't control everyone."

He bowed his head before pulling me to him. I was surprised when he hugged me, burying his massive face in my neck. "You're exactly everything pride has ever needed, and I've been a beast. Thank you for all the good you've done. For dealing with things that I haven't been able to. For saving lives that I couldn't. And though you didn't do it for me, thank you for bringing Hayt back. I don't always show it well, but my demons – they're everything to me. It would have destroyed me if he'd died. The guilt at knowing I'd caused it would have eaten at me for the rest of time."

It wasn't just his words. Words were nice and all. But I could hear the emotion in his voice. How heavy and filled with sorrow it was when he thanked me for helping pride.

And then how it broke, over and over, when he spoke of Hayt. I could feel them in that strange ethereal thing that now ran through me. Connecting me to Malak?

I hugged him tightly, letting my eyes fill with tears for an eventuality that didn't happen.

"I love my demons," he said quietly. I felt him tremble a little. "Even Kingsley, though he's more of a pain in the ass than anything."

Quiet laughter surrounded us as I smiled. "How did you find me?" I asked. I couldn't deal with this much emotion right now.

"Your watcher led us," Rhyl said.

I recognized his voice, even if I didn't recognize most of the demons around us. I assumed, based on numbers alone, they were the four demons that were Malak's and my three. And on Revan's shoulder was my watcher, staring at me. I smiled.

"And you finally have the magic," Kingsley said.

That surprised me and I pulled back from Malak's arms. "You do? How?"

"I think you and I both let go of something today," he said. "And when you put your trust in me to catch you, the magic came flowing in, tethering us together."

"Just as mine was stolen," I said, sighing.

He tilted his head. He turned me and I felt his claw run down my spine, starting at my neck. When it touched the sensitive spot on my back where I'd been hit in the air, my breath was taken from me as he removed the pressure. And my wings came blazing back to life.

I turned around with a wide smile. "How did you-" I didn't need to finish the question. There was a small thing between his fingers that he was staring at shrewdly. Then he handed it off to who I thought was Zyphon. I hadn't seen his demon, but this hellish dog thing had three tails and I remember him when I first got here with three tails as I irritated them all by walking out to find my own help.

"Can we go home now?" Malak asked me.

I raised a brow, amused that he was asking me. But I nodded and found myself once more in his arms. Since he was more realistically sized, I didn't feel like a rag doll. Though I still felt incredibly small.

We weren't far from home and there were bridges that connected all the city blocks that we needed to reach. A little too conveniently. Behind Malak and I was a trail of our demons. And as we passed through the buildings, there were quiet cheers and voices of relief and excitement.

My eyes drifted shut as my body throbbed with aches. Too much strenuous exercise. We should outlaw rock climbing.

With the sound of doors opening, I looked around. This wasn't my room. I was a little perplexed when we walked through the enormous doors of Malak's room to reveal nothing but a wide empty space save for a large bed.

"Really?" I asked.

He smirked. His features were fading from the demon. He was man-shaped for the most part now. The bulk and oddly proportioned features having melted away. But his skin was still that of the demon and his horns hadn't gone anywhere, either. I actually rather liked them there. Like ginormous handles...

My thoughts drifted off when he sat me down. We were in a closet now. A closet filled with clothes. Running down the middle was a bank of drawers that Malak had put me on. He turned away and threw open a set of cabinet doors, revealing more clothes. Shoving them aside, he pushed on the back panel.

I shifted so I could get a better view. When the panel opened and a soft purple light flickered on, I could barely make out some dark, pointy shapes. He turned with it in his hand, and I grinned at the crown.

There was nothing feminine or dainty about it. It was a full circle with many points, and it was black. He paused so I could study it. When I met his eyes again, he moved closer and set it on my head.

"My queen," he said, taking a step back and bowing his head.

"*Our* queen," Hayt corrected.

I looked at him in time to see that he and all the other demons with us got down to one knee and bowed their heads, too.

I shivered, smiling stupidly with pleasure and pride. Also, now that the demons were melting back into their man shapes, though some of their demonic features remained behind, I could tell who was who.

Revan looked up, his eyes still glowing and his wings fluttering in an invisible wind. But I knew what I saw in his eyes. Hunger.

"Think you can keep that on while I take you to bed, my queen?" he asked.

I reached up to touch it, pleased that it managed to fit on my head with my horns. Smirking at him, I shrugged. "That depends. Think you can keep the wings?"

The heat that flared in his eyes was accompanied by a low growl. "Anything you want, sweet girl."

I laughed. Sweet girl. Pfft.

Malak's hand on my knee had me facing him. And though there was arousal there, too, he studied me intently.

"Where's your crown?" I asked.

A smile climbed up his lips, sexy and sinful. Behind him,

Bael lowered a crown similar to mine on his head. It was the same shape and color, but his was larger and thicker. I mean, he needed a larger one to sit properly over his enormous ego.

"Not bad," I said. "You look good with a crown."

He chuckled. Then his hands were on either side of my face. I wasn't sure who moved after that but the next thing I knew, he was kissing me. He pressed his lips hard against mine and pushed his tongue into my mouth. Encircling me in his arms, I found myself pulled against him, our mouths caressing each other.

The taste of his tongue against mine, his lips, the taste of his skin, the smell of him. I didn't expect to like it. To enjoy anything about him. Yet, everything shifted in the last hour. I wasn't sure it was all mental, either.

I was partially convinced that something fundamental inside me changed. Malak was still the demon who murdered me, but it no longer pissed me off in quite the same way. Did saving my life alter my feelings about it? Maybe it was something else entirely.

All I know is that I did not despise him at this moment. Quite different, really. Now, I was kinda craving his touch. Not rough or demanding, but gentle, each kiss he gave was like a caress, and you can't ask for more.

His lips were dry and warm against mine. He pulled me close to him and I could feel his heart beating in his chest. Racing. When he pulled away, I could still feel the sensation of his lips for a few seconds after.

The feel of his skin against mine, the curve of his lips, the roughness of his hands, the scrape of his facial hair against my cheek. It was all different than I expected.

"My crown looks good on you," he said, his voice husky, his breath warm on my neck. Before I could speak he had laid another kiss on my lips, this one even more demanding than the first.

"I want you to…" His words trailed off, his tone growly.

His hands began to move over me. One slid down the small of my back then back up to my forehead, his fingers threading through my hair. The other hand followed the contour of my body, down my arm, sliding down my back and to my ass. The second he touched me there, I felt a jolt of electricity shoot through me.

Not painful, but intense.

It was as if I could feel him right through my clothes and skin. I gasped, inhaling his scent, my body responding to his touch. His fingers ran along my back then dipped into the cleft of my ass.

The next moment, he was pressing against me, pulling me to the edge of the drawers so that I was flush against the hard planes of his body. He covered my mouth with his, kissing me like we hadn't kissed before.

His lips were still soft, but the kiss was hard. Demanding. Urgent. The hem of my shirt lifted but I wasn't sure it was his hands moving it. I slipped out of it easily, pulling my arms out of the sleeves, tossing it aside.

He stared at my breasts appreciatively, caressing me with his hot gaze. He looked up at my face and smiled, then leaned forward and began to kiss and suckle my nipples.

"I've always been a fan of the closet but I can think of a dozen better places for this," Kingsley said.

Malak sighed, his eyes narrowing as he glared. But Kingsley grinned. He took a step back and made a flourishing motion with his hand, encouraging Malak to bring me back into the bedroom.

Rolling his eyes, Malak scooped me up with his hands under my ass. I hid my grin by leaning my chin on his shoulder and bit my lip. A train of hungry demons followed, eyes glowing with hunger and cocks standing straight, hard, and dripping.

I shivered in appreciation.

There was no longer a separation between my demons and Malak's. His demons were mine, too. Even though I'd only began a relationship somewhat officially with Hayt, I knew that Zy, Kingsley, and Bael were mine as well.

However, whether Eko, Rhyl, and Revan belonged to Malak now, too, was up for debate. I wasn't sure they'd agree to that.

My observations were cut short when Malak moved across the bed on his knees before bringing us both down so I was on my back and he lay over me.

His hands were everywhere. Hips, ass, legs, waist. I could feel the heat of him against my core, sense him throbbing and hard.

"I'm willing to bet this will be explosively good," he said.

That was a sentiment I could agree with. I was hungry, too, and his words were like an injection of lust in my blood.

Its pulsing waves crashing against me, drowning me in a dark sea of something that I didn't even know what to call.

I gripped Malak by the ass, pulling him to me. My kisses were frantic. Deep. I wanted to taste him, touch him, smell him. Hear him growl and moan.

His hands continued to roam. My hair, my breasts, my stomach, my ass. Making up for all the time we hadn't been together.

Not that we were together. I wasn't sure I was agreeing

to that yet. But I think we were more together now than before.

He kissed me again. Long and deep. His hand slid down my body, caressing my stomach, my hips, my thighs. He parted my legs and settled between them. The heat between my thighs was intense. Only as he pressed against me did I realize my pants were gone. The curiosity of that only lasted a minute before I was focused on Malak again.

I was wet and aching. My body thrilled that he was home.

The thought made me pause. Where had that come from?

His body pressed against me, the hard length of his cock pushing on my thigh. I yearned for the moment when he would thrust into me. His right hand slid up my body until he was gripping my hair, pulling my head back. He leaned his forehead against mine, his eyes shut.

And then, as if he sensed my urgency, he moved to kiss me again, his hand no longer teasing, but instead rubbing me, slipping his fingers inside me. Pleasure tore through me as he found the spot I needed him to touch. Intense and almost painful, but in the best possible way.

I gasped and writhed beneath him, my pleasure so great I thought I might shatter.

He kissed me again, his tongue thrusting into my mouth as he finger fucked me. My heart was pounding, my entire body on fire. At that moment, I wanted nothing more than to feel him inside me.

There was no need for him to ask twice.

He kissed me, his hand sliding down my body, his fingertips not rubbing the walls of my pussy finding my clit. As he rubbed me there, every nerve in my body pulsed. His cock throbbed against my thigh as I began to tremble. I was close, so close.

"Fuck's sake, Malak. If you don't get inside her already, I'm going to help you," Bael muttered as he came up behind Malak, hovering over us.

"This isn't going to be just you and I," Malak told me, frowning.

I grinned, feeling a ridiculous amount of giddiness fill me. They were mine. All of them.

"Another time," I told him.

That seemed to please him. Malak grinned, his teeth taking my lip as he nibbled and chewed as if trying to distract me from him taking his hand away from my pussy. It was less than a grumble later that it was replaced with the head of his cock.

"This is going to be the best fucking time," Malak told me. The last thing I heard was his voice, a growl soft in my ear.

He slid into me in one smooth and hard motion, ignoring any resistance his size caused and pushing through it.

I cried out, my body arching as he filled me. Pleasure and pain washed through me. The intensity of the sensation was almost too much. But I arched as much as I could, taking him all the way down to the base.

He only managed less than a handful of thrusts before Bael was on top of him, pressing him down and still. I thought Bael was coming for me. But it was clear in the next several seconds as Malak's hips jerked and he groaned in my ear, that Bael was making himself at home in Malak's ass.

I grinned; Bael winked at me.

"Our mighty leader is a bottom," he said. "Much rather take a dick than an ass."

A giggle escaped my mouth but it was soon replaced with moans of my own as Bael set a hard, steady rhythm. The beat of it traveled through Malak and into me, bringing my pleasure up as if a snare drum was building the anticipation of what was to come.

It was building an orgasm.

"Nuke."

My eyes fluttered open and I found a dick hovered over my face, a bead of precum ready to drop. I licked my lips before looking beyond the cock to the man above.

Hayt still looked remarkably like his demon more than man. Red, red skin with matching eyes. Massive horns that curled and bent. A long tail made of vertebrae whipped behind him like a pissed off snake.

I nodded, opening my mouth.

He dragged the length of his cock over my tongue, easing his way to the back of my throat. He remained still for a minute before matching the pace of Bael's thrusts.

Around me, wet squelching noises filled the air. The slapping of skin that wasn't in time with what was going on with me. Moans, groans, and growls.

It all filled me with more arousal, bringing it to a tipping point and ready to flow over. The scent of sweat and the musk of an aroused male.

The air was filled with the scents of sex, orgasm, and sweat. Sex was the strongest, because each person who orgasmed sprayed their seed into the air like a fine mist. The other smells were complements to the air with their own unique spice and flavor.

The wet slapping of flesh on flesh, the growls and grunts of pleasure, and moans.

At some point, I noted a particular guttural moan and realized it was mine as the cock in my mouth found the back of my throat and pressed against it. Feeling it there only brought me to the brink quicker.

The salty tang of cum, the faint hint of Hell, and the bitter taste of sweat and musk touched my tongue. It was all a heady feeling as it spurred my orgasm to build, making my head foggy with desperate need.

The slick feel of a cock sliding down the back of my throat, the ache created by being filled by cock. It was only matched with the same yet different feeling of Malak's filling my pussy.

All across my body, against my skin, and inside me, every surface and way to stimulate was being taken advantage of. I felt hands across my skin, something working in my ass, my nipples tweaked, and my hair and scalp were rubbed and pulled.

I was saturated in sex.

It was only at the last second when I was on the edge of my orgasm that it all came together, as if cradled by the thousands of sex scents and sounds to carry me off.

A wave of pleasure tore through me, a tsunami of orgasms that shattered the world into a million pieces. All I knew was the thousands of sensations that came with the half dozen touches, and the blackness of my own orgasm sweeping me up into it.

I felt the pressure of a cock in my ass. It had nothing to do with me and everything to do with the subtle vibrations that had been put into the air by these demons. It was a thick and long thing, but it carried the sensation of the cock, the heat of it, and the girth of it through the air.

It was enough to push me off the edge and take me over

again. How many orgasms were possible? It seemed that perhaps I was going to find out.

I was so lost in my own pleasure that I barely registered my body being shifted until it was free from dicks, only to have them replaced with another set.

They moved me around like I was a doll. When my mind cleared from the sex haze, I was sitting on Kingsley as he slammed his hips upwards, his cock smashing into me so deep, I saw stars of desire flash before my eyes.

Zyphon and Revan's cocks were both in front of my face, on either side of me. They looked down with excited grins, waiting for me to take hold.

I did, wrapping both their lengths in my hands. Two very different demon's dicks, the feel of them strange, enticing, and nothing like the other. I took a lick of each, catching the beads of cum as they dribbled before taking Zy in my mouth.

I took him deep, my jaw aching from trying to swallow him. He was thick. Something hard and strong wrapped around my torso and I had to think it was a tail. The rough tip messed with my nipples.

I closed my eyes as I turned my head for Revan's dick. Humming around it, hands wrapped around my throat as someone came behind me and began working his cock into my ass. By the sound of his praise, I was confident that it was Rhyl.

My mind was a storm of heat. Desire so thick that I could barely breathe. Hands, mouths and cocks were everywhere - two dicks in my mouth, another stuffed in my ass, the fifth hand on my shoulder, the sixth smacking my cheek or tugging at my hair, the seventh teasing my neck and the eight teasing my waist. I was surrounded with flesh, and sweat, and heat, and so much want.

Revan's eyes flashed a glow of green. Rhyl's jawline rippled with muscle, his fanged grin a promise of pain as his hands were locked around my throat, as if he was about to choke me. The dark mass that was Zy's head filled my vision. His eyes closed and his groan of pleasure was the only sound in the room.

Sweat dripped along my spine, coating my skin in a sheen of salt. I smelled of sex. The thick musk of arousal and cum, the aroma of hot bodies covered with it, of humid air and sun.

And then a tongue landed on my clit and everything around me erupted as if I were a volcano. It wasn't just my own climax. I could feel others filling me and landing on me, dripping between my breasts, along my neck, down my thigh. I cried out as my orgasm churned on, these men - these demons - pleasing me like no human was capable of.

My body was gently pressed into the bed as the men rearranged. Tails, claws, wings everywhere. I grinned through my exhaustion, pleased at having this sight. Hands on each other as they took cocks in mouths and asses for me to see. Letting me catch my breath.

But I only had a minute before eyes turned to me. Wanting, possessive, filled with passion, heat, and affection.

Smiling, I reached for them, too sore and tired to do much else. Oh, I wanted everything they had for me. But after the day I've had, they were going to have to do the work.

Next time, I would tell them exactly what I expected of them. Where they needed to be and what they ought to be doing. But right now, I would let them be in charge.

Hands gently and caring moved me among them and I was pressed into Malak's embrace as Hayt this time, slammed his ass with cock. I didn't miss the pleasure that shined in his red eyes as he looked down at me, his hands soft and feather-like as he traced a finger along my jaw.

"You're the queen I've always waited for. The one I wanted but was too afraid to seek out. Nuke, I will worship you until the end of time," he said.

I shivered. "What about the throne of Hell?" I murmured, feeling hands on me again, spreading my legs, touching my clit and nipples, sliding into my pussy. It was already almost too much sensation to hear his response. But I heard it.

"Fuck Hell. You, these demons, and pride is all I care about. You, my queen, are far more important than any throne."

His mouth covered mine, and my demon orgy carried on.

CHAPTER TWENTY-FIVE
RHYL

Was it weird living in Malak's house? Yes. However, being with Nuke was worth any weirdness I had to endure. Like when she wanted us all to join Malak and her demons in his room.

What made that more interesting was that every time she stepped into Malak's room, a little more of the room was furnished. She hadn't caught on quite yet as to what was happening.

Malak is a salos. He sees the desires of any living creature. But his desire for his room has always been to please his queen. Whatever his queen wants, the room will change based on that desire. Why was it completely empty when she was carried in the first time? Because she was a blank canvas concerning Malak.

There was a tentative friendship. A cautious trust and budding relationship. Nuke wasn't sure what to think about him or anything else after the events that had just taken place. Though she was kept occupied in the moments (hours) after Malak placed the crown on her head, all around the room, furniture and color began popping up as her heart's desires shifted and changed.

Nuke didn't take any downtime from her kidnapping ordeal, and she didn't let Malak, either. He was still angry. His eyes were still fiery, and his horns had become a permanent fixture.

Actually, all of us kept something of our demons out. Primarily because keeping them stuffed away for long periods of time is exhausting. But also, because our pretty little queen enjoyed them.

Enjoyed looking at them, touching them, and stroking them. It was enough encouragement to keep them visible.

Anyway, the first thing Nuke demanded the next day was that they take a look at the foggy and swampy areas of Pride to see what they could do now that Malak had his magic. And now that he had his magic, he could also teach Nuke how to use hers properly.

A week later, the east end of Pride was still getting fixed up, being brought back to life, but it was happening. It was coming back.

Now that Nuke was convinced pride was going to be standing and healing, she was planning a trip for me and her. Something Malak was not at all pleased about.

"I think we should all go," Malak argued.

"No," Nuke said without anything further. I loved that about her. Seriously adored that she didn't feel the need to argue her stance. It was simply, 'this is how I feel/what I'm doing.' Period.

Malak did not hold the same amount of appreciation for it as I did.

"Nuke-"

"No," she repeated. "Rhyl and I have business. You'll be fine here until we get back."

He stared at her, pressing his lips together. I could almost visibly see the war raging inside him. He was who he was. And letting someone do something he didn't want them to, especially when they were a part of his circle, was difficult for him.

But he was trying hard to make a relationship with Anuka work. Part of that was not controlling her. Something he wasn't always aware he did with his demons but was becoming more mindful of. The confrontation that eventually came between he and Zyphon had almost been explosive.

I think he knew he was going to lose Zyphon for good if he didn't back down. I didn't think he even wanted to withdraw. It was his pride that made him continue to fight.

We watched him stop his argument abruptly and take a step back. His expression was slightly surprised as he stared at Zyphon with wide eyes as if he'd said something. He hadn't spoken in almost three minutes while Malak regained his jerk facade.

But then he suddenly had a change of heart. There wasn't even any begrudging in his voice when he apologized and more or less gave his blessing on Zyphon and Revan's relationship. I might have rolled my eyes at the 'blessing' part but like Zy at the time, the sudden change had everyone in the room staring at him in confusion and surprise.

Except Anuka, who grinned maniacally. Whatever had just happened, she'd known.

The minutes in which Malak continued to fight his instincts droned on until Nuke sighed and stood from where she was sitting nonchalantly on the stool in the kitchen where we'd all gathered. She stood in his space, placing her hands on his chest, and looked up at him.

"I'm coming back," she said.

And just like that, the tension in his shoulders fell away. There was just a brief moment of vulnerability that he let the room see when he asked, "Yeah?"

Nuke smiled, nodding. She reached up on her toes to press a soft kiss to his lips. "Yes. We'll be home before dinner."

Taking a breath, Malak nodded. He rested his forehead on hers for a moment before backing away. "Alright. Be safe. The magic can turn a little weird in the world."

Nuke smiled and turned toward me. I held out my hand, pleased when she placed hers in mine and let me lead her away.

She hadn't gotten a handle on how the doors worked so when I opened the pantry door and it dropped us into a mall bathroom stall, she looked at me with comical confusion. "We'll teach you later," I told her. "For now, let's get a ride to your mother's house."

"Did you get the key?" she asked as I followed her out.

There were eyes on us as we left the ladies' room together. Scandalized and also giggling. Oh, to be a weird human.

Reaching into my pocket, I pulled out the keys on a keyring and passed them to her. "Financial arrangements have also been secured."

Nuke sighed as we stepped into the sunlight. She frowned as she looked around. "I love New York but I'm already missing the cool breeze that comes off the water in Pride."

"We've been here for thirty seconds."

She frowned again, squinting into the parking lot. We crossed it and grabbed the subway, changing several times until it dumped us into a more suburban neighborhood where the houses were small and crammed in tight.

We hiked up the street as Nuke continued to frown at her surroundings. "I'm glad I don't live here anymore, but I think we ought to check on my condo. Do something with it."

"Give it to your sister," I suggested.

Finally, Nuke smiled, rewarding me by turning that dazzling look my way. "I like that idea."

That was the end of our conversation as we stepped up to the door of a tiny house. We're talking barely bigger than a true tiny house. She knocked on the door and waited.

It opened with a young version of her staring out at us. The girl's eyes went wide with disbelief. Tears gathered on her lashes. "Anuka?" she whispered.

"Hi, Jessie."

A sob left Jessie's throat as she threw herself at Nuke, wrapping her arms tight. I watched as they clung to each other for many long minutes, tears tracking down my queen's cheeks just as quickly as they did her sister's.

I was concentrating on them so fully that I missed when the older woman wrapped them both tightly, blabbering about how this was a miracle from heaven.

Yes, I rolled my eyes. Heaven had nothing to do with this. Heaven wasn't good enough for our queen. She belonged in Hell with the demons who worshiped her.

It was a long time before they split apart, and their mother dragged them inside. No one had noticed me yet, but I followed, shutting the door quietly behind me.

"Where have you been?" her mother demanded. "The cops-" She trailed off, tears still trickling down her face.

Nuke sighed. "You're really not going to believe me if I

tell you, so I really need you to trust me. I'm okay, but I'm only here for a visit."

"But Nuke," Jessie started.

"I promise, everything is okay. It wasn't at first, but sometimes people grow, and situations change. I'm happy where I am."

It was obvious that neither of them knew what to think.

"I'm sorry I couldn't get here sooner. There were extenuating circumstances that needed to be overcome. And I promise, now that they're on track, I can come visit."

"Often," her mother said, leaving no room for argument.

Nuke smiled. "Often," she agreed. Then she took her sister's hand. "Your tuition is set for the next three years. If you want grad school, just let me know and I'll make it happen."

"You don't have to."

"I know that." Nuke pulled her in for another hug. "I'm so incredibly proud of you. I have the means to help, and I want to. All you have to do is keep your grades up. Okay? Make it worth my investment."

"I promise," Jessie said, her voice cracking.

"I didn't bring my keys, but my apartment is yours now, too. I'll drop them off in a couple weeks."

Jessie shook her head, but Nuke took her chin and looked at her sternly. "You're not getting a choice. I don't need it, but I have no desire to sell."

It was clear that her sister knew better than to argue further. It was cute to see that same look in Malak. It must be a universal expression. Knowing which battle to fight. Fortunately, I don't even engage in battle. I remain heavily on the winning side all the time.

Nuke turned to her mother, who was looking at her

with the same unyielding expression that Nuke had given to her sister. And as with her sister, Nuke didn't engage in battle. Instead, she held up the key I'd handed her.

Her mother stared at it, the severity in her face falling away as her brows knit together.

"One of the biggest goals I have always worked for is being able to take care of you and Jessie the way you've always taken care of us. Before you tell me that wasn't my job, I know. But sometimes, you need to be taken care of, too, Momma. This is for you."

Her mother continued to look at the key. She reached for it, her hand trembling. We watched as she examined it, turning the tag around and reading the address.

"Mortgage is all paid off. Land tax is set for the year. Insurance is set for the year, too. All you have is normal utilities and living expenses."

"What is this? I didn't know you owned a home."

Anuka smiled. "I don't, Momma. You do."

The tears that fell from her mother's face were like a faucet. I watched more hugging and babbling before I examined the tiny room I was in. Tiny didn't cover it. Whatever the room was supposed to be, it barely fit the four of us and a small rectangle table against the wall.

Anuka assured her family for several more minutes before she could pull us away. Only as we were walking out did they notice me. Jessie grinned, almost knowingly. Her mother looked at me with suspicion.

We hopped onto the subway again and headed back downtown. Everything was so close together and stuffy, I immediately wanted to break out of my skin. Too much. Too many people. Strangers touching me. I felt myself growl in response several times and enjoyed when people innately moved away or avoided me.

"That was miserable," I muttered as we stepped out onto the street again. Taking a breath, I scowled. It wasn't exactly fresh air.

Nuke grinned and dragged me along. The sign on the door read 'Nuke Studio'. She pushed the doors open and then paused.

The room was large and mostly empty save for a long table down the middle. Across it lay several headshots. A man leaned over them, shaking his head.

Nuke grinned.

The man looked up, wiping a hand over his face. He turned and stopped short when he saw Nuke standing there. I could see him try to figure out if he was hallucinating or not. But then it seemed he would welcome it if he were.

"Anuka!" Like her sister, he flung his arms around her and squeezed her tightly. "I've been so terrified. They found your phone in the museum bathroom! Broken glass. Blood. And literally nothing else!"

I scowled. Yeah, they should have at least cleaned that mess up. That was just sloppy.

"I'm sorry. I was detained for a while but I'm here now."

Malcolm took a step back, wiping the tears from his eyes. "I'm so relieved you're okay. I tried like Hell to keep it running as you would want but I don't know what I'm doing."

"You know exactly what you're doing, which is good. I'm going to be an absentee business owner now and need you to take up the weight of the company."

Malcolm's eyes went wide. "But I can't-"

"You can and you will. Your eye is perfect. You know what sells and who won't. Besides, I won't vanish, and you can call me any time."

At his further hesitation, Anuka grinned and grabbed my hand, pulling me forward. "Besides. I've brought you the model you're going to need to take us to a $1 million revenue this year. All you have to do is make it happen. You know the steps. So, let's see what you can do."

And that's how I became a demon parading around as a human model that was drooled over for years. It didn't matter though. I made strategic appearances as Malcolm thought I should but otherwise, he had me going through shoots and avoiding as much interaction as possible.

As it turned out, that made the public hungrier for me. Mysterious Rhyl showed up out of nowhere and is exactly nowhere. Paparazzi were going crazy searching for me. It was a blast.

Meanwhile, I spent my days with my queen, her many lovers, and enjoying the best place to be – the prideful circle of Hell. Watching my queen rule with compassion and pride, keeping Malak in proper balance.

I wouldn't change this for the world. And thankfully, neither would Anuka, who chose to stay with us instead of returning home after all.

READ THE REST OF SONS OF SATAN!

Corrupting Lust by Lyra Winters
Draining Sloth by Holly Hanzo
Possessing Greed by SA Mackenzie
Consuming Gluttony by Novel Blake
Courting Envy by Mile Sin
Taming Wrath by S Lucas

ACKNOWLEDGMENTS

Let me start by saying this is a standalone and there will be nothing further. That doesn't mean you have to leave this world, though. Make sure you check out the rest of the Sons of Satan. Those demons are hot, hot, hot and the women are badass! I'm not even going to talk about the authors.

Okay, I'm going to talk about the authors. It has been a blast working with you ladies. You've made the experience fun and hassle-free. I am more than happy to share more worlds with you in the future.

I've had a lot of fun with Nuke and her demons. I hope you enjoyed her journey into Pride and the way she dominated that magic! She's one of my strongest, feistiest characters to date and I certainly adore her.

Now let's talk about my patreon readers. Lauren - did you see your part?!?! I've been waiting for just the right moment for this and I finally found it. And my other pretties - Sarah, Shyla, Chelsi, Kylee, Miriam, Jen M, Fawn, and my Savage Jennifer! Your support means the world to me. I adore you and am thankful for you every single day!

My beta team also needs a very loud shot out for keeping me consistent with P/pride, Q/queen, etc. I still don't think we're there yet but you know, we gave it a good effort. As with everything I throw at you, I appreciate your receptiveness to all the weird and your enthusiasm. You make me a better writer.

And my dragons. Without you, nothing would get done.

More than that, you make my writing shine. I fluff you so much.

But more than anything, my readers are the best. I appreciate you in a way I can never explain. You grab everything I throw out there with excitement. Thank you so, so very much.

ABOUT THE AUTHOR

Crea lives in upstate New York with her dog and husband. She has been writing since grade school, when her second grade teacher had her class keep writing journals. She has a habit of creating secondary, and often time tertiary, characters that take over her stories. When she can't fall asleep at night, she thinks up new scenes for her characters to act out. This, of course, is how most of her meant-to-be-thrown-away characters tend to end up front and center - and utterly swoon-worthy! Don't ask her how many book boyfriends she has...

When not writing, Crea is an avid reader. Her TBR pile is several hundred books high (don't even look at her kindle wish list or the unread books on her tablet). Sometimes, she enjoys crafting; sometimes, exploring nature; sometimes, traveling. Mostly, she enjoys putting her characters on paper and breathing life into them. Oh, and sleeping. Crea *loves* to sleep!

BOOKS BY CREA REITAN

THE IMMORTAL CODEX

Immortal Stream: Children of the Gods

Mortal Souls

The God of Perfect Radiance

The Hidden God

The God Who Controls Death

Gods of the Dead

Gods of Blood

Gods of Idols

Gods of Fire

Gods of Enoch

INFECTED FAIRY TALES

Wonderland: Chronicles of Blood

Toxic Wonderland

Magical Wonderland

Dying Wonderland

Bloody Wonderland

Wonderland: Chronicles of Madness

The Search for Nonsense

The Queen Trials

Veins of Shade

Finding Time

Neverland: Chronicles of Red

Neverwith

Nevershade

Neverblood

Nevermore

OTHER/STANDALONES

Hellish Ones Novels

Blood of the Devil

House of the Devil (2022)

Harem Project Novels

House of Daemon

House of Aves

House of Wyn (2022)

Paranormal Holiday Novel

12 Days

Satan's Touch Academy

A Lick of Magic

Fae Lords

Karou

Sweet Omegaverse

Alpha Hunted

Beta Haunted (2022)

The Princess and Her Alphaholes Anthology (excerpt of *Wrecked)*

Wrecked

Unsolicited

Hell View Manor

Stroking Pride (2022)

THANK YOU

Thank you for reading *Stroking Pride* and joining Nuke as she faces her murderers. One of my favorite things about Anuka is that she isn't afraid to get her hands dirty. Whether she's seeking a new thirst trap or looking to harness wild magic, Nuke is sure she can do it and doesn't stop until she does. But even the biggest badasses know when they need help and aren't afraid to ask for it.

Would you be so kind as to take a moment and leave a review? Reviews play a big role in a book's success and you can help with just a few sentences.

Review on Amazon, Goodreads, and Bookbub

Thank you!!
Crea Reitan
PS - If you find any errors, spelling or the like, please do not use your kindle/Amazon to mark them. Amazon's algorithms pull the book! Instead, please reach out to me on Facebook at https://www.facebook.com/Crea.Reitan or via email at LadyCreaAuthor@gmail.com. Thank you!!